DARK PROPHECY

■

A little over twenty years ago, on *Walpurgisnacht,* Anton Szandor LaVey, former lion tamer and police photographer, shaved his head in the tradition of black magicians and medieval executioners, announced the establishment of the world's first Church of Satan, and declared 1966 to be "Year One, Anno Satanas," the first year of the Satanic Age. In the light of a recent rash of media accounts, many believe his prophecy may finally be coming true.

■

SATAN WANTS YOU

SATAN WANTS YOU

THE CULT OF DEVIL WORSHIP IN AMERICA

ARTHUR LYONS

THE MYSTERIOUS PRESS

New York • London • Tokyo • Sweden

MYSTERIOUS PRESS EDITION

Cover design and illustration by Stanislaw Fernandes

Mysterious Press books are published in association with
Warner Books, Inc.
666 Fifth Avenue
New York, N.Y. 10103
A Warner Communications Company

Printed in the United States of America

Originally published in hardcover by The Mysterious Press.
First Mysterious Press Paperback Printing: July, 1989

10 9 8 7 6 5 4 3 2 1

To Arthur Lyons, Sr.,
who still lives in the double helix.

TABLE OF CONTENTS

SATAN
WANTS YOU

FOREWORD

by Marcello Truzzi, Ph.D.

With this new examination of contemporary Satanism in America, Arthur Lyons brings us a much needed antidote to the extremist writings that have either decried or simply intellectually dismissed the many recent and usually sensationalist accounts the public has been presented through the mass media. On the one hand, we continue to be exposed to the horrified concerns about the devil and his minions expressed by television evangelists, ranging from the hard sell anguish of Oral Roberts who claims to have physically wrestled with Satan to the softer warning of Billy Graham that "The Devil is making his pitch!" But, as Lyons demonstrates, concern with the devil and his purported followers has recently turned into a growth industry. This includes religious best sellers like Hal Lindsey's *Satan Is Alive and Well on Planet Earth* and an apparently growing number of self-styled "occult experts." Some of these claim to be "ex-Satanists" and make the rounds on the TV and radio talk shows and earn a living as lecturers and consultants, mainly on the religious speakers' circuit but also giving seminars for law enforcement personnel and others interested.

On the other hand, academic scholars of religion have displayed very limited interest in our contemporary forms of devil worship. As Jeffrey Burton Russell, our premier historian of the devil concept put it in speaking with some disdain about the popular culture Satanism that emerged as part of the occult revival that began in the 1960's: "The Devil no doubt has some interest in cultural despair, Satan chic, and demonic rock groups, but he must be much more enthusiastic about nuclear armament, gulgags, and exploitative imperialism, and it is to such problems as these that the serious philosophy and theol-

ogy of the latter twentieth century has properly been
directed."[1] Since most educated scholars today are unlikely to accept the traditional, corporeal view of Satan, they
have typically either dismissed Satan as myth or concerned themselves with the deeper issue of evil in the
world. Yet, even if Freud was right in writing that demons
are merely "the products of the psychic activity of man,"[2]
Denis de Rougemont was surely also correct in saying of
the devil: "A myth, hence he exists and continues to be
active. A myth is a story which describes and illustrates in
dramatic form certain deep structures of society."[3] Dos-
toyevski reminds us that "If the devil doesn't exist, but
man created him, he has created him in his own image."[4]
Bertrand Russell went even further by pointing out that
"God and Satan alike are essentially human figures, the
one a projection of ourselves, the other of our enemies."[5]
By looking at the images of the devil found today, we may
learn a great deal about people's current fears and values.
Lyon's investigative research, by attempting to give us an
objective and detailed ethnographic picture of modern
Satanism, as found in what he terms its "outlaw" cults
and Neo-Satanic churches, is an important first step in
helping us understand not only these maverick believers
but ultimately ourselves.

In dealing with modern Satanism, we need to separate
three questions. The first is: Does Satan actually exist?
This metaphysical question is clearly beyond the scope of
any empirical investigation. The second is: What is the
extent of belief in Satan in modern society? The answer to
this question determines the cultural context and frequency of both devil fear and devil worship. The third question
is: What are the actual practices, and their frequencies,
among those practicing some form of Satanism? The
answers to the second and third question have too frequently been colored by analysts' views on the first, but

[1]Jeffrey Burton Russell, *Mephistopheles: The Devil in the Modern World* (Ithaca N.Y.: Cornell University Press, 1986), p. 257.
[2]S. Freud, quoted in Eugene E. Brussell, editor, *Dictionary of Quotable Defini-tions* (Englewood Cliffs, N.J.: Prentice-Hall, 1970), p. 139.
[3]D. de Rougemont, quoted in *ibid.*, p. 142.
[4]F. Dostoyevsky, quoted in George Seldes, compiler, *The Great Thoughts* (N.Y.: Ballantine Books, 1985), p. 111
[5]B. Russell, quoted in *ibid.*, p. 362.

objective social science can be concerned with the second and third questions.

Most analysts would probably agree with Professor Russell, author of the monumental and probably definitive four volume history of the devil concept, who noted, "the belief in both Devil and God has declined drastically since the eighteenth century. Though the doctrine of belief in evil has not been accompanied by any decline of the action of evil in the world, by the 1980s belief in the devil had disappeared except among conservative Catholics, charismatics, conservative Protestants, Eastern Orthodox, Muslims—and a few occultists."[6] Yet, public opinion polls on American beliefs about the devil—though somewhat unclear and apparently affected by the times and ways the questions were asked—suggest a stronger affirmation. Thus, in 1982 George Gallup, Jr., reported that 34% of adult Americans believe in the devil as a "personal being who directs evil forces and influences people to do wrong" and another 36% believe in the devil as "an impersonal force that influences people to do wrong." Only 20% said they did not believe in the devil at all, and the remaining 10% said they were undecided.[7] Interestingly, this 70% affirmation seems to apply only to Satan himself, for Gallup found that only 39% of his 1978 sample said that they believed in a host or entourage of devils or demons (the percentage going up to a mere 50% for those who said that religious beliefs are very important in their lives).[8] Aside from such generally stated belief, the strength of such views may be on the rise. Thus, in a 1974 report from the Center for Policy Research, sociologist Clyde Z. Nunn reported finding that those who expressed certainty that the devil exists had risen from 37% in 1964 to 48% in 1973. (Oddly, during the overlapping time period between 1952 and 1980, this increase in belief in the devil contrasts with a 5% decline in belief in the existence of hell.[9]) These sorts of figures are markedly unusual when compared to public beliefs in most other Western countries. Thus, when

---

[6]Jeffrey Burton Russell, op.cit., p. 253.
[7]George Gallup, Jr., with William Proctor, Adventures in Immortality (M.Y.: McGraw Hill, 1982), p. 97.
[8]The Gallup Poll Release of 15 June 1978 (Field Enterprises).
[9]Clyde Z. Nunn, "Casting Out the Devil," prepublication draft, (New York: Center for Policy Research, 1974).

Gallup asked the question "Do you believe in the devil?" 60% of Americans replied "yes" in contrast to substantially lower percentages in France (17%), Great Britain (21%) or West Germany (25%). The only European country polled that surpassed the United States in the percentage of citizens expressing belief in the devil was Greece (67%), and the next highest percentage was found in Norway (38%).[10]

Generalizations about the American public can easily be misleading, however, in that they obscure the great variation in such beliefs found when we look at different segments of our society. Thus Nunn's 1974 study, which examined correlations between devil beliefs and other social psychological variables, found that people who are more likely to believe in the devil also are more likely to view communists and radical students as a threat, are less likely to indicate support of civil liberties, and are less tolerant of nonconformity. He also found that among the general population, those who believed life will be worse in the next few years, those more active religious service attenders, those who lived in the South and Mid-America, those less educated, and those who were more authoritarian, were all more likely to believe the devil exists.[11] Also, despite what has probably been greater contemporary media attention to Catholic devil beliefs (exemplified in such films as *The Exorcist*), these also remain a largely Protestant phenomenon. Thus, in their 1968 report, sociologists Rodney Stark and Charles Glock found that although 66% of Roman Catholics compared to 38% of Protestants agreed with a statement that it is "completely true" that "the Devil actually exists," the response varied greatly between different Protestant denominations with a range going from lows of 6% among Congregationalists and 13% among Methodists up to 77% among Missouri Lutherans and 92% among Southern Baptists.[12]

As regards the question of what Satanists actually do, Lyons' book goes a long way towards dispelling much of the nonsense that has been written on that subject. Lyons'

[10]George Gallup, Jr., *op.cit.*, p. 98.
[11]Nunn, *op.cit.*
[12]Reported in Rodney Stark and William Sims Brainbridge, *The Future of Religion* (Berkeley: University of California Press, 1985), p. 44.

analysis strongly supports the view of our leading scholar of religious cults, religious historian Dr. J. Gordon Melton of the Institute for the Study of American Religion, who recently surveyed the evidence of Satan in contemporary America and concluded:

> Satanism remains a twofold phenomenon: First, the public [or] open Satanic groups remain, though their relative size had changed, such groups remain relatively small and harmless. They pose no public threat. Secondly, small ephemeral Satanic groups, most consisting primarily of young adults and/or teenagers, some led by psychopaths and/or sociopaths continue to come and go. While they pose no threat to the larger society, they do pose an immediate danger to those involved in them and are frequently involved in criminal activity, from dealing in drugs to rape and murder. Where ever they appear, they should be carefully monitored by local authorities. Further, personnel and energy currently devoted to the protection of children from proven physical threats should not be diverted to a crusade against an evil whose very existence must be considered dubious at best.[13]

As regards the recent reports by children told to family members of purported Satanic cult activities, as members of a free society we should heed Dr. Melton's additional advice: "Given the difficulty of maintaining a secret occult society over a period of time, a skeptical approach must accompany any conclusions drawn from the children's stories until and unless substantial evidence, independently obtained, is made public."[14]

—Department of Sociology
Eastern Michigan University

[13]J. Gordon Melton, "The Evidences of Satan in Contemporary America: A Survey," paper presented at the meeting of the Pacific Division of the American Philosophical Association, Los Angeles, California, March 27–28, 1986, p. 12.
[14]J. Gordon Melton, *Encyclopedic Handbook of Cults in America* (N.Y.: Garland Publishing Co., 1986), p. 79.

CHAPTER I

A Question of Conspiracy

The blood-dimmed tide is loosed, and everywhere
The ceremony of innocence is drowned;
The best lack all conviction, while the worst
Are full of passionate intensity.

. . . And what rough beast, its hour come round at last,
Slouches towards Bethlehem to be born?
         —William Butler Yeats, "The Second Coming"

A little over twenty years ago, on Walpurgisnacht, Anton Szandor LaVey, former lion tamer and police photographer, shaved his head in the tradition of black magicians and medieval executioners, announced the establishment of the world's first Church of Satan, and declared 1966 to be "Year One, Anno Satanas," the first year of the Satanic Age. In the light of a recent rash of media accounts, many believe his prophecy may finally be coming true.

Since 1983, the country has been shocked by the epidemic of allegations, coming from parent groups and law enforcement spokesmen, that American children in day-care centers and preschools are being sexually molested and forced to take part in barbaric rites. The villains are identified as the adult followers of a nationwide secret Satanic cult who have worked themselves into teaching and administrative positions to gain access to the children.

The testimony of kids in these cases is astonishingly similar in content—too similar to have been fabricated, some experts say. They tell of being forced to commit sexual acts with robed, chanting adults, of being made to drink blood, eat feces, witness animal and human sacrifice, and taste the flesh of roasted babies. Special task forces have been set up within police departments to investigate Satanic and occult-related crimes, parent groups have formed to combat the "conspiracy," and Phil Donahue, Oprah Winfrey, *20/20*, and *Nightwatch*, among others, have devoted segments to the phenomenon. At the time of this writing, official police investigations of at least thirty cases of ritualistic child abuse have been conducted in nine states, resulting in thirteen coming to trial. But despite all the attention, no physical evidence has been unearthed and no convictions secured that bolster the Satanic conspiracy theory.

Still, many concerned parents and professionals—police, social workers, and religious leaders—remain convinced that the children are telling the truth and that society is being victimized by a plot of sinister and unprecedented proportions. As corroboration, they cite the current popularity of "heavy metal" rock groups that flaunt Satanic symbols and anti-Christian messages in their music, as well as a wave of crimes across the country over the past few years claimed to be "Satanically related."

Since 1980, cemeteries from Vancouver, British Columbia, to Sarasota, Florida, have reported graves being opened and bodies stolen, apparently for use in Satanic rituals. From California to Maine, police have reported a wave of church and school vandalism, burglaries, arson, and animal mutilations by gangs of Satanic "heavy metal rockers" who have labeled themselves "stoners."

In El Paso, Texas, allegations in 1986 by "ex-Satan cultists" that they had participated in rituals involving the murder of newborn infants and transients set off a full-scale investigation by sheriffs, yet no evidence to corroborate the stories was ever developed. Authorities in eastern Tennessee say they have been "run ragged" by similar reports.

In June 1985, police conducted a two-day dig of a wooded area near Toledo, Ohio, after several informants claimed to have attended human sacrifices there on several Halloweens. Lucas County Sheriff James Telb speculated that some eighty victims had been sacrificed during the past sixteen years by a Satanic cult. Although the dig turned up some odd and interesting items, such as a headless doll with nails driven through its feet and a pentagram attached to its arm, a nine-foot wooden cross with ligatures attached, sacks of folded children's clothing, sixty male children's left shoes, assorted hatchets and knives, and an anatomy dissection book, no human or animal remains, or any other evidence of murder, were found.

Evidence of murder *was* found in 1987, when a pair of severed female legs identified as having belonged to a twenty-one-year-old Cincinnati waitress, Monica Lemen, were found behind a church in Brookville, Indiana. A few days later, John Fryman, a paroled felon, was arrested for the murder, and a search of his mobile home turned up a black ritual room containing a gravestone altar, Satanic literature, black candles, and other ritual paraphernalia. There was widespread speculation that the killing was linked to a rash of animal mutilations in nearby Fayette County over the past two years and that Lemen had been the ritual sacrifice of a Satanic cult of which Fryman was a member. No cult was ever turned up, however.

Authorities in Union County, Ohio, have blamed Satanic cultists for the mutilation and killing of more than two hundred dogs, cats, and pigs in that area since 1982, and law enforcement officials in Guntersville, Alabama, have deemed a similar group responsible for a rash of cattle mutilations that occurred there in 1986. Two years before, in nearby Walnut Grove, Alabama, a fire containing animal bones, along with a crude Satanic altar, was found after a group of juveniles was interrupted conducting a ritual in a vacant lot used for Easter sunrise services.

In that same summer of 1984, in Northport, New York, Richard Kasso, seventeen, a self-proclaimed Satanist, and James Triano, eighteen, both high school dropouts, were arrested for the murder of seventeen-year-old Gary Lauwers. All three had belonged to a group of local youths called the Knights of the Black Circle, which dabbled in Satanism, and whose gatherings included such social activities as drug use, blood drinking and animal sacrifice, and listening to the music of such heavy metal groups as AC/DC, Black Sabbath, and Judas Priest. Lauwers, it was revealed, had been taken by the pair into the woods and tortured for four hours, then forced to proclaim his "love for Satan," before being stabbed to death. Kasso later

3

hanged himself in his jail cell. At first, it was speculated that Lauwers had been offered up as a human sacrifice, but further investigation determined the murder to be the result of a falling-out over a drug rip-off, and the "Knights" seem to have been more interested in PCP and AC/DC than Satanism.

That rock group also seems to have played an inadvertent role in the murder spree of Richard Ramirez, the so-called Night Stalker, who spread terror throughout Southern California in the summer of 1985 by sneaking into homes during the dead of night and mutilating and murdering the inhabitants. Ramirez, who spray-painted Satanic pentagrams on the walls of some of his victims, was a self-styled Satanist and an avid AC/DC fan, and it is said that he took their song "Night Prowler" as the inspiration for his nocturnal blood orgies.

More terrifying were the stories of Henry Lee Lucas, who confessed to the killing of over 360 youths after luring them to his Texas ranch for sexual purposes. Lucas told FBI agents that he belonged to an international Satanic cult called the Hands of Death, which had a training camp in the Everglades. The rites of the cult allegedly included animal crucifixions, the drinking of urine and the blood of decapitated victims, and cannibalism; on the more prosaic side, its activities included contract hits, child trafficking, and kiddie porn. Neither the training camp nor any other members of the Hands of Death have been found, and FBI agents have openly expressed skepticism about Lucas's claims.

Even the Soviet bloc countries, which many biblical literalists see as being the citadel of Satan himself, have reported incidents of demonic disobedience. In February 1987, two members of a cult called Worshipers of Satan were arrested on charges of desecrating human remains and torturing an animal in a Roman Catholic cemetery in Jarocin, Poland, as part of a Lammas Day (August 1) Mass. During the Mass, which was attended by about twenty young people following a rock concert in nearby Kalisz, a dog was killed upon an altar made from a casket that had been removed from a tomb. According to PAP, Poland's official news agency, the incident was the first publicly reported account of Satanic activity in that country. Little is known about the cult, since it failed to register with the Ministry of Religion, as required by Polish law.

There are several problems with this current rash of media accounts. Because "Satanism" is a buzzword that captures the public's imagination and therefore sells newspapers, there is a tendency to mislabel and print such claims unskeptically. One example is the 1987 case of the Finders, in which newspapers from coast to coast carried the story that Tallahassee police had arrested two members of a "bizarre Satanic cult" on felony child molestation charges. The charges were later dropped and the Finders was found to be not Satanic, but a pacifistic Taoist cult. Nonetheless, most of the newspapers that originally carried the "Satanic" headlines did not bother to update developments in the story, thus perpetuating in the public's mind the growing menace.

Another instance showing that retractions do not sell was stories carried in the mid-1970s by all the major news wires about a rash of mysterious cattle mutilations in the Midwest. It was widely speculated that the mutilations were the work of a network of Satanic cults, a fact which was later challenged by animal pathologists who determined that in almost every case they investigated, the animals had died of natural causes, and the mutilation had been uniformly the work of predators. Their findings, however, failed to surface in the media, and the myth of the cattle mutilation epidemic persists today, and has begun to surface in other parts of the country.

In San Diego County, California, for example, animal-control officials have refuted claims by San Diego police and sheriffs' spokesmen that Satanic cults have been responsible for the ritualistic mutilation of numerous animals in that area over the past two years. They contend that, despite increasing news stories giving credence to the claims, they have not seen a single case in the past five years attributable to a ritualistic killing. As in the Midwest, animal investigators have found the mutilation in almost every case to be the work of predators, yet their conclusions have been ignored by law enforcement proponents of a Satanic conspiracy.

Those spokesmen point to several incidents that have shown the work of a human hand—a disemboweled cat found on Halloween night, 1986, and a rat with its heart cut out, both at San Diego junior high schools—as evidence of the growing magnitude of the problem. The magnitude of the problem is the primary question. No one is disputing that a tiny number of adolescents are spray-painting Satanic graffiti on walls and even sadistically killing small animals in haphazardly concocted Satanic rituals, but the reports of such incidents far outnumber their reality. Moreover, much of what is being submitted to the public through the media by law enforcement "experts" as evidence of livestock-ripping Satanic ritual is nothing more than the work of coyotes.

A second problem is that even when an individual or group claiming to worship the Devil is involved in a crime, motivations are often not easy to sort out. The Cincinnati murder of Monica Lemen is an example. At first, it was speculated that because the killer, John Fryman, was a self-proclaimed Satanist, he had picked out Lemen as a sacrificial victim. Then it was revealed that Lemen had begun corresponding with Fryman, a convicted armed robber, while he was in prison, and arranged to meet him when he got out. According to police investigators, the waitress's legs had been cut off not as a part of any ritualistic dismemberment, but for the more mundane reason that the body would not otherwise fit into Fryman's Pinto station wagon.

Authorities on serial and mass murderers say one must be careful drawing conclusions about a killer's motivations even on the basis of his own claims. Commenting on the case of Richard Ramirez, U.C.-Berkeley sociologist Richard Ofshe, a specialist in thought control in extremist organizations, was recently quoted: "Anybody who is going to serially murder a number of people is probably a little unusual, and what he develops an interest in isn't going to automatically connect."[1]

San Diego State University sociologist R. George Kirkpatrick, who has studied modern pagan and witchcraft cults, concurs, saying, "There is no lack of bizarre crimes in this culture, but to link them to any conspiracy is farfetched."[2]

[1]"Satanism: Overtones in Other Slayings," Los Angeles Times, Sept. 2, 1986, I-2.
[2]Conversation with the author.

A third problem is that the media, already biased in favor of sensationalism, is being fed by a recently developed information network based on the Satanic conspiracy message. Economics has become involved. Psychologists and social workers are making the rounds of the talk shows and commanding hefty fees for their views on Satanic child abuse. Police and probation officers have gained publicity, prestige, and supplementary income giving training seminars in their new field of expertise, "Satanic crime." Christian fundamentalists claiming to have been "ex-Satanic priests" are packing in audiences who come to listen to how they escaped from the clutches of the Devil.

The cycle is self-perpetuating and has infected the information base. The media unskeptically prints rumor, which is thus given the media stamp of approval and fed back to the believers as "corroboration." Claims by informants, which a few years ago would have been passed off by police as flights of fancy or attempts to bargain away other charges, are now being swallowed whole by investigators. As Lieutenant Curt Surprise, of the Toledo Police Department, who was involved in the abortive dig there, told me: "I'd never heard of any of this stuff before, but now I see it everywhere. I don't know if it's real, or it's like buying a red car and suddenly seeing red cars everywhere."

Theologian Aidan Kelly, of Holy Family College, believes that "very little of what is currently being called Satanism is actually religious phenomena, let alone a religious movement. It is almost all media hype and hysteria." To illustrate, Kelly mentioned a wire-service story that asserted there were "250 covens of Satanist teenagers" in a certain western city. "The story might just as well have claimed that the teenagers were cruising Main Street in 250 flying saucers," he points out, "because a lowrider is no more a flying saucer than a clique of teenagers is a coven."[3]

But the fact is, such assertions have been promoted by the media and eagerly accepted by those who see in them proof of the coming of the Antichrist, as biblically prophesied in *Revelations*. Books have been burned and records

[3]Kelly, Aidan A., "Looking Reasonably at Outrageous Religions: Satanism as a Stage of Religious Maturation," paper, 1986, p. 1.

7

smashed by Christian groups concerned about the reputed
Satanic plot. In some communities, the hysteria has come
to infect the political process in less obvious ways, ones
which up to a few years ago would have been regarded
unthinkable. In 1986, for example, parent groups succeeded in pressuring high schools in East Jordan, Michigan, and Palm Desert, California, into changing the names
of their football teams—the Red Devils and Sun Devils
respectively—claiming that the teams were winning by
being in league with the Powers of Darkness.

Just what *is* going on out there, anyway? Are we being
murdered and our children being kidnaped and sodom-
ized by an infernal conspiracy of international scope, or
are the demonic forces that are terrorizing us merely the
hobgoblins of hysteria, invoked by religious alarmists, an
opportunistic media, and our own night fears? According
to Dr. J. Gordon Melton, director of the Institute for the
Study of American Religion:

> Satanism as it now exists and has existed during
> the past two centuries has been a most unusual
> cult. It has produced almost no literature and
> individual groups have come and gone without
> connecting with previously existing Satanic
> groups or leaving behind any progeny. The Sa-
> tanic tradition has been carried almost totally by
> the imaginative literature of non-Satanists—
> primarily conservative Christians, who describe
> the practices in vivid detail in the process of
> denouncing them. That is to say, the Satanic
> tradition has been created by generation after
> generation of anti-Satan writers. Sporadically,
> groups and individuals have tried to create
> groups which more or less conform to the Satan-
> ism portrayed in Christian literature.[4]

Historically, there has been much popular confusion as
to what "Satanism" is. Partially, this is the result of the
work of Christian theologians, who have had a tendency to
label all individuals and groups perceived as religious or
political enemies as "Satanic." Pagans, Moslems, Freema-

[4]Melton, J. Gordon, *Encyclopedia Handbook of Cults in America*, New York:
Garland, 1986, p. 76.

sons, and Communists have all, at one time or another, been tagged "Satanists" by church leaders. There has also been a tendency to lump together all occultists, voodooists, and, in particular, practitioners of witchcraft in the same package with Satanists.

Most modern "witches" consider themselves to be the practitioners of a pre-Christian, pagan, fertility religion (described by Margaret Murray and others) and resent the label "Satanists." As revived by Gerald Gardner on the Isle of Man in the 1950s and picked up by the counterculture in America in the late 1960s, these witches worship a "horned god" of fertility, not the Devil, and claim not to believe in a Christian God, Hell, or Satan. They believe that their magic and spells are derived from supranormal laws of nature, not from demonic entities, and that their rituals enable them to tap into that source. Because they found themselves being lumped together in the public mind with Satanists, many witches in the 1960s began to distinguish their brand of magic as being "white," or "good," saying that they only used it for the purpose of helping others, never for self-benefit. Satanists, by contrast, practiced "black magic," not only because they used it for their own selfish goals but also because its source was allegedly evil.

In this book, the term "Satanist" refers to anyone who sincerely describes himself as a worshiper of the Christian Devil, *whatever he perceives that to mean.* As we will see, what it does mean to the individual worshiper can vary drastically. Because many modern groups have picked up their practices from horror movies or fictional accounts of Black Masses, there is a great latitude among modern cults in both practice and belief. Only in Dennis Wheatley novels is there such a thing as a "traditional Satanist."

As it emerged in the mid-1960s, a contemporary Satanism can be divided into three distinct realities: (1) solitary Satanists, (2) "outlaw" cults, and (3) neo-Satanic churches.

Solitary Satanists belong to no cult and employ their own made-up brand, which they usually procure from books on the subject. For the most part, these Satanists are alienated teenagers who have a difficult time socializing, and the rituals they perform usually involve some sort of wish fulfillment, such as the acquisition of money, popularity, romance, or sex. Often the practices of these individuals are tied to drug use and a fanatical devotion to rock music—particularly heavy metal rock—and their Satanic "rituals" consist of little more than getting stoned, lighting candles, and reading a passage aloud from Anton LaVey's *The Satanic Bible*, to the accompaniment of an Ozzy Osbourne tape.

Since they hold their rituals in private, not much is known about how many of these solitary Satanists are around or how long they cling to their belief system. My impression, from the few I have talked to, is that the seriousness of such dabblers is not deep, lasting only as long as it takes this person to realize that Satan is not going to make his or her dreams come true. Aidan Kelly, rather than viewing such dabblings with alarm, sees them as part of a process of "religious maturation." Occasionally, however, the symbolism of evil can become enmeshed with antisocial rage and psychotic impulses, and become a rationalization for violence.

A typical case was that of seventeen-year-old Sean Sellers, who was sentenced to death for the 1986 Oklahoma City slayings of his mother, stepfather, and a convenience store clerk. Sellers, a self-proclaimed Satanist, described at his trial as an "alienated youth suffering from a deep sense of rejection," allegedly began to become interested in the occult at the age of twelve, and became more deeply involved after discovering the role-playing game "Dungeons and Dragons." In 1983, after becoming embittered by the breakup with his girlfriend, Sellers began to drink and take drugs and "dedicated his life to Satan." He constructed an altar in his bedroom, read works on Satanism, and held his own, private candlelit ceremonies.

At school, he purposely fueled his reputation for being strange by growing his left pinkie fingernail long and painting it black, and carrying vials of his own blood, which he made a show of drinking in the school cafeteria. With his only close friend, Richard, Sean managed to attract several other high school students into his "coven," and held blood-drinking ceremonies in an abandoned farmhouse, but the "cult" met infrequently, and did not last long. Eventually, Sellers's heavy use of amphetamines, alcohol, and marijuana, led to prolonged periods of sleeplessness, and he began to suffer from blackouts.

Although Sellers claimed he had killed "in homage to

Satan," it seems that his homicidal urges were more the result of drug use and a deep-seated rage. His relationship with his mother and stepfather was described by relatives as extremely strained, and, at the time of the murders, he was mad at them for forcing him to break off relations with his new girlfriend. The convenience store clerk had been picked as the sacrificial victim because of a personal grudge stemming from the man's refusal to sell Sellers beer.

Sellers had difficulty making friends, felt alienated and inadequate, unable to "fit in." His attempts to look bizarre and to shock with his blood drinking were blatant cries for attention. But the attention he got was not the kind he really wanted; it only increased his alienation. An outcast, he sought out the King of the Outcasts, the Prince of Darkness, as his source of strength. Since nobody liked Sean Sellers, Sean Sellers would hate them back.

The main interest of this book is in groups; and in determining the myth and reality of a Satanic *human* (vs. supernatural) conspiracy, the focus will be on the remaining two categories of cults, rather than on the solitary Satanists, like Sellers.

"Outlaw" groups worship Satan as the Evil One of the New Testament, and their practices reflect that orientation. Historically, such groups were primarily made up of sadomasochists and other sexual deviants, and their *raison d'être* was orgiastic, a la the old British Hellfire Club. Since the emergence of the counterculture in the late 1960s, however, and the easing of sexual taboos by society, the focus of such groups has tended to be more on drugs, music, and vandalism than sex.

The members are usually young (fifteen to twenty-five), socially alienated, and held together by a charismatic leader. Meetings are generally sporadic and lack any coherent theology; the rituals, like those of solitary Satanists, tend to be slapped together from movies and books on black magic. Since feelings of alienation are the Krazy Glue that holds these groups together, the rituals often include socially deviant, and sometimes violent, acts.

A typical example was uncovered in 1972 in the Denver suburb of Northglenn, as a result of an investigation of the theft of thirteen choir robes from a local church. The group, which called itself the Black Magic Cult, was made up of students from two nearby high schools, and had

11

stolen the robes for use in rituals that included animal sacrifice, blood drinking, and drug use.

In such "outlaw" groups, the practice of Satanism is often secondary to the acting out of deviant impulses. As sociologist Howard Becker puts it: "Instead of the deviant motives leading to deviant behavior, the deviant behavior in time produces the deviant motivation."[5]

In stark contrast to such groups are the neo-Satanic churches like the Church of Satan and its splinter organizations. These groups—which constitute the overwhelming bulk of the current Satanic membership—strictly prohibit the ritualistic harming of any living thing, and enjoin members from participating in illegal activities. These cults have adopted an unorthodox theological reconstruction of the Devil quite different from that of Christianity. Satan is perceived not as evil, but as a Miltonian symbol of man's carnality and rationality. They advocate egotism, indulgence, and the acquisition and use of personal and political power, have well-defined theologies and authority structures, and recruit members openly—to the point where two such groups, the Church of Satan and the Temple of Set, maintain listings in the San Francisco yellow pages under the heading "Churches— Satanic."

Most other churches either are splinters of the Church of Satan, founded in San Francisco in 1966 by erstwhile lion tamer Anton Szandor LaVey, or rely heavily on LaVey's works, *The Satanic Bible* and *The Satanic Rituals*, which are the only two popularly published works in print that lay out Satanic doctrine and philosophy. In spite of the fact that some current Satanists dismiss LaVey as a carnival huckster, he began the movement and remains by far its most influential spokesman.

The size and growth of the current Satanic movement is difficult to gauge accurately, for several reasons. One is that most of the so-called outlaw groups, as well as the solitary Satanists, hold their rituals in secret. Often, their presence is known by circumstantial evidence (sacrificial animal remains, for example), or when members of such a cult are arrested for a crime. Another is that both Satanists and anti-Satanists, as I've stated, have inten-

[5]Becker, Howard, *Outsiders*, New York Free Press of Glencoe, 1963, p 42

tionally and unintentionally distorted facts, for reasons of economics and self-aggrandizement.

One example I ran into was a "cult" called the Third Temple of Baal. The "temple," which advertises its literature in magazines like *Fate* and *Gnostica*, claims to be a "spiritual organization dedicated to dominance, conquest, murder, and slavery," as well as the downfall of Christianity. A sister cult asserted by temple literature to be closely affiliated is the Warlords of Satan, whose espoused goals are "nothing less than to turn human beings into prey." "Justice, equality, or world-harmony should be forgotten," the Warlords' mimeographed pamphlets proclaim. "The coming rule of Satan means power to the leaders, and slavery for the followers."[6] To facilitate its aims, the cult claims to have a "hidden chapter" within the Russian KGB.

With a little effort, I managed to track down the twin bloodthirsty cults and found them to be the fictitious creations of a Minneapolis accountant, "Jeremy Rollins."[7] Rollins, an unexpectedly soft-spoken, college-educated, sane-sounding man, told me that he had become interested in the "Semitic and pagan tradition of God as a warlord" in college while working with the civil rights movement. That experience had convinced him that "at some higher level, there is a force which likes to invoke bloodshed." He put an ad in *Fate* to try to locate others who shared his beliefs and eventually began to use the ads to sell political tracts—power-oriented, Spenglerian material—and currently has a mailing list of two hundred.

Another "cult" that conducts business through magazines is the Continental Association of Satan's Hope, headquartered in Montreal, Canada. Ads in occult and true-detective magazines in the United States and Canada encourage readers to "turn your fantasies into reality and discover for yourself the infernal power of mighty Satan!" For a fee of twenty-three dollars, the association will send subscribers a newsletter called *The Rage*, prescribed for curing illness, achieving wealth, or getting a girl in the sack. "'The Magic Power of Satan' will reveal to you rituals by which you can conjure up the infernal powers of

[6]"Warlords of Satan: A Cult of Blackness and Power," pamphlet, n.d.
[7]A pseudonym.

the Mighty Satan and hold them in servitude," the ads proclaim. "Find out how good it feels to have security in life, to know if anything goes wrong in your life you will always have someone to turn to in order to help you out of the toughest jams!" To find out, all one has to do is send money, a cashier's check, or money order to (step right up, folks!) CASH.

CASH is the brainchild of British-born Eric McAllister, who claims that the "organization" has been in business for seventeen years and has a worldwide membership of 45,000. When I called Montreal information for a phone number for the cult, I was told that there are twenty-three different companies with the abbreviation CASH, proving that Satan has not cornered the market on suckers.

Not that he hasn't tried. A recent glaring example was the case of Derry Knight, a con man who in 1986 was convicted of fraud in a British court after bilking a group of gullible Anglican churchmen and landed gentry out of $313,000 to aid him in his battle against a fictitious two-thousand-member cult called the Sons of Lucifer, to which Knight claimed to have been introduced by his grandmother when he was twenty. Despite his conviction, and despite Knight's previous record for fraud and rape, the victims of the swindle insisted they still believed his devilish story.

Just what is fact and what is fantasy? How many Satanists are there in the world, and what kind of a threat do they pose to society? Is there a network of real "Warlords of Satan" out there, just waiting for the opportune moment to pull our children into the shadows?

Discounting distortions due to hype and hysteria, and a tradition by neo-Satanic churches of inflating membership figures for publicity purposes, I would estimate the total number of Satanists of all types, worldwide, to be no more than five thousand. That is not a tremendously impressive figure until you begin to deal with it in terms of a murderous, child-molesting, cannibalistic conspiracy.

And from that standpoint, the question of the reality of the conspiracy takes on a double significance: One, if the conspiracy is real, we had better find out about it but quick, or we are all going to be in deep trouble. Two, if it does not exist, and Melton's picture of contemporary and historical Satanism is correct, the significance of the existence of Satanists in such numbers is not that they are part of a centralized conspiracy, but that they are not. If such cults have evolved simultaneously and independently, it must be because they fulfill certain psychological and emotional needs on the part of their members. As sociologists Orrin Klapp puts it: "If cults are booming in the twentieth century, we presume it is because identity problems are also booming."[8]

Folklorists and anthropologists have long assumed that in order for a myth to survive, it must serve some sociological and psychological function. Professor Mircea Eliade has stated his belief that certain mythologies have repeated themselves in disguised forms. "While recognizing that the great mythical themes continue to repeat themselves in the obscure depths of the psyche," he wrote, "we still wonder whether the myth, as an exemplary pattern of human behavior, may not also survive among our contemporaries in more or less degraded forms. It seems that a myth itself, as well as the symbols it brings into play, never quite disappears from the present world of the psyche; it only changes its aspect and disguises its operations."[9]

J. Gordon Melton has explained the new rash of Satanic stories as a disguised form of a myth centuries old, of a baby-stealing, orgiastic, cannibalistic secret society that preys on humanity from subterranean cellars. Historian Norman Cohn has noted that this myth has its origins in certain apocalyptic beliefs of early Christianity; he puts its most recent appearance, in secularized form, in Nazi Germany.

If the current evidence fails to validate the reality of a Satanic conspiracy, and if the new set of stories is found to be a recycled version of an old myth, as Melton says, its persistence in some way must be functional for society and the individuals who adhere to it. To determine that, it will be necessary to transport the reader back across the centuries, to the Devil's birthplace.

[8]Klapp, Orrin, *Collective Search for Identity*, New York: Holt, Rinehart & Winston, 1969, p. 142.
[9]Eliade, Mircea, *Myths, Dreams, and Mysteries*. New York: Harper & Row, 1960, p. 27.

CHAPTER II

The Birth of Satan

> Satan is an individualist. He upsets the command-
> ments of Heaven which enforce a definite moral
> conduct. He inspires us with dreams and hopes. He
> endows us with bitterness and discontent, but in the
> end he leads us to the Better, and thus he mainly
> serves the Good. He is that "force which strives for the
> evil yet causes the good."
>
> —Kurt Seligmann,
> *Magic, Supernaturalism, and Religion*

Just as modern man has inherited his ideas of God and
the universe from his Christian predecessors, so has he
inherited the Devil. Satan is an archetype, a force embedded in man's unconscious, a remnant of his psychological evolution. Satan is the child of fear, and fear is innate
in all men.

Evil, as it has appeared throughout man's history, has
had a schizoid development, manifesting itself in two
forms. The most elementary of these forms is purely
internal, deriving from man's instinctual drive toward
self-preservation, the concept "self" here including man's
own physical being and the physical beings of related
others. The object of this type of fear is anything that man
might see as impairing his fight for survival.

As the primitive man sits in a jungle clearing by his fire
at night and hears the sounds of animals stirring in the
bushes around him, he fears for his safety. He feels
powerless and is overcome by a seemingly unbridgeable
gap between knowledge and environment. He feels himself to be a mere pawn, a plaything, victimized by nature's
capricious ways. Drowned by nature's angry waters,
baked by her merciless sun, attacked by her vicious

animals, starved, beaten, bullied, he is at a loss for an explanation. Though fully aware mentally, he finds himself totally blind in the face of her inscrutable ways.

What recourse does he have? He must attempt in some way to make these strange and wondrous forces less capricious and more subject to his control. So he re-creates them in his own mind, makes them more tangible, more related to his own experience. He takes them out of their detached state to give them more personal meaning. Once he has done this, he has some recourse for his grievances: now he may make offerings, get down on his knees and ask the god for a good crop or an abundant herd, attempt to cajole or coerce the god into granting his requests. Those deities that man has traditionally created to represent evil have stemmed from those forces of nature that he has found to be most uncontrollable; the shapes into which they have been cast being those shapes and forms that he has feared the most. Primitive man saw hideous demons with six heads and fierce claws waiting for him in the darkness, and he was forced to respond to the danger.

In Chinese mythology, there are tales of an evil sky dragon that threatened to swallow up the sun, obviously an explanation of solar eclipse, an event that must have struck fear in even the most stouthearted Chinese. In Babylonia, the creation of evil was attributed to Tiamat, the horned and winged god of unbounded salt water, a force of darkness and chaos. The ancient Assyrians saw the desert wastes populated with horrible creatures, waiting to devour any man foolish enough to venture into their domain. The most terrible of all these Assyrian demons was the dragonlike demon, the god of the southwest wind, who had an almost fleshless dog's skull for a head, a serpent's tail, and who, with his fiery breath, spread devastating diseases among mankind. The Egyptian god Set came the closest of all the early deities, perhaps, to becoming the complete personification of evil. Locked in a life-and-death struggle with Horus, the hawk-headed sun-god, he, like many of the evil deities of other cultures, threatened to extinguish the life-giving sun, and was thus born out of man's timeless fear of darkness.

The early demons, however, were never complete personifications of evil in the social sense. They were always incomplete in their evilness, due to their rather personal nature. For the most part, they were projections of man on nature and, as such, most of them had at least some of man's character in them, rendered both consciously and unconsciously. This can be seen in the recurrent theme in many Eastern and Western mythologies of the winged serpent, for, in fact, man's ambivalence toward himself and nature is reflected in his casting of his many demons and gods in this shape. The wings are symbolic, at an unconscious level, of a loftier striving, an attempt at spiritual transcendence, while the snake has always been an object of instinctual fascination for man. Man's ancient dichotomy of intellect versus instinct is apparent in this symbolism.

The old gods, then, were oddly like men, so that they could either heal or destroy, aid man or plague him, depending on whether he awoke in the morning with heartburn or had had a satisfying night with his wife. Thus the Indian goddess of destruction, Kali, spreader of diseases and devourer of men and animals, is infinitely kind and generous to those she loves.

The second type of evil traditionally defined by man is less spontaneous and more highly structuralized, for its sources lie not within the wrath of nature, but within society itself. These ideas of evil are indigenous to culture and aim at the maintenance and stabilization of culture. The evil here is what is socially harmful, what threatens social rather than personal disintegration. The evils defined are negativisms, inversions, and usually take the form of cultural taboos.

In many cases, both kinds of evil are intertwined, the social type, through inculcation, inspiring fear and awe and thus assuming the proportions of a force of nature. After being handed down from generation to generation, the reasons for certain social laws are often forgotten and they become elevated to the stature of natural laws, the breaking of which is felt by man to be detrimental to his survival as an organic entity. The laws begin to work independently of the reasons for their existence and in the process assume greater force. The dietary prohibitions against eating pork, very possibly instituted in early Judaism as a protection against trichinosis, have assumed for many Orthodox Jews the proportions of a cosmic law, even the *thought* of consuming pork eliciting in some people pyschosomatic reactions such as nausea.

"Thou shalt not" is the basis of the concept of social evil. Thou shalt not kill, thou shalt not steal, thou shalt not covet they neighbor's wife—all these are examples of social evils. Such acts are evil in that, if indulged in, they would facilitate the breakdown of ties within the culture; they are prohibitions aimed at maintenance and control. Seldom have these evils been personified by any particular god, since they act in the capacity of universal laws and, as such, are mechanical, impersonal. Satan has not personified these social taboos in the sense that Set personified the night and Horus personified the sun; he rather has skillfully manipulated these moral edicts in an attempt to undermine the forces of righteousness and good.

Satan as a personification of evil has beaten a consistent and clear path through the religious history of Western man and in each guise has been representative of the social type of evil. He has been uniformly antisocial, antihumanity, anti-God throughout all the religious systems in which he has appeared, at least according to the tenets of the opposing side. But only under one of the religions in which he appears, Christianity, did a separate movement materialize devoted to his worship as a symbol of the anti-God.

The reason for this has been stated many times by writers and historians: historically, Satanism as a religion was the anomalous child of Christian repression. The reason that Devil worship reached the degree or organization and the size that it did under Christianity, and not under other monotheistic religious systems, is the Christian definition of evil. The idea of social evil for the Christians soon became aligned and synonymous with self-indulgence. The Christian idea of the Seven Deadly Sins (greed, pride, envy, anger, gluttony, lust, and sloth) is indicative of this aversion to self-indulgence. Pleasure came to be looked upon as being tainted.

Man found it hard, nevertheless, to dissociate himself intellectually from self-indulgence and from his own carnality, from his emotions and from his physical delights. His self became divided and he found that he was being led in two directions at once. A gulf widened between man's conscious and unconscious mind, and he found himself obsessed by images of his instinctual nature, his animal being. The Devil, conceived and cast in the form of the ubiquitous chthonic snake, functioning at an unconscious level as man's animal being, was looked upon by the Christian theologians with stern foreboding.

The people were told that the Devil was evil, that he represented carnality, pride, lust, gluttony, rebelliousness, all those centrifugal forces that would tend toward atomization and social disintegration. They were told that Satan was evil because he had dared to oppose God, the perfect and omnipotent creator of the universe. The people nodded in agreement, for they knew that this was correct, but at a deeper level of consciousness something squirmed uncomfortably. It all struck a chord that was just a bit too familiar, for the Devil reminded them of somebody they knew very well—themselves. He was self-indulgent and so were they; he had great pride and so did they; he rebelled against tyrannical authority and so did they often wish to. He painted a colorful picture, to be sure, much more attractive than the one of an overpowering, intolerant, faultless God whom none could ever hope to approach in perfection. So the Devil remained intact as a symbol under Christianity; he was humanity in all its weaknesses, and it was from this manifestation that he originally derived all his strength. In other religions in which he had played a major role, Satan had never achieved any great following simply because the theologians, in their mythmaking functions, were more careful in their social definitions of evil.

All those religious systems in which Satan has appeared share one common trait: they are all monotheistic and, as such, need a negative balance for the positive construct of an all-powerful, all-good, and merciful God. Satan is necessary because there is no other way to dispose of the evil realities constantly confronting humanity. Since pestilence, famine, and death are formidable evils faced by all men, and since it is difficult, to say the least, to attribute their origin to pure goodness, an evil source must be assumed to exist.

Satan first appeared in the sixth century B.C., in Persia, under the name of Angra Mainyu. He was usually represented as a snake, or as part lion, part snake, which points up once again the recurring symbolism of the serpent and cat. The Zoroastrian religion was the official religion of Persia at that time, and it spread with the extension of the Empire until the Persian military might was crushed by the Muslim invasion of A.D. 652. The teachings of the prophet Zoroaster served as a vehicle by which the doctrine of ethical dualism, the eternal battle between good and evil, was to spread to the rest of the world.

Zoroastrianism taught that there were two forces or spirits in the universe from which all else emanated: Ahura Mazda, the Principle of Light, the source of all good, and Angra Mainyu, the Principle of Darkness, the source of all evil. These two were supposed to be carrying on a constant battle, each attempting to destroy the other, until the coming of the Judgment, at which time the forces of Light would triumph. The earth and all the material universe were created by Ahura Mazda to be used as a weapon by which to ensnare and defeat Angra Mainyu. Man was created by Ahura Mazda for the same purpose, but having the faculty of free will, he could choose between good and evil.

In preparation for the oncoming battle, both spirits created subsidiary spirits to help them in their fight, these sides being organized into vast military organizations, efficient and terrible. The development of this military hierarchy, with Satan commanding legions of horrible demons, was to have a tremendous impact on the thinking of Judaic, Christian, and even Islamic cosmologies, the idea coming into special prominence at times when each of the cultures was making moves toward military expansion.

In 586 B.C., Jerusalem was taken by King Nebuchadnezzar after a long and bloody war, the Hebrews being deported to Babylonia. In 538 B.C., Cyrus the Great of Persia conquered Babylonia and issued a decree giving the Jews there a privileged status in the new social order. But Cyrus was not only the harbinger of political freedom but also the carrier of a new spiritual awakening in the form of Zoroastrianism.

The Jews came to know the Zoroastrian faith firsthand, and to many Hebrew scholars of the time, the Persian religion seemed to supply many of the answers to troublesome theological questions. Satan had appeared in the holy books of the Jews long before their contact with the

Persians, but only in a very limited role. Satan translated from Hebrew means "accuser" or "adversary," and that was precisely the role Satan played in Judaic angelology before the Persian influence. Satan was at the time, at the very most, slightly rebellious and resentful, perhaps wishing to work evil but forced to promote good due to the overriding influence of God. His function was to accuse men before God, expose their infidelity, and then bring about their punishment—but only under the auspices of God himself. To the ancient Jews, who were hard-core realists, Satan symbolized man's evil inclinations. It is very likely, in fact, that the introduction of Satan into Judaism was intended only in a figurative sense, and that he was not supposed to function as a distinct spiritual being at all.

The early Jews viewed man as a microcosm of the vaster universe, in which the duality of good and evil was reflected. The opposition of two forces, Yetzer Tob, the inclination toward good, and Yetzer ha-Rah, the inclination toward evil, existed not only in the external universe but also in man. In view of these facts, the Devil could possibly have been merely a symbolic externalization of the Yetzer ha-Rah in man, and was not supposed to have assumed the proportion of a concrete entity at all. The more superstitious among the Jews, taking his existence literally and forgetting the original purpose for his introduction, might have promoted the belief in an anthropomorphized deity.

The contact with the Zoroastrians, at any rate, brought drastic changes in Jewish literature. The Jewish Sheol, once a place of eternal peace and sleep, was transformed into Hell, a place of damnation and punishment for the wicked. The serpent that tempted Eve became Satan in disguise, and the Devil became the originator of all evil, the author of death, a complete contradiction of the earlier Book of Isaiah, in which God proclaimed himself to be responsible for all good and evil in the world, the creator of life and death.

The Judaic demonology, which had been up to that time relatively unimportant, took on a fresh look, and Satan as the archfiend came to head up a formalized hierarchy of storm troopers dedicated to the overthrow of the heavenly forces. Demons consorted with humans to produce nonhuman offspring. Men went to bed at night fearing the coming of the bloodsucking she-demon Lilith or her consort, Samael, the Angel of Death, who cut men down in their prime and carried them off to Hell.

It was in such a condition that Satan was transferred to the emerging Christian sect. In the New Testament, he became the "Old Serpent," the "Great Dragon," upholding his snaky image. Considering later developments, these reptilian descriptions are very relevant, for nowhere in Zoroastrian, Judaic, or Christian mythology was Satan described as a goat, as he was later portrayed by the Inquisitors.

The Devil in early Christianity was primarily the same Devil as in Judaism: he was the tempter, the adversary, leading men astray in order to exact their punishment. His attributes get a little worse than this until much later. The Devil was a cosmic element to be taken seriously by any right-thinking Christian, of course, but at the time, Christianity was much too busy fighting for its own survival to search out Satan in any lair in which he might be hiding.

In the fifth century, in his treatise *The City of God*, Saint Augustine described the legions of demons that are active on earth and the powers that they exert over men. But he went on to say that evil was a creation not of the Devil, but of God, in order to select the "elect" from the damned. In stating, "For we cannot call the devil a fornicator or drunkard or ascribe him any sensual indulgence though he is the secret instigator and prompter of those who sin in these ways," he reflected an image of Satan far different from the one that was to emerge later on the Continent. The picture of Satan as sort of an immoral dope-pusher, getting weak persons hooked on his "junk" while he himself abstained and reaped the profits, was a far cry from the later lecherous goat, the Prince of Fornication, who at the witches' Sabbats copulated with every woman present.

From its inception until Constantine's rise to power and its subsequent acceptance in A.D. 383 as the official religion of Rome, Christianity underwent a series of persecutions, due to the Roman fear of the rapidly spreading sect. Soon after its acceptance, the new Church found itself in mortal danger from a series of barbaric invasions. Teutonic hordes from the north and later

Muslims during the seventh century divided the Empire into fragments and threatened to break the back of Roman power. Until the reconsolidation under Pepin the Short and his son, Charlemagne, who was crowned Holy Roman Emperor in 800, Christians could only relate to the external threat. Their attention was so fixed on the threat of extinction at the hands of the barbarians that were assaulting the holy walls of Rome that they could not pay any heed to the threat from within, from the Devil that was in their midst.

But as the Church gained power and spread across the landmass of Europe, it found itself obliged to incorporate many elements into itself that were in conflict with Christian orthodoxy. The conquerors sent their missionaries into the pagan lands in an attempt to "civilize" their new subjects, and there these emissaries of God encountered primitive peoples praying to strange and vile images.

In the gray Celtic mists of Wales and Scotland, they found the remains of Druidism, a mysterious religious group that claimed to be able, by certain strange, magical rituals, to make rain, to bring down fire from the sky, and to perform other wondrous and miraculous acts. They met deep in the darkness of the forests, these sorcerers, among their sacred trees.

In the ruins of the once Egyptian culture, the Romans found the strange cults of Osiris, the god of vegetation and regeneration, the god of fertility, the tree spirit.

In Greece, they found the bloody rites of Dionysus, the goat-god, the god of vegetation. There also, in beautiful gardens, they discovered the people making offerings to Priapus, who bore the horns of a goat and who displayed proudly a huge phallus, a deity of productive power who protected the fields and the bees and the sheep.

They encountered the god Pan waiting for them deep in the black forests, waiting for the transformation that would increase the limits of his kingdom a thousandfold.

Wherever the Christian missionaries turned, they found the peasantry worshiping many animal gods, primary among them being the bull, the ram, and the stag. Among the northern Teutonic peoples, there were the war gods Thor and Odin, and the evil Loki, all wearing horned helmets as they went to battle. Freyja, the Scandinavian

24

May queen and counterpart of the southern Diana, donned antlers and was responsible for the revival of life in the spring. Dionysus, Isis, Priapus, Cernunnos, all were horned gods of fertility. The woods and glades were populated with nymphs and goatlike satyrs, lesser spirits who played gleefully and licentiously in the summer sun. The horned god was spread over the entire continent, and it was he who was to resist the oncoming Christian tide, become miraculously transformed into Satan, the ruler of the earth in all its glory.

With the conquest of the new pagan territories, the Christians launched a spiritual assault on their new captives in an attempt to spread the gospel. Once rolling, however, the military machine moved so fast that the efforts at proselytizing were more superficial than had been hoped. It is said that Charlemagne, in order to speed up the conversion process to fit his busy schedule, conducted mass baptisms of Saxons by driving them through rivers that had been previously blessed upstream by bishops.

This type of conversion failed to bring any long-lasting results, needless to say, and the participants usually reverted immediately to the old gods. Often when Christianity did make inroads into the minds of the people, it did not succeed in displacing the old beliefs, but merely assumed a place beside them. Redwald, King of the East Saxons, reportedly had a temple in which existed twin altars, one on which he made sacrifices to Christ, and the other on which he made sacrifices to the nature gods.

Most of the missionaries underestimated the power of the nature religions of the pagans. They viewed the holding of such religious beliefs to be due merely to error and believed that once such errors were revealed, the pagans would be blinded by the light of truth and embrace Jesus as their Savior. But the pagans found the teachings of the Nazarene to be a little too distant and mystical for their liking. Thus, when the initial attempt at conversion failed, the missionaries found it necessary to change their views, and they began to incorporate many elements of the old religions into Christian doctrine in an attempt to kill them by subversion. Many of the pagan deities were transformed overnight into Christian saints, adding new pages to the growing Christian mythology. Elements of pagan rituals and ceremonies found their way into Christian services as each parish soaked up local traditions. As late as 1282, a priest at Inverkeithing was found to be leading fertility dances at Easter around the phallic figure of a god, and the Catholic hierarchy, after investigation, allowed him to keep his benefice.

From the sixth century, as more territory became opened to Christianity, the pagan kings began to convert one by one. Introduced from the ruling classes, it was slow to penetrate to the lower classes of peasants. Moving slowly, as water through thickly encrusted layers of mud, it met stubborn resistance all the way. But even in areas where conversions were accomplished, the peasantry frequently relapsed to the pagan ways of the past. Many of the conversions soon showed signs of strain, and the Church awoke to find the tenuous grip that it held on its newly found members to be slipping. Christian dignitaries, worried about their recently claimed souls, began to institute new policies. Turning their attention from the outside to within, searching desperately for a cause for their failure, they came upon the Devil himself.

The laws at the time against witchcraft were vague and ambiguous, reflecting the general skepticism among ecclesiasts about such matters. Punishment for sorcery was usually light, unless the lives of important clerical or secular officials were threatened, and although between the ninth and twelfth centuries there were several cases of women being burned as witches, these were for the most part irregularities, incited by the excitement of mobs, rather than executions carried out in the pursuance of any formal edicts. In the ninth century, an official Church document attributed to the Council of Ancyra stated:

> Certain wicked women, reverting to Satan, and seduced by the *illusions* and phantasms of demons, believe and profess that they ride at night with Diana on certain beasts, with an innumerable multitude of women, passing over immense distances, obeying her commands as their mistress, and evoked by her on certain nights.

Tales of nocturnal gatherings of witches who flew on animals to hilltop meetings were common enough to have been included in Boccaccio's *Decameron* in 1350, but most of the high Christian officials saw these women not as practitioners of the abominations to which they confessed, but only as the unwilling victims of demonic tricksters.

In the tenth century, the laws of King Athelstan declared that anyone convicted of witchcraft was to be sentenced to 120 days in prison. King Cnut in the eleventh century issued a proclamation "earnestly forbidding" the worship of the sun and moon, of trees and stones, and "other forms of heathenism." No general law was found in Europe concerning witches, for European power was fragmented at that time, broken up into many separate feudal states of various sizes. But by the time the twelfth century rolled around, the old attitude of leniency on the part of officials in Rome began to change and the laws began to harden.

The reasons for the drastic change were not only to be found in the persistent resistance to conversion by the pagans but also in the intrinsic attitudes within the Church itself. Inspired by the teachings of Saint Paul, Christianity began to splinter off into sects that were dedicated to the principles of asceticism. Convinced that concern for bodily comfort was a distraction from the true means of attaining spiritual salvation, these ascetics set forth into the desert wastes to live in seclusion and discomfort. They denied the flesh by tormenting it, inflicting lacerations and periodic self-whippings on their bodies, purposely festering and scratching the wounds to prevent them from healing. The Christian heroes of the day, the paragons of piety and adored by the Church, were men such as Saint Simon Stylites, who lived most of his life either in a pig sty or standing on one leg, and as Saint Anthony, the founder of Christian monasticism, who took a bizarre delight in being tormented almost to the point of insanity by his own sexual fantasies.

Spurred on by the pessimistic view that the world was purposely created and maintained as a living Hell, existing solely to prepare man for his future heavenly existence, the pious conducted a "holier than thou" contest to see who could inflict the most self-abuse. They measured earthly success in terms of how much pain they could force themselves to endure, or how many lice they were able to nurture in their hair.

27

The craze caught on, monastical orders began springing up everywhere, and celibacy became a new of life within the Catholic priesthood. But with the change in Catholic attitudes came changes in perception, and as the sensory data that came in from the outside was now being filtered through a different cognitive system, the world suddenly became a different place. As asceticism came to be incorporated into Church dogma, all of nature came to be looked upon as something vile and corrupt.

The material world was condemned as a carefully laid trap, set up by the Devil for the purpose of deluding and ensnaring man. Christians were warned by the priesthood to beware of the delights of material existence, lest they be sidetracked from their true earthly purpose, the preparation for a spiritual afterlife. All joys came under the rule of the Church, to be dispensed as the clergy saw fit. Sex, people were informed, was to be indulged in solely for the purpose of propagating Christian babies and nothing else. The ecclesiastical severance of man from nature went so far that in the twelfth century a book entitled *Hortus Deliciarum* issued an ominous warning that the joys of gardening might well be harmful to the redemption of the soul.

But while these ideals of asceticism and self-denial were taking root in Christian dogma, the inequities of administration were apparent for all who had eyes to see. The hypocrisy of the clergy was flagrantly displayed, and, on this account, many had ceased to listen to long, tedious sermons dealing with the inevitable damnation of sinners. Priests were constantly seducing female members of their own laities, and as early as the eighth century, many convents had been condemned by high ecclesiastical figures as being "hotbeds of filthy conversation, drunkenness, and vice."

As the peasant masses were considered to be the property of the feudal lords whose lands they occupied, they found themselves subject to the caprice of these lords and felt crushed beneath the injustices of the system. The serfs were taxed unmercifully and were subject to the foraging raids that were frequently made by the soldiers of the nobility, who came to carry off their grain or their women, depending on their inclination. One feudal law went to the extreme of declaring that before a peasant could consummate his marriage, he had to bring his bride to his lord in order that the lord might have the "first fruits" of the marriage. The peasant might forestall this, thereby preserving his wife's virginity (at least temporarily), by making a prescribed payment to the noble, but the payment was usually too large for the peasant to afford.

These injustices usually had the weight of the Church behind them, for the Church was a *de facto* part of the aristocracy. The social order was presented to the people as being ordained by Heaven and therefore immutable; the Church took the attitude that if God had wanted the situation changed, then He would change it. As long as they were on top of the heap, the Church and the nobility had little impetus to rock the boat.

But soon the peasantry became resentful of the oppression forced on them from above. Peasant revolts spread across Europe and one by one were put down by force of arms. The Church backed up the efforts of the aristocracy to quell the rebels, deeming them to be anarchists inspired by the forces of Hell trying to topple God's empire. The result was that the lower classes had ceased to listen to a God who had become in their eyes a solemn and unfeeling hypocrite, who dealt fortune to those least deserving and inflicted punishment on those most virtuous. God was the friend and ally of the corrupt nobility, the enemy of the common man.

The disaffection with the Christian hypocrisy was not only widespread among the peasantry but was shared by many members of the nobility themselves. It was no wonder, then, that the organized heretical movements that had begun to trickle into the Empire from the south had taken root in the minds of many. New ideas, carried from the east and south by the Crusaders, who had been sent, ironically enough, to stamp them out, began to take seed in certain Christian circles. Many of these movements, such as the Knights Templar and the various Gnostic heresies, were clear-cut reactions against the corruption rampant in the Church, and they instituted strict vows of chastity and poverty among their priesthoods.

By the thirteenth century, the officials in Rome, exhausted from the senseless bloodshed and humiliating defeats in the Holy Land, began to call the troops home and turn their attention to more domestic problems. When they opened their eyes, they not only found blasphemous idolatry being carried on by the peasant masses but also saw their own position being undermined by heresies that had grown too big to be considered lightly. Christianity was rotting beneath its own weight, and these devout and pious men saw that something would have to be done, and done quickly, if the kingdom of God were to be saved from the jaws of Hell. The laws grew steadily tougher.

One of the first targets was the Manichaean sects, which had been brought into northern and central Europe from Bulgaria. Some of these groups, such as the Albigenses and the Cathari, had attained such power that they had managed to send out missionaries to various parts of Europe in order to gather converts, and in many areas they had been quite successful. Manichaeism taught its followers that there were two coeternal forces at work in the universe, good and evil. The good was a purely spiritual force and the evil was a purely carnal one; in physical matter, both these principles have become inextricably intertwined. They felt that the only possibility man had for redemption was to expurgate evil by denying all forms of carnality. Christianity to them was a corrupt force, leading men into sin and degradation, and the rabid opposition they expressed to the Church caused the papacy grave concern.

The Church responded to the crises by establishing, by a series of papal bulls, the Holy Office of the Inquisition, an investigatory board put under the control of the Dominicans, an order of mendicant friars founded in the early thirteenth century. The Holy Office soon moved against the Albigenses, the Cathari, and the Waldenses, sparing no brutality in stamping out the heretics.

The meetings of the Cathari were given the rather ominous title of *synagoga Satanae* by the Dominicans, the reports of the proceedings being similar to the accounts later to emerge of the witches' Sabbats, complete with anti-Christian symbolism and wanton sexuality. Although many of the charges levied against the sects were obviously trumped up, there may have been, in fact, some basis of truth in the accounts. Considering the contempt the groups held for the Christian fathers, there seems a great likelihood that some anti-Christian behavior may have been included in the ceremonies.

As for the accusations that the Cathari and Albigenses practiced homosexuality and unnatural acts of sodomy, including intercourse with animals, this may have occurred in certain instances, for the priesthoods of these groups frowned upon any type of sexual union that would result in childbirth. To the Manichaeans, procreation was the ultimate sin, since it was the propagation of materiality. Realizing that the lower elements of the movement would not be able to expunge their animalistic drives entirely, the elect of these sects may have given their unofficial sanction to sexuality that would not result in reproduction. At any rate, under the direction of Innocent III, these pockets of dissension were exterminated, many of the groups going underground to carry on their opposition to Christianity.

By the time of the suppression of the Manichaeans, the death penalty had come to be used freely in cases of heresy. In 1312 the powerful Knights Templar, a fraternal organization of Christian Crusaders, which had ostensibly formed as a response to what its leaders saw as corruption in the Church, was declared heretical by the Church, and its members imprisoned. Many disciples of the group cracked under the strain of torture and confessed to having practiced a variety of abominable rites, including the worship of a deity called Baphomet, described alternately as a bearded man's head with one or three faces, a human skull, or a monstrous figure with human hands and the head of a goat, a candle sputtering between its horns. Initiates were forced to spit and trample upon the cross, renounce Christ as a false prophet, gird themselves with cords that had been tied to pagan idols, and perform homosexual acts with group leaders.

Since the Templars were a wealthy order and since the wealth of all those convicted of heretical crimes became the property of the state, it is possible that the entire episode was fabricated by King Philip of France to fill his badly depleted treasury. But considering the fact that as Crusaders the Templars had come in contact with Moslems and followers of the Gnostism, it is possible that there was some truth in the charges brought against them. The denial of Christ, for instance, was common to all the accounts, which vary widely in detail, as was the wearing of the cord, a practice of the Cathari. Another possibility, ignored by most historians, is that the initiations were part of POW training. The Templars were fighting the Saracens, and the inquisitors took Baphomet to be a corruption of Mahomet. Mohammedan practice at the time was to offer Christian prisoners their lives if they renounced their religion and converted to the Moslem Faith. The horrible Baphomet image could have been a piece of wartime propaganda meant to reveal the true disgusting nature of the enemy. Unfortunately, the Templars failed to develop a survival course geared to an unexpected enemy—their own church—and the last Grand Master of the Templars, Jacques de Molay, was burned outside Paris in 1314.

Regardless of the reality of the Satanic charges against them, the Templar legend would play an important role in Western magical tradition and in the belief systems of other secret societies—Satanic and non-Satanic—which traced their own practices to those of the Knights.

In 1275, not long before Jacques de Molay's execution, the first official execution for witchcraft (as opposed to heresy) had taken place when a woman was burned at the stake in Toulouse. Other executions followed. With most of the powerful heretical movements stamped out by the fourteenth century, the Christian fathers, intoxicated by the smell of burning flesh, searched frantically for new victims. The early witch executions set a valuable precedent, and the pantheon of nature gods of the peasant farmers was opened up for attack.

By this time the concepts of heresy and witchcraft had become thoroughly confused, and the Inqusitors saw demons everywhere. The biblical edict "Thou shalt not suffer a witch to live" came into literal use on a grand scale. By the time that Pope Innocent VIII gave official sanction by a papal bull in 1484 for the witch prosecutions, executions for witchcraft had been in full swing in parts of the Continent for two hundred years. But in 1485, a more detailed account of the dealings of witches was published by the Dominican Inquisitors Henry Kramer and Jacob Sprenger, entitled the *Malleus Maleficarum*. This work, which became a manual for Inquisitors and witch-hunters for the next two centuries, spelled out in great detail the methods and workings of witches, their treacherous league with the Devil, and described methods for securing convictions of the accused. The doors were thrown open for the bloodbath.

The frenzy that shook Europe was monumental. The witch became for the European Christian, as H.R. Trevor-Roper terms it, the "stereotype of noncomformity," a convenient scapegoat for jealousy and self-hatred. The craze reached such paranoiac proportions that between 1120 and 1741, when the madness finally subsided, ninety domestic animals had been tried before courts of law for murder and witchcraft. In 1314 at Valois, a bull that had gored a man to death was sentenced to death by strangulation. All of Europe was under the dark cloud of Satan, as neighbors and friends viewed each other with suspicion and familes turned on one another in blind fear.

The Reformation of the sixteenth century made Catholics even more certain that the Satanic forces were everywhere trying to undermine the authority of the Church. The Thirty Years War was seen as Armageddon, the Infernal Hierarchy more than ever assuming the aspects of a well-oiled military machine, with Satan leading Luther and his demonic Protestant hordes in a bloody assault on the City of God.

The Lutherans entered the proceedings with vigor, for they were revolting against the corruption and laxity they saw in the Church, this decay being due to Satanic influences. Luther viewed his adversaries as being inspired by the Devil, and even his own bodily ailments he attributed to demonic activity. The spiral of executions soared ever upward, each side trying to outdo the other to meet the challenge. One Protestant reformer by the name of Carpzov claimed personal responsibility for the deaths of 20,000 people.

One reason for the mass executions was that for Catholic and Protestant alike, they had created much prosperity. The property seized from the witches was a valuable source of capital with which to finance the war effort. Besides this, there were many carpenters, judges, jailers, exorcists, woodcutters, and executioners who had an economic reason to see the bloodbath continue. By the time the people had regained their senses and the Inquisition had come to a screeching halt in the late seventeenth century, an untold number of victims had been burned, strangled, hanged, or tortured to death.[1]

But while the tragic farce had been conducted, a strange metamorphosis had taken place. The Inquisition, which had convicted a multitude of peasants for worshiping the Devil, had found itself caught up in a self-fulfilling prophecy; it had created a new vision.

Satan had begun to change in appearance by the time of the first mass executions for witchcraft in the fifteenth century. He had shed his snakeskin and had grown a coat of fur and horns. He had become hoofed and shaggy. He had become Pan and Priapus and Cernunnos and Loki and Odin and Thor and Dionysus and Isis and Diana. He had become the god of fertility and abundance and lust. He was the lascivious goat, the mysterious black ram. He was all of nature and indeed life itself to the peasant, who had often lived on the verge of starvation due to the crushing taxes of the feudal aristocracy. He was sex, and since to the peasant sex was identical to creation itself, and was one of the few pleasures not open to taxation, he was their god.

The Church's fanatical asceticism, its rabid identification of sex with evil, added to the Devil's strength. The Inquisitors, with an image of Satan and his hellish activities imprinted on their brains, slowly managed to stamp the image on the minds of the peasantry. It was through their dogged efforts that Satan became the savior of man.

[1]Estimates range from several hundred thousand to 9 million.

CHAPTER III

The Sabbat and the Esbat

Underneath all the tales there does lie something different from the tales. How different? In this—that the thing which is invoked is a thing of a different nature, however it may put on a human appearance or indulge in its servants their human appetites. It is cold, it is hungry, it is violent, it is illusory. The warm blood of children and intercourse at the Sabbath do not satisfy it. It wants something more and other; it wants "obedience," it wants "souls," and yet it pines for matter. It never was, and yet it always is.

—Charles Williams, *Witchcraft*

The texts of the Inquisition all gave serious consideration to those meetings held in desolate and lonely places, usually on isolated mountaintops or in forest clearings, to which Satanists and witches flocked in great numbers. By the fourteenth century, the Inquisitors no longer felt that these meetings with Diana and Hecate were imaginary, but that they were all too real. The witches were supposed to have arrived by the thousands to pay homage to Satan, to report on their own latest evil accomplishments, and to partake in the most heated debaucheries of the ceremonies.

The festivals were called Sabbat and were held on regularly appointed days, the big dates being Roodmas Day, or Walpurgisnacht (April 30), All Hallows' Eve (October 31), Candlemas (February 2), and Lammas Day (August 1). It has been postulated by Margaret Murray and others that these celebrations were pre-Christian and, in fact, pre-agricultural in orgin, because the dates follow a May-November year, a division of time that corresponds to neither the solstices nor any known planting season. This points to the probability that these festivals were remnants of fertility celebrations, held during the livestock-breeding seasons to promote fecundity among the animal herds. This theory would also help to explain the presence of much of the animal symbolism during the ceremonies.

Since the festivals were concerned primarily with fertility, and since in the primitive mind the entire universe revolves around the cosmic law of imitation, likes attracting and opposites repelling, it is only natural that the basis of the festivals was sex. Sexual acts were performed publicly by the actors, who were often dressed in masks and animal skins, in order to ensure fertility among the herds. Since the main food sources for the peasant were sheep and cattle, the principle actors in the drama would appear in the guise of a bull or a ram—the horned god!

Some experts, like historian Norman Cohn, fail to believe in the reality of the witch cult at all, terming the four centuries of the Inquisition a tragic, paranoid fantasy dreamed up by the Inquisitors and confirmed by torture. As evidence, he cites the fact that the stories of the Sabbat did not appear in eastern Europe at all, a curious absence if a fertility religion was as widespread as claimed.

Others, like Richard Cavendish, point out that in England, one of the last bastions of paganism in western Europe, there is no evidence that the pagan cults survived later than 1035, and that on the Continent, they seemed to have died out long before that. Cavendish believes that the witch cult existed, but identifies it as a new sect on the scene. "The principal beliefs and rituals of medieval witches," he asserts, "seem to have come from the Cathars, the Luciferans and other sects accused of worshipping the Devil. It is also likely that the persecutions of Satanist sects and the witch trials themselves stimulated the activities they were intended to suppress."[1]

Whatever their origin, the rites were attributed by the Inquisitors to the Devil, and immediate steps were taken to stamp them out.

Undoubtedly, the orgiastic abominations practiced at the Sabbats were fueled and embellished by the repressed sexual fantasies of the Inquisitors themselves. The fan-

[1]Cavendish, Richard, *The Black Arts*, New York: Capricorn, 1968, p.

tasies were "proof" that they were on the right track, that Satan himself was punishing them for their righteousness, for was that not the way the Devil worked, tormenting man and hoping to secure his fall through his own carnal appetites?

The Dominicans viewed their hallucinations as an affidavit that Satan was running scared, that he was trying desperately to corrupt them, to fatigue their spiritual purity by working on their bodies. After a day of testimony, hearing detailed descriptions of the sexual orgies of the Sabbats, the Inquisitors would retire to their chambers and attempt to sleep, but they found themselves unable to close their eyes, still tormented by visions of the hellish congregations indulging in the most perverted sexual practices. When sleep finally did come, it was not peaceful, but filled with demons in the shape of succulent young maidens shedding their clothing. The Inquisitors were certain that they had uncovered Satan's lair, else why would they be tormented so by succubi?

According to Inquisition testimony, Satanist meetings followed two forms, that of the Sabbat and the more local meeting known as the Esbat. The two types differed mainly in function and size. The Esbat was primarily held for the purpose of transacting business, which usually meant the working of magic, either to accomplish some act of Satanic mischief or to perform a magical rite for an outside, paying customer. Since the Satanists found themselves surrounded by enemies, it is natural that most of this magic was for the purpose of working *maleficium*, or harm, to their persecutors; but occasionally magic was practiced in order to aid a friend or ally.

The magical nature of Esbats contrasted with the more religious function of the Sabbat. At the Esbat, the coven master appeared among the congregation in the normal dress of the day, not in costume as he appeared at the Sabbat. There was much less ceremony involved, the performance of the religious ceremony and the obsequious adoration of the Devil being supplanted by the working of spells and charms. Few of the meetings were ever strictly business, religious elements always being present. The meetings often concluded, like the Sabbat, with feasting, dancing, and sometimes sexual indulgence.

There is still much debate among experts as to the size

of the Esbat meetings. Some, like Margaret Murray, argue that the number in a coven never varied, always being thirteen—twelve in the congregation, plus a master. Catholic scholars, such as Montague Summers, are quick to agree with this theory, seeing the scheme as a blasphemous parody of Christ and the twelve apostles. Other researches insist just as emphatically that the number in the covens was never fixed at thirteen, or at any other number.

The number 13 has undoubtedly possessed great fascination for man throughout his historic and prehistoric past, and has taken on the aspects of a mystical number, embedded in his collective unconscious, just as the number 7 has been for time immemorial a number possessed of magical properties.

Since 13 is the number following the perfect cycle of 12, it is symbolic of death or the unknown. In cartomancy, the ace of spades, the thirteenth card in the suit, is in many cases a symbol of death. Triskaidekaphobia, the neurotic fear of the number 13, is obviously a manifestation at an unconscious level of this representation. Many hotels and office buildings, in an effort to allay any such fears on the part of their inhabitants, eliminate the thirteenth floor. Many judicial systems, including our own, involve the number 13—a judge and twelve jurors. King Arthur and his twelve knights, Robin Hood and his twelve Merry Men are both indicative of the pattern. Lastly, Pennethorne Hughes points out that in Granada, Spain, anthropologists recently uncovered a Neolithic "Cave of Bats," in which were found twelve skeletons seated in a circle around another skeleton, which was dressed in a leather skin.

Thus the number 13 does not appear to be a parody of Christian mythology, as it was later believed, but seems to share a singular place in man's collective unconscious. It is quite possible, therefore, that some covens might have been fixed at thirteen members. But the evidence from the witch trials tends to corroborate the view that the number of members in covens varied, depending on how many members showed up.

The Esbats were held in or around the village where its members lived, sometimes at a member's house, or in a graveyard, or at a crossroads near the village, in accordance with the old Thessalian cults of Hecate. Unlike the Sabbats, which were fixed calendrically, Esbats were not established as to day, or even hour. Though held quite regularly, at least once a week in most villages, Esbats could be held during the day or night, the Grand Master letting the members know of the meeting's date, place, and time by sending word through an officer.

The Sabbat, however, due to its function and size, was specified as to time and date. Accounts vary greatly as to the number of witches in attendance at these festivals, but most agree that they were large. Some witches stated that the numbers were in the thousands for some ceremonies, but these estimates are almost surely high. The large numbers involved, at any rate, imposed certain restrictions on the meetings, forcing them to be held at night and in isolated locations. Secrecy was imperative, for discovery meant certain death.

The Devil himself invariably presided at the important Sabbats, in the personage of the Grand Master of the region. Appearing in the guise of a black ram, he was an awesome sight, hoofed and often taloned, wearing a great goat mask, a consecrated candle glowing between his horns. Some accounts have him appearing in the likeness of a bull or as a tall, black man (an effect probably accomplished with charcoal or greasepaint), but the goat costume seems to have been the favorite guise.

Seated on a black throne, Satan began the meeting by reading the roll call of members from a book he had in his possession. As their names were pronounced, witches reported their activities—their magical successes or failures—since the last Sabbat. If the number of participants was exceedingly large, it is most likely that the report would have been made by the different coven masters, as a large roll call would have imposed a time problem. The coven master was responsible for his coven's behavior at the Sabbat and acted as the enforcer of discipline on the individual members.

After the roll call, the Devil admitted new members. The initiation proceedings were not unique in conception, the symbolism of the rite recurring time and time again throughout man's religious history; in this respect, they serve to point up the psychological motivations of joiners of all religious secret societies and thus help link the Satanism of the past with that of the present.

First, the initiate had to enter the cult of his own free will. This requirement was misleading, however, for the methods of recruitment employed by the groups varied according to necessity. Many had been brought up into the religion from childhood by relatives or friends who were already Satanists, for the Devil demanded at the meetings that the witches bring children to the Sabbats for conversion.

All members were brought into the movement by other members; lovers brought lovers, relatives brought relatives, the recruits being lured by the promises made them by the recruiters. Sex, money, power, all those things that man might wish for, that were denied him by the social structure, acted as bait. But force was not unknown in the recruitment process, and in cases of vacillation, beatings, barn burnings, and extortion were powerful weapons in securing members.

Second, the initiate had to make an explicit disavowal of the Christian faith. The symbolic quality of this disavowal is obvious, for being an anti-Christian movement, Satanism deprecated Christian belief. At another level, this practice served a further purpose, for in defiling certain holy relics, in trampling or defecating on the crucifix, in blaspheming God and the Church, a clear break was made with the old way of life. Any latent feelings the initiate felt for the old religion were quickly erased; he had nowhere to go but in.

The third initiation requirement was that the initiate had to make a pact with the Devil, which usually involved signing a contract to do Satan's work for a specified period of time. This vow of obedience usually employed as a writing fluid the blood of the signer, which was extracted from the arm or the finger. The symbolism behind this part of the ceremony is clear, blood being a traditional symbol for the life force, or the soul.

Fourth, the initiate had to receive the "witches' mark," a permanent scar, probably a form of tattoo, which was placed somewhere on the initiate's body that was not readily visible, usually under the arm or on the genitals. This mark was not unique to Satanism, but has its counterpart all over the world in the subincision rites of initiation on primitive societies, mutilation of the initiate's body seemingly functioning as a symbol of regeneration or rebirth. Before being born into a new life, in which higher mysteries will be revealed to him, the initiate must first "die," the mutilation serving in this capacity as a partial or substitute death.

Some interesting theories of the psychological nature of circumcision have been forwarded in recent years, throwing a new cast on such practices. Mircea Eliade states that subincision functions symbolically in two ways: as a means of obtaining new blood (blood being a universal symbol of fertility), and second, to symbolically give the male neophyte a female sex organ so that he will resemble the tribal divinities, who were, in many cases, bisexual. This possibly has some validity, taking into consideration the fact that Satan is often pictured as a hermaphroditic deity, having a male phallus and the breasts of a woman. One apparent flaw in the hypothesis is that it would not readily apply to female members. In many cases, however, the "mark" did not exist as such for the female witches, but was replaced by a wart or teat, by which she was supposed to feed her demon familiars.

Aside from the psychological possibilities, there are more likely sociological reasons for the occurrence of the mark. Scarring the members in such a fashion would provide an easy method of identification, and this would necessarily act as a deterrent to informers from within. The potential informer would be reluctant to go to the authorities, knowing that his mark would provide him with a surefire ticket to the executioner. Certain Inquisitional testimony tends to show that this was foremost in the minds of the Satanic masters, for in several cases testimony was offered stating that the Devil only marked those members whose fidelity he was not sure of.

Following the admission of new members, the formal business was concluded and the religious service began. An animal was sacrificed at the altar—a goat or hen, always pure black in color. The the participants lined up in order to pay homage to Satan. The traditional bowing and scraping was followed by the *osculum infame*, or "Kiss of Shame," a ritual kiss planted on the Devil's buttocks.

It is often said by experts that such accounts were

invented by the Inquisitors to make the proceedings appear more degenerate than they in fact were, but in reality such acts of self abasement are common among secret societies, since they serve not only to demonstrate the member's unbounding loyalty to the cause but also to carry the member one step further beyond the limits of conventional morality. The Mau Mau, for example, used such self-abasement rituals, the repulsiveness of the rite increasing proportionally to the degree of initiation. One of the final Mau Mau initiation degrees, the *batuni*, required the neophyte to put his penis through a hole that had been made in the skinned thorax of a goat. In light of such barbaric practices, the kiss of shame, as it later came to be called by the Inquisitors, was a relatively mild swearing of fealty.

There is considerable speculation as to whether any ritualized parodies of the Christian Mass occurred during the Sabbat, but it is not unreasonable to suppose that there did, at least in limited form.

After the Mass, the feast began. Some accounts state that the food was abundant and delicious, consisting of succulent meats, bread, and wine. Others, primarily the Inquisitional authorities, again probably in an attempt to play down the pleasurable aspects of the Sabbat, testified that the food was only the most nauseating substance. However, the former is more likely, considering that most of the people had gorged themselves with food and drink before leaving the feast to dance.

The dancing was an important part of the ceremony, the particular ones performed likely being those of the local peasantry. It was wild and sensual, often obscene, and served to work the dancers up into a frenzy. When a fever pitch had been reached, the orgy began, Satan commencing the proceedings by copulating with every woman present. Since this feat would have been impossible even for the most virile man, and since many of the women participating described intercourse with the Devil as being painful, his penis being invariably large and cold, it is supposed by most authorities that a dildo made of leather or some other material was attached to the costume as a phallic fertility symbol and as an instrument of fornication.

After the Devil took his due, the men and women fell

madly upon each other, enacting the most extreme forms of debauchery, partaking in every possible heterosexual act.

Pennethorne Hughes describes the scene in vivid detail:

> Whoever stumbled on the occasion of a real Sabbat must have seen something very terrible. . . . They saw processions of rich and poor persons, perhaps naked, perhaps masked, bearing torches glowing with sulfurous flames. They saw it might be, the Hand of Glory itself—the human hand with the fingers ignited as candles. They saw even a devil god, monstrously masked, with a candle spluttering between its horns. They were seeing a degenerate form of the saturnalia of the classical world—a barbaric release into an even earlier worship.[2]

The Satanic rituals had been born out of the old pagan ways and had grown into something different with the passage of time. The pagan symbols had been twisted and wrenched violently into something negative, something *anti*. The old horned god had been converted into a symbol of hate and hope simultaneously. Through the smoke of the smoldering campfires, through the drifting odors of roasting lamb and deer, over the ecstatic cries of sexual release, the chanting of hatred had come to dominate all, until the reasons for the chanting had disappeared.

But even after the movement had died, something it had spawned lived on, and the chanting could still be heard echoing through the subterranean caverns of European society.

[2]Hughes, Pennethorne, *Witchcraft*, Hammondsworth: Penguin, 1970, p. 135.

CHAPTER IV

The Black Mass

> The madness of desire, insane murders, the most
> unreasonable passions—all are wisdom and reason,
> since they are a part of the order of nature. Every-
> thing that morality and religion, everything that a
> clumsy society has stifled in man, revives in the castle
> of murders. There man is finally attuned to his own
> nature. . . .
> —Michel Foucault, *Madness and Civilization*

The Black Mass, the Catholic Mass perverted for the
purpose of defiling the image of God and worshiping
Satan, turned out to be the residue left in the crucible of
the burned-out Satanic movement by the end of the
seventeenth century. The scientific rationality then sweep-
ing European intellectual circles numbered the days of the
dreaded Inquisition. A latent result of the demise of
religious repression was the wasting away of the rebellious Satanist movement, which it had triggered. The
mountaintops and meadows at Walpurgisnacht and All
Hallows' Eve lay silent and still, no longer spotted by
flickering fires, no longer echoing the cries of laughter and
orgiastic rebellion. But a part of the ceremony remained.
The nature of its practice changed and its location moved
indoors, but the Mass remained in certain social circles,
its ritual hideous or ridiculous, depending on its practitioners.

In the more publicized variety of Black Mass, the
Catholic missal is read backward in Latin or, more
commonly, with parts excluded, and with word substitutions such as "Satan" for "God" and "evil" for "good." The
altar is either a naked woman or a coffin, and all the
religious artifacts, including the ritual chamber, are

black. The priests wear black robes, usually with cowls. Frequently there are substitutions for the consecrated wine—sometimes human urine. The Host is usually a holy sacrament that has been stolen from a church, but sometimes it is made of some obnoxious substance, such as dried feces, which is either eaten or smeared on the face. The significance of these sacramental materials lies in the fact that they are bodily products, as opposed to spiritual, and, as such, are pleasing to Satan, who is a carnal deity.

Some students of the subject reject the presence of the Mass in Satanism before the advent of the eighteenth century. Rossell Hope Robbins expresses the belief that the Mass was a "literary creation," inspired by such writers as the Marquis de Sade, who popularized such abominations in his famous novel *Justine*. Robbins admits that isolated practices, such as desecration of the Host, occurred as early as the fourteenth century, but denies that these were a regular part of the Sabbat. Later, imaginative authors such as de Sade picked up the ideas for these practices from biased Inquisitional testimony, he asserts, and used them in their works. Thus the ritual Black Mass was born not out of early Satanism, but out of horror fiction.

It must be kept in mind that the Inquisitors were so firmly convinced that certain horrendous activities took place at the Sabbats that they refused to admit evidence to the contrary. Devil worship was entirely antithetical to Christian belief and ritual, with the ceremonies complete inversions of Christian practices; this was apparent and indisputable to them. Any accused witch who denied the facts sought by the Inquisitors was proclaimed to be lying and was tortured until a "confession" was acquired.

Granting this fact, evidence indicates that the Mass really did exist, and was not a dream created by the Dominican friars, or a concept from the fertile imaginations of fiction writers. For example, in England torture was not allowed officially, and while it did exist *sub rosa*, it was in no extent comparable to that of the Continent. But still, even there, reports of early rituals that parodied the Mass and mocked God flowed from the mouths of the accused. Second, the nature of the Satanic movement—a violent reaction against the brutal and hypocritical practices of Christianity—would dictate the necessity of such a ritual in one form or another. Since *Justine* was not written until 1791, and since evidence is present of purely anti-Christian liturgy in Satanic ceremonies well before that in too great a frequency to label them "isolated occurrences," it is necessary to conclude that Robbins's theory is too simple and totally inadequate.

The only conclusion that would take into account all the facts is that the Black Mass not only existed, at least in shortened form, in early Satanic ritual, but that it existed on a dual plane, with two different frames of social reference both in practice and in function. Among the peasantry at the Sabbats, it was born out of ritual rebellion and fulfilled a cathartic function for the performer, while for the group as a whole it preserved group solidarity by providing a means of alienating members from the external Christian world. In the upper classes, on the other hand, it was born out of the early Catholic Amatory and Death Masses, and was performed usually for magical purposes, in order to secure some benefit for the celebrant. Only later, when the Inquisition had taken public credibility to its limits, did the Black Mass become an amusement, a plaything by which the aristocracy institutionalized its own sexual perversions.

As performed at the Sabbat, the Black Mass was clearly a case of ritual rebellion. Probably the earliest evidence of such happenings was brought to light in Ireland in 1324, with the trial of Lady Alice Kyteler. She was accused of practicing witchcraft, of denying the Christ by defiling certain holy articles, of sacrificing animals at crossroads, and of having had sexual intercourse with an incubus (a demon appearing in the form of a man). In her possession was found a holy wafer on which Jesus' name had been replaced by that of the Devil.

As time went on, the Mass portion of the Sabbat became more formalized, reaching a peak at the time of the severest persecutions, in the late sixteenth and early seventeenth centuries. Although there is a wide geographical separation of the witch trials, the accounts of the Mass that spewed from the pens of the Inquisitors showed great similarities. These accounts usually involved reading the Lord's Prayer backward, partaking of an infernal sacrament, and sometimes carrying out a rebaptism in the Devil's name.

The reversal of word order that occurred in early diabolic rites, for the purpose of unworking that which had already been done, is a common practice in imitative magic, and is encountered quite often in psychotic patients. As puerile and absurd as the practice might seem to scientific man, to a primitive who believes that the tying of a knot means the casting of a spell, and the untying of the knot signifies the breaking of the spell, this reversal of rite must have seemed altogether logical. In fact, modern man has not lost all his contacts with the imitative world of the magician, for he practices this ritual when he curses someone for whom he feels an intense dislike; the curse is merely a reversal of a blessing, the words "God damn him" being substituted for "God bless him."

At Aix, in 1610, Madeleine de Demandoix spoke of a Mass being celebrated at the Sabbat by an officiating priest, who consecrated the sacrament and blessed the congregation by sprinkling them with wine. Henri Boguet in 1590 described a Mass in which the rite performed by the priest involved placing water in the chalice instead of wine, turning his back to the altar, and elevating a black turnip slice instead of a wafer. At this point, the witches were supposed to have said in unison, "Master, help us!" This ritual was reflective of the nocturnal rites of the older Luciferans. In Scotland and Sweden, the Devil who presided over the Sabbat and performed the baptism and sacramental rites was supposed to have been a defrocked priest. Communion in these instances consisted of wafers made from bread and drink that was sometimes blood, sometimes black moss-water.

The meaning of all these practices becomes more apparent when viewed in an anthropological context, for the Black Mass, as practiced by the peasantry, was basically a reversal of rite, comparable to instances of ritual rebellion found more infrequently among primitive societies. Such behavior helps to canalize feelings of resentment toward conventional norms and social customs that a primitive people may find alien to them. A passage recorded in 1881 demonstrates this:

The dancers suddenly wheeled into line, threw themselves on their knees before my table, and with extravagant beatings of their breast began an outlandish and fanciful mockery of a Mexican Catholic congregation at vespers. One bawled out a parody upon the pater-noster, another mumbled along in the manner of an old man reciting the rosary, while the fellow with the India-rubber coat jumped up and began a passionate exhortation of a sermon, which for its mimetic fidelity was incomparable.[1]

This particular ceremony ended with the actors swallowing large quantities of human urine.

This is not an eyewitness account of a medieval Black Mass, but a description of a ritual rebellion performed by Zuni Indians. Nor is it unique in its execution, for ritual burlesque and reversal of normal behavior are common practices among certain North American Indian tribes, especially those bearing natural resentment for the white man and his ways. It is significant, perhaps, to note that around the time this ceremony was witnessed, the resentment for white culture and Catholic missionaries was particularly acute, a time when old social patterns were rapidly breaking down in many tribes, a time when the Ghost Dance, a messianic religious movement, was spreading among the Western Plains Indians.

Although it is obviously dangerous, due to vast cultural differences, to draw an analogy between the social positions of the American Indian in the 1880s and the European serf of the fourteenth century, the crisis period of tradition experienced by both might be legitimately compared in certain respects.

Both groups found themselves stifled by an encroaching, alien force that spelled out death for their old way of life. Ways of life die hard, and seldom without a fight. If the odds are greatly uneven, as they were for the American Indian and the European serf, and physical combat is not practical, then man is forced to go underground with his pent-up emotions to carry on the fight from there. Frequently, the struggle appears to those on the outside to be

[1]Norbeck, Edward, *Religion in Primitive Society*, London· Harper & Row, 1961, p. 208.

merely protest for the sake of protest, and often it is just that. But it is a means of striking back, nevertheless, and, as such, is a valuable possession for a man depossessed.

For the peasant, who saw himself victimized by Church, the Mass served such a purpose. It was a way of venting hatred, of outpouring all the frustrated energy accumulated by the years of humiliation suffered at the hands of the Church. It was a way of asserting his individuality, a way of thumbing his nose at God. Second, it served a social function, as said, by adding an extra binding force on the participants. By institutionalizing blasphemy, the Satanists provided a feeling of estrangement from the outer Christian world. By partaking in such a ceremony, the initiate broke claim to any Christian heritage by which he might have felt bounds, and became fully a part of the deviant culture that he entered. The Black Mass was a repeated denial of Christian dogma and a continual affirmation of the new faith.

But in the upper strata of society, another form of Mass was being performed, much different, much more complete and formalized, and more monstrous in its execution than its peasant counterpart. These were the rites that were to serve as the prototypes for the Black Masses of later fiction writers such as de Sade and Dennis Wheatley.

Some of the early instances of the Mass being employed for purposes other than worshiping God were in the Gnostic cults. The Cathari were reputed to have conducted parodies of the Mass and to have participated in perverted sexual acts during their rituals. The Luciferans, a group that flourished in the thirteenth century, were also accused of such practices. They, like the Gnostics, proclaimed the duality of the universe, the unresolvable and coeternal schism between light and darkness, good and evil. They worshiped Lucifer as the "bringer of light," the one true God, and considered the Christian God to be the supreme evil God, who had successfully tricked the world into believing that he represented goodness.

Certain charges leveled against the Luciferans by their Christian persecutors were obvious fabrications, but other accusations seem to have had an element of truth in them. They were reputed to have attended Christian Masses to partake of the sacrament; keeping the wafers in their mouths, they later spit them into a cesspool or in other ways defiled them. At their nocturnal meetings, the initiates were supposed to have for some obscure reason first kissed a toad, and then a tall, thin man who was described as having had cold lips. This man was reported by ecclesiasts to have been the Devil. A feast followed this, after which the lights were extinguished and an orgy ensued.

Those members who were interrogated described a curious symbol that they worshiped at the ceremonies. This was a human figure, its body being half gold, half black, obviously representing the dual nature of the universe, Lucifer being the gold or "light" side. It is not certain whether the figure was a statue or a real human being, since the accounts of the proceedings are so vague, but at any rate all the initiates tore off a piece of their clothing and presented it to the figure as a token of fealty.

The Knights Templar, also accused by the Church of having blasphemed the Mass, trampling the cross, rejecting Jesus as a "false prophet," and indulging in homosexual and onanistic acts during their ceremonies.

The Church did its best to suppress these heresies, but it had considerable difficulty, because the seeds from which they sprang were firmly planted within the Church itself. Superstition was rampant within the Church, and this superstition, coupled with the widespread corruption of the clergy, provided fertile soil for the growth of such illicit practices.

The efficacy of magic was widely believed among the clergy from the earliest times, and higher Christian officials, alarmed by the extent of such practices within the Church, often found it necessary to clamp down. In the thirteenth century, Pope Gregory IX passed a canon law forbidding priests to indulge in sorcery. But these edicts did little to curb the belief on the part of the clergy that magic really did work. People still made the long pilgrimage to the shrine of Saint Vitus to procure the touch of the saint who cured the disease named after him. Pope Gregory the Great in the sixth century had promoted such beliefs by recommending that penitents seek the help of the saints. Such superstitions were played upon by the priesthood, who saw in them a powerful means of manipulating the peasant masses.

The atmosphere of childish superstition pervaded the

Church, and even high officials were accused of practicing the black arts. In 1343, the bishop of Coventry was accused before the Pope of paying homage to the Devil. Pope Sylvester II, in the tenth century, was said to have been a sorcerer and was accused by many of having attained the papacy by magic. Pope Honorius III was rumored to have been a dabbler in magic, this assertion causing his name to be used later on a manual of black magic of doubtful authenticity, the *Constitution of Honorius the Great*. In 1401, Boniface IX absolved a priest named Otto Syboden for being concerned in an incantation to discover the location of some stolen money; the thief had supposedly died from the spell.

It was only natural that the Mass should become the vehicle for later Satanists, for the Mass was believed by all good Christians to be the ultimate magical ritual. During the ceremony, the priest was supposed to be possessed by the spirit of Christ, thus establishing direct contact with the secret powers of the heavens. But these powers were not exclusive; they could be used and abused, just like other magical forces. By reversal and substitution, such powers could be twisted to fit the needs of the performer. Thus as early as 681, the Council of Toledo prohibited the so-called Mass of the Dead, which was performed by priests for the purpose of securing someone's death.

The magical tradition of the Church was consistent, but the fruit was not to become truly ripe until economics came to play a major role in the drama. Many of the lesser priests came to be envious of their ecclesiastical superiors, whom they saw glutting themselves on the riches accumulated by the Church. In seeking to better their own lot, many of these lesser members of the clergy sought outside means of bolstering their support, even though the price of discovery was often excommunication.

By the sixteenth century, the practices of sorcery within the Church had become so widespread that Christianity found itself in the precarious position of having to separate, doctrinally, heretical from nonheretical sorcery. A long list of canons forbade the use of sacraments or holy objects in magical rituals or divination with holy water or blessed candles. The practice of sorcery with profane objects, it was decided, did not come under the jurisdiction of the Inquisition but was to be handled by secular authorities.

With the growth of the mercantile class, Masses performed for individuals who had the proper fee were common. To fill this growing need, a body of Mass priests was created who were hired to say these private Masses for an annual tribute. This group of priests were especially noted for its corruption and for its singular devotion to money. Members of the group were often found to be conducting rites too wild for the Catholic hierarchy to condone and were excommunicated. It was from this body of clergy that the modern Black Mass was to emerge.

In the sixteenth century, J. G. Sepúlveda, in his *De Vita Aegidii Albornotti*, described an order of priests called the Fraticelli, who were renegades of the Franciscan order. These monks were reported to have held nocturnal conventicles at which, after the service, indiscriminate intercourse was practiced. When a baby was the inadvertent product of one of these gatherings, its body was supposedly burned, the ashes being mixed in with wine that was served as a sacrament during the admission ceremonies of new members. Such reports of disaffected renegade priests conducting illicit Masses were not infrequent at the time.

One of the most notorious instances of the celebration of the Black Mass took place in France in the fifteenth century. Gilles de Rais, the original Bluebeard, was marshal of France and personal escort of Joan of Arc. After squandering away his vast fortune, he fell in with a Paduan alchemist by the name of Prelati, who promised to help him regain his lost wealth. According to the instructions of the magician, he began holding rituals in which he sacrificed young children to Satan. The sacrifices took place, however, only after he had satisfied his pedophilic desires by assaulting the children in the most brutal fashion. The victims were obtained either by outright abduction or by buying them from their peasant parents, who were glad enough to sell the children, thinking that they were being taken as servants and would have a much easier life on the estate of a rich nobleman than plowing the fields.

On the testimony of his wife, an investigation was conducted in 1440, and then the full horrendous nature of de Rais's activities was brought into the open. On his premises was found a chapel, complete with inverted cross and black candles. At the altar stood a statue of a hideous demon, presumably Satan. But that was not all that was found, for Gilles had been, among other things, a very systematic killer. One room contained copper vessels filled with the blood of his sacrificial victims, the vessels all bearing neat labels revealing the dates of execution. In the center of the room was a black marble table, upon which was the body of a child who had been freshly slaughtered. Breaking down under examination, de Rais confessed to having slain eight children and having plotted to take his ninth by tearing his own baby from his pregnant wife's womb. Later estimates put the number of boys he sacrificed to be much greater than eight, but there is little agreement on the number. After expressing his conviction that God would forgive him for his sins, he was burned at the stake.

Another case which achieved great notoriety in its day was that of Abbé Guiboug, which scandalized the royal court of Louis XIV and shook Paris social circles to their very core. Fearing an attempt on his life, Louis set up a special royal commission in 1679 to investigate certain cases of poisoning in the city. Arrests were made, one of the detained being a woman by the name of Catherine Deshayes, a self-proclaimed clairvoyant, whose house was a prominent social center in Paris. She was burned to death in 1680; soon after, more evidence began to surface, a rotting stench released from the depths of Parisian high society.

One of the most seriously implicated was the Marquise de Montespan, who had been for twelve years the King's mistress. Seeking to rise in the King's favor, and fearing to lose him as a lover, she had invoked the magical aid of Deshayes. Deshayes, in turn, had invested the aid of a priest named Mariette and another priest, Abbé Guibourg, who promised to help her in her quest in return for an ecclesiastical living.

Guibourg proceeded to conduct ritual Masses that called for blood sacrifice to Astaroth and Asmodeus, demons of love and lust. In the Mass, a child was sacrificed by cutting its throat and letting the blood pour into a chalice. To that blood, flour was added and a wafer made,

53

which was slipped to the unaware Louis by Madame de Montespan. This Love Mass was held three times. Later, in 1676, the Mass was held three more times, with Madame de Montespan acting as a naked altar. She was stretched out with a cross and chalice laid on her belly, while Guibourg consummated the child sacrifice over her. The children were obtained either by purchase or by kidnaping.

The marquise, despite her magical efforts, soon felt the pressures of competition and saw her firm grasp on the King's love slipping, as he went in search of younger liaisons. Jealousy turned her head, and the Amatory Masses, designed to bind love, were replaced by the Mass of Death. Finally, after repeated failure, more material means were tried, and an attempt was made on Louis's life by the use of a poison petition. This attempt was also abortive and an investigation was begun.

The investigatory council established by the King uncovered the vastness of the plot, and during the inquiry 367 persons were arrested, many of the accused being members of the Catholic priesthood. Only 74 of the offenders were sentenced, for Louis, learning the facts, stifled the inquiry in an attempt to keep the public from becoming aware of the corruption of his own court. Madame de Montespan was given her freedom and Guibourg was sentenced to prison, where he died three years later.

The fact that this plot had been so widespread and that many of the legitimate clergy had been involved suggests that these practices were more than merely "isolated instances." The operators, seeking personal gain, sought to get what they wished from any source that would give it to them, and they were willing to prostrate themselves before any deity, good or evil, to accomplish their goals. It can hardly be said that the Guibourg Masses were a direct outgrowth of the fiction of de Sade, for *Justine* was not to be written for over a hundred years yet. Nor could it be said that this occurrence of the Black Mass was original in its conception, for although Guibourg did add his own personal touches to the ceremony, such as using Madame de Montespan as a naked altar, the rite had its counterparts elsewhere.

Jean Bodin, in his *Démonomanie des Sorciers*, wrote of a

Black Mass that was performed by Catherine de Médicis in order to save the life of her son Charles IX. The ritual was analogous to the one of Guibourg—the sacramental elements being black, the Host white; a young child being sacrificed by cutting his throat, then catching the warm blood in a chalice. It seems obvious that officials within the Church and without believed in the existence of such practices by renegade priests.

The dark tradition of the Church has been so consistent that even today, in areas where religious pressure is still strong, reports of religious oddities occasionally come to the attention of the authorities. It is said that in parts of Normandy a blasphemous rite known as the Mass of the Holy Ghost is performed for the purpose of fulfilling a personal request. In the Isle of Man, in the 1940s, legal proceedings were brought against certain priests for singing psalms of destruction against people.

By the eighteenth century, another form of Black Mass had evolved. With the dawn of The Enlightenment, the ascendance of science, and the popularization of such cynics as Voltaire and Swift, a sharp break in man's attitude toward man and toward religion occurred. For the first time in centuries he began to look at himself and his society less seriously. With this new perspective, man's religions also changed, and Satanism did, too.

The colossal, ominous figure of Satan, which had struck men dumb with terror and awe, had by the eighteenth century acquired the status of a carnival freak. As popular cynicism negated belief in his actual material existence, he became less a godhead through which man increased his own power of manipulating the environment—less a godhead that was actually summoned and employed.

Instead, Satan became the plaything of aristocratic rakes who were searching for a neo-religious creed with which to intertwine their sexual practices. These men were seeking the assistance of Satan to institutionalize their perversions, to give them that extra touch of unique-ness without which they would quickly seem insipid and boring. These were the infamous Hellfire Clubs.

There were several Hellfire Clubs in existence by the 1730s. A Mr. Connally held Satanic orgies at his hunting lodge on Mount Pelier in Ireland, where, it was rumored, mock crucifixions were held. There was a Hellfire Club in Dublin and one in London, but the most famous was the one organized at West Wycombe in the 1750s under the leadership of Sir Francis Dashwood.

These Black Masses were held in an elaborate abbey built especially for the purpose; processions of white-and-red-robed, torch-bearing monks were seen, floating down the misty Thames at night on rafts toward the abbey. Women were imported and dressed in "nuns' robes" to complete the sacrilege. The ubiquitous inverted crucifix and black candles were present, the Mass being performed over an altar consisting of a naked girl. Sacrificial wine was poured and tasted from the girl's navel.

The Hellfire Clubs were merely an excuse for sexual debauchery and little else. Blood sacrifice and other of the more abominable practices of earlier Satanic groups were not employed, and there is little evidence that members actually took the religious part of the ceremony seriously. For instance, one of the tools used by the "nuns" was a device called the *idolum tentiginis*, or "lustful toy." This essentially was a hobbyhorse with the head of a bird, the head turned around so that the phallus-shaped beak was on its back. The women would mount and ride the "toy" until they were sufficiently aroused for the mass orgy that would inevitably follow. Incest was a common practice at the meetings. Many of the male participants reached impotency at a very early age, and several died of venereal diseases.

The monks of the group, known as the Unholy Twelve (the number present at the ceremonies always being thirteen—Dashwood and twelve others—in this case definitely a parody of Christ and the twelve apostles), included some of the most influential political and literary figures of the day: the Earl of Sandwich, First Lord of the Admiralty; the Earl of Bute, Prime Minister of England; poet Charles Churchill; Thomas Potter, son of the archbishop of Canterbury; John Wilkes, member of Parliament and vocal proponent of democracy; satirist George Selwyn; and famed novelist Laurence Sterne. It is even said that Benjamin Franklin, a personal friend of Dashwood's, visited the abbey during his brief stay in England. In its heyday, from 1745 to 1768, the club was a significant force in English politics, and the length of its existence demonstrates the extent to which public tolerance was stretched by the Enlightenment.

After the decline of the Hellfire Clubs in England, Satanism also went into decline, or rather a state of temporary hibernation. When it reemerged toward the latter part of the nineteenth century, Lucifer had regained at least a part of his terrifying majesty, and the name of Satan was again to shake the world.

In 1848, Pope Gregory XVI condemned the widely publicized sect of Eugène Vintras, a Catholic prophet who, at his Church at Carmel, in France, held "White Masses" at which certain miraculous events took place, such as chalices overflowing with blood and blood appearing on the Host. Vintras claimed that he was holding these rites in order to counteract the evil effects engendered by Satanists, who were performing Black Masses for magical purposes. Vintras conducted these Masses for the benefit of clients who felt themselves to be plagued by evil forces.

The fact that the sect was proclaimed heretical by the papacy does not mean that the Masses being held were Black, but, interestingly enough, the famous magician Eliphas Levi, who later visited the group, reported that the Host used in the ceremonies was of a reddish color, triangular in shape, and most definitely Satanic, while the robes worn bore an inverted cross.

After the death of Vintras, the cult was taken over by Abbé Boullan, a defrocked priest who also claimed to be a white magician. The Masses were said before an altar surmounted by a cross, on top of which was the sign of the tetragram, a traditional magical symbol representing the four elements and used in the conjuration of elementary spirits.

If Vintras's Satanism was suspect, there seems little doubt about Boullan's. In 1859, he and his mistress, Adèle Chevalier, a former nun, had founded the Society for the Reparation of Souls, which specialized in exorcism rites. Part of these bizarre rites consisted of force-feeding the "possessed" consecrated Hosts that had been mixed with human feces, and the performance of Black Masses, during one of which Boullan and Chevalier sacrificed their own bastard son.

When he met Vintras, Boullan became a convert, but after Vintras's death the new self-appointed Supreme Pontiff began to introduce new elements into the church services. He taught his followers that the road to salvation lay in fornicating with angels, this being done mainly through a combination of imagination and masturbation, with sexual intercourse between members and a little bestiality thrown in for good measure.

To the public, Boullan promoted himself as a lone crusader of good, locked in a life-and-death struggle with evil, embodied in the personage of Stanislas de Guaita, head of the Rosicrucian Society in Paris. After being accused by de Guaita of being a Satanist, Boullan publicly returned the accusation, and when Boullan died in 1893, his followers claimed it had been the result of a "psychic attack" launched by de Guaita and his fellow Rosicrucians.

The death of Boullan did not bring the affair to a close, however, for matters were confused by the publication of a book by J. K. Huysmans, called *Là-Bas*. The book was written as fiction, yet it was also claimed by Huysmans to have been based on fact. The author boasted that he had attended a real Black Mass, although this has never been verified.

In *Là-Bas*, evil is represented by Canon Docre, a priest who is believed by some to have been in real life a man by the name of Roca. Opposing him is a Dr. Johannes, supposedly a characterization of Boullan. There are some who believe, however, that the Roca figure, the antagonist of the book, was really the good man, locked in spiritual combat with the malevolent Boullan. Boullan was said by these critics to have preached that sex was the road to salvation, and he supposedly conducted obscene rites, at which female members were encouraged to indulge in sexual intercourse with spirits and even with Christ himself.

The theory that Boullan was Dr. Johannes in the book and represented the forces of good is most likely, considering that Huysmans knew Boullan and, apparently, from the tone of some of his letters, sympathized with him.

The important thing to note about the Boullan episode is not the actual culprits involved, but rather the conception of the Mass. The Boullan rituals were far toward the magical end of the continuum, the forces invoked being more mechanical and more certain than those in the old religious services. The Mass was conceived, even by its "white" practitioners, as a manipulative tool, a vehicle for the harnessing of magical powers rather than as a calling upon the Christ for aid and intervention. It was part of the arsenal of weapons to be used by either side in the eternal battle between good and evil.

The Black Masses performed by Docre in *Là-Bas* were held in a deserted chapel. On the altar was a crucifix bearing a twisted figure with a peculiarly elongated neck, his mouth shaped in a hideous grin. Black candles were used, and hallucinogenic substances were burned in place of incense. Docre wore a red biretta with bison horns and a red chasuble. During the proceedings, the Host was thrown on the floor by the priest, the congregation rushing in a frenzy to trample and otherwise mutilate it. The evil Docre also reportedly fed consecrated Hosts to animals that had been simultaneously given graduated doses of poison. Once the animal's bloodstream had become completely polluted, the blood was extracted and used as poison by which to kill unfortunate victims.

Another Mass described by Huysmans was a Death Mass called the Mass of Saint Sécaire. In the rite, the sign of the cross was made on the ground, with the left foot. The Host was triangular and black, and water was substituted for wine in the ceremony, the preferred fluid being well water in which an unbaptized baby had been drowned.

Such accounts have been scoffed at, but it is more than likely that part of the ceremonies that Huysmans described did have basis in fact. Around the time he was writing *Là-Bas*, some very strange reports began to surface. In 1889, in the newspaper *Le Matin*, a writer described a Black Mass that he had attended: The altar was surrounded by six black candles, above which there was a painting of a goat trampling on a crucifix. The priest wore a red robe and performed the ceremony over a naked woman. Black Hosts were consumed, and the congregation, after chanting a series of hymns praising the Devil, fell upon one another in a frantic orgy.

In 1895, in the Palazzo Borghese in Rome, an odd chapel was discovered. The walls of the chapel were done in scarlet and black, and black candles surrounded the altar, on which a figure of Satan majestically sat. The decorations were extravagant, thus forcing the conclusion that

Satan had wealthy followers in the holy city. Thefts of wafers from churches were common during this period and church vandalism was widespread.

Things once more quieted down with the turning of the century, but not for long. In the 1920s, new reports of Satanism began to spread. Rumors of a reborn Hellfire Club began to circulate in London. William Seabrook, an American author, claimed to have attended Black Masses several times during the twenties and thirties in Lyons, Paris, London, and New York. The Satanists he encountered worshiped Lucifer, the fallen angel, who they believed had always had more power on earth than God. Their goal was to restore him to the "throne of the universe," these strains echoing the tenets of the old Luciferans. Although the cults were seven hundred years apart, they were both born out of the same need; they were both nativistic, seeking restoration in a time of social turmoil.

The four essentials of the ceremony as described by Seabrook are: an apostate priest, a consecrated Host, a prostitute, and a virgin. In front of the altar, which is surmounted by an inverted crucifix on which lies a naked virgin, a black-robed priest recites the Lord's Prayer backward in Latin. The prostitute, in a red robe, serves as an acolyte, and the chalice of wine is placed between the breasts of the virgin altar, part of it being spilled over her body. The Host is then debased instead of being elevated, and is defiled. Although Seabrook makes no mention of how the Host is defiled, it was most likely placed in the vagina of the prostitute, or urinated upon by her.

This version of the Mass is recurrent throughout the period, and in many cases, with variations, is the form followed today. In many areas, the ceremony has degenerated into a racket, in which tourists, for example, are brought to "authentic" rituals for a price. Princess Irene of Greece recently said she had attended such a ceremony in a Paris cellar. Gerald Gardner, the famous white witch of the Isle of Man, claimed that he had been invited in 1952, for a price, to attend a Black Mass in Rome. The ritual was supposed to have been performed by defrocked priests and nuns.

In the early 1960s, in the British Isles, evidence of Satanist groups operating there began to crop up.

Churches were vandalized, graves disturbed, and mysterious magical symbols were inscribed on church walls. In Ayrshire, Scotland, in 1964, a minister reported that he had found that Black Masses were being held in a ruined seventeenth-century church. Among the pieces of evidence he found were a partially destroyed Bible, a broken chalice, and an inverted cross inscribed above the altar. Similar events took place a year earlier in a church in Essex. Weird animal sacrifices began to turn up with alarming frequency, pointing to the possibility of a Satanic tie-in.

In Switzerland, in 1966, in the little town of Helikon, a so-called religious group known as the Seekers of Mercy was broken up by police when a young girl who had been under its care mysteriously died. The Seekers' "church" was fully equipped, right down to a torture chamber, and the investigation revealed that the girl had been sexually assaulted and brutally whipped while tied to an inverted cross. Black candles were found on the premises, and the ceremonies that had been held there were apparently akin to the Black Masses a la the Marquis de Sade.

But such practices of the Mass have been largely isolated incidents, particularly in recent years. This seems to be corroborated in recent newspaper accounts of youthful rituals. Even among the violent cults, the formal, stylized elements of the Mass are absent. Rituals today are more apt to be influenced by horror movies and Stephen King novels, and accompanied by the strains of heavy metal music rather than Church hymns sung backward.

CHAPTER V

The Journey to America

> By the sympathy of your human hearts for sin ye shall scent out all the places—whether in church, bed chamber, street, field, or forest—where crime has been committed, and shall exult to behold the whole earth one stain of guilt, one mighty blood spot. Far more than this. It shall be yours to penetrate, in every bosom, the deep mystery of sin, the fountain of all wicked arts, and which inexhaustively supplies more evil impulses than human power—than my power at its utmost—can make manifest in deeds. And now, my children, look upon each other.
>
> —Nathaniel Hawthorne, "Young Goodman Brown"

In America, from the beginning, the witchcraft cases were more sporadic and less clearly of a religious nature than those in Europe. That the practice of witchcraft existed among the more superstitious settlers (who were considerable in number) is obvious, but it is unlikely that Satanism in its European forms—that is, as an organized religious movement—found its way into the early colonies.

Laws defining witchcraft as having league with the Devil and prescribing the death penalty for such offenders cropped up in the colonies as early as 1636 in Plymouth. Other colonies soon followed suit—Connecticut in 1642 and Rhode Island in 1647. The first executions took place in Boston in 1648 and in Hartford, Connecticut, in that same year. The executions were carried out by hanging, in contrast to the European practice of burning witches, which probably stemmed from the widespread fear among the European peasantry of vampires, the dead who return from their graves to suck the blood from the living.

The vampire myths never took root in America, so the necessity of destroying the bodies of the witches was not deemed urgent.

Throughout the 1650s, there appeared prosecutions and attempted prosecutions in America, but these cases were infrequent, and all of them were based on the fear of *maleficium*, the witch's working of evil, the accusations coming from frustrated and jealous neighbors.

Few confessions were recorded in the early cases, and none that had any real validity. The few that did confess mentioned having had dealings with Satan, but for the most part these admissions were confused and incoherent, and the details of the accounts differed greatly from the confessions of the witches in Europe.

For example, in 1669, in Connecticut, a woman named Greensmith confessed to trafficking with the Devil, but made no mention of the all-important Covenant, or pact. She further stated that the Devil had appeared to her in the form of a deer (not a goat) and that she had attended meetings at a place not far from her house. The mention of "meetings" occurred in some early confessions, but the word "Sabbat" or "Sabbath," commonly used by European witches, did not come up until later, aparently at the suggestion of the Salem judges.

There appeared to have been little witch activity in New York, the reason being that New York was a Dutch settlement and the Dutch were noted for their skepticism. There had been no witch trials in Holland since 1610 and the Dutch mentality was not about to allow them to begin in the New World. There were later trials in New York for witchcraft, but these occurred only after the King of England had given his brother, the duke of York, the Dutch territory in America, allowing the more superstitious New Englanders a chance to move in.

In Pennsylvania, only two cases were brought to trial, but these were not brought up by the tolerant Quaker settlers but rather by the Swedish peasants who had begun to move into Pennsylvania territory from Delaware. Under the rule of William Penn, however, the cases were never allowed to turn into full-fledged legal proceedings, and in 1684, he directed the jury to return the verdict "not guilty."

It was strange that in Pennsylvania, one of the most

tolerant of the New World colonies, the only early form of organized witchcraft existed and flourished. This was the PowWow, which was brought to the colony by the German immigrants who had begun to settle there. In Germany, many of the smaller villages had white-witch groups, which served as healers of the sick and as protectors of the village from black magic. These magical vigilante committees in the New World were soon to become syncretisms of German superstitions and Indian magical practices, and were entrusted with the task of seeking out and breaking the spells of black witches.

The pattern of the courts during the early period was erratic, sometimes convicting, sometimes throwing cases out of court for lack of evidence, sometimes awarding damages for slander to those who had been maligned as witches by accusers. This vacillation sprang from the fact that the judicial bodies that heard the cases were not religious but secular, and therefore had little competence in dealing with matters that were primarily religious.

As the church authority had bound its own hands in New England, as far as control was concerned, in adhering to the principles of congregationalism, the responsibility for suppressing heresy and enforcing religious behavior within the communities went to the state. The trial judges were not the sure, steadfast, confident Dominican Inquisitors or Protestant prosecutors of the Old World, but merely secular officials of the colonies who had been forced into the position of trying heresy for lack of anyone else to do it.

But the trials went on. Mary Johnson admitted having had "familiarity with the Devil" in 1648 and was executed. She confessed to murdering a child and having had intercourse with men and demons. She made no mention of mass meetings; rather, her Devil seems to have been a personal one, coming to her aid when needed.

A prelude to the Salem outbreak of 1692 occurred in Boston in 1688. Cotton Mather, the influential Protestant preacher who was to play so great a role in the Salem prosecutions, investigated a case of possession in the Goodwin family. The woman accused of bewitchment was an old Irish washerwoman who apparently spoke little English. She finally confessed to having used dolls as a means of projecting curses, and said she had attended meetings with Satan and his consorts. Mather expressed complete belief in the existence of the witches' pact with Satan and attributed it to part of God's inscrutable plan of the universe.

The Puritan settlers in America believed in the doctrine of Original Sin wholeheartedly; their pessimistic outlook proclaimed that all men were unworthy until God saw fit to bestow his grace upon them. They believed that God allowed the Devil to afflict not only the guilty but also anybody else that might happen to get in the way. He might punish an entire community for the sins of the most wicked in that community if he had it in mind to teach the misguided humans a lesson. And at that time it appeared to the God-fearing Puritans that he was doing just that.

Being a sect that had been subjected to much derision in England because of their self-righteousness and virulent attacks on the corruption within the Anglican Church, the Puritans were highly intolerant and had a paranoiac distrust of other religious groups that differed in doctrine or ritual. They had particular hatred for the Quaker settlers who were landing in the colonies, seeking refuge from the persecution they had experienced in England. Moreover, Quakers entering the colonies were often under suspicion of witchcraft. The case of a woman tried in 1660 by the general court of Massachusetts demonstrates the Puritan distrust of the invaders, for the court, upon hearing the case, acquitted the woman of the charge of witchcraft but convicted her of being a Quaker and banished her from the colony.

The Puritans had come to America to seek refuge from the corruption they saw in the Church of England, to establish a utopia—a true kingdom of God on earth— where the "elect" could live peacefully in his glory and guidance. What they found upon arriving was something entirely different. They found a land of bitter cold winters and inhospitable terrain. They found themselves in a wilderness, surrounded by savage Indian tribes whom they considered to be the legions of Hell incarnate. Having come to settle in the last stronghold of the Devil, they were plagued by him constantly for the very reason that they were God's chosen people, thus the most likely target for unholy temptation.

The fact that the new settlers in New England were

being attacked by Satan seemed incontestable. Increase Mather, the father of Cotton and one of the most respected theologians in the New World, in 1679 had called the clergy in Massachusetts together to determine what had brought the Lord's wrath down upon New England. The colony, ravaged by smallpox, had suffered constant harassment by the French and Indians during King Philip's War. In 1684, King James II revoked the charter of the Massachusetts Bay Colony, and Governor Andros, a spitefully hated man, was in power. Churchmen asked themselves what they had done to offend God that he should allow the Devil such free rein.

Cotton Mather had the answer: Judgment day was at hand and Satan was therefore stepping up his activities in one last desperate move. It was simply the nova-like burst of fire from a dying star. He glibly stated that "there will again be an unusual Range of the Devil among us, a little before the Second Coming of our Lord, which will be to give the last stroke in destroying the works of the Devil."

This theory found wide acceptance among the clergy and laity of the colony, for not only did it offer a simple explanation for all their maladies and misfortunes, but it also gave them hope, promising cooly a quick end to their hardships. The fact of the matter is that Mather probably came a lot closer to stating the truth in the same treatise, without realizing it, when he said that Satan is most able to seduce men in periods of great discontent, for men, in times of poverty and affliction, will turn knowingly to whatever hand will feed them.

The colonies had had a difficult time of it up to that time, and famines had reduced the population drastically. But, as if laboring under the most severe environmental handicaps was not enough, Puritan perfectionism went even further in making life unbearable. In seeking to establish a holy kingdom, according to Heaven's law, self-indulgence in any form was strictly repressed. Severe punishments were meted out for drinking, swearing, and licentiousness; in Massachusetts it was a punishable offense to walk on the street on Sunday, except when going to and from church.

On top of it all, there stood the Calvinistic doctrine of election, holding that as soon as man was born he was judged to be headed for either Heaven or Hell, this choice being made according to God's immutable law. But even if a man thought himself to be damned, the civil punishments for his indulgence were still exacted upon him.

It was into this environment that the waters of the witchcraft flood would soon pour. The year was 1692, the place was Salem. It began when the young daughter and female cousin of a Salem minister began to act strangely: they ranted and raved, contorting their bodies into awkward positions and crying out that they were bewitched. The good people of Salem clearly saw signs of Satanic activity in their midst, and so an investigation was launched.

The first to be accused was a Negro servant of the minister's family, by the name of Tituba. Brought before the court, she confessed to having attended witches' Sabbaths and of having met with the Devil, who was a tall, black man from Boston. Soon the witch fever spread, more children of the village becoming possessed by demons. The belief was common among theologians at the time that witches, when entering into a Covenant with Satan, became the owners of specters, with the help of which they could do harm to any person of their choosing.

The children next burst forth with unified voice, their accusations flying right and left. They pointed fingers at those witches whose spectres had come to torment them. The new governor from England, William Phipps, bewildered by the excitement in Salem village, authorized the beginnings of legal prosecutions.

Soon the possessions reached epidemic proportions, spreading to other young people in outlying areas near the village. Hundreds were rounded up for questioning, and many cracked under the strain of imprisonment and began to confess. The confessions for the most part were conflicting and vague, and in many cases obvious fabrications, but they were taken literally by the court. The Satanism that had emerged in the New World was very different from its European counterpart.

According to the confessions, the witches met in a pasture outside the village at midnight. A trumpet was sounded, audible to all witches within Essex County, but never heard by those of good conscience. The witches, thus signaled, mounted their broomsticks and flew to the meeting. Once there, they all sat in an orderly congregation, partaking of the sacrament in the usual manner, except for the fact that both the bread and wine were red. Then they heard a sermon delivered by the Devil, whom eight of the confessors later claimed to have been George Burroughs, a minister who once presided at the Salem church.

The sermon usually dealt with the overthrow of the theocratic system then in existence and the abolition of strict social laws; the new system that would follow would bring with it greater abundance and a more pleasurable life. All would be well once the Church was destroyed. Afterwards, cockfights, gambling, and other forbidden delights went on until the break of day. There was no mention of copulation in any form, either within the congregation itself or with the Devil, no mention of defiling holy relics, nor of animal sacrifice, nor the administering of the witches' mark, no mention of a glorious feast. The signing of the Devil's book was present, but the initiates differed as to the method of signing. Few of the confessors said they had signed the book in the traditional manner, with their own blood, but most of them had signed with plain pen and ink.

As for the possessed girls, the events in Salem were indicative of a pattern repeated frequently in religious history. Such epidemics of possession have tended to occur most frequently in times of social tension. Since a person possessed is no longer responsible for his or her actions, such outbreaks function psychologically as a release, as a means of casting off authority with impunity, as well as a method of projecting repressed doubts or guilt. "The Devil made me do it."

It is not surprising, then, that outbreaks of mysterical contagion have historically taken place in areas where authority, manifested in an overpowering social structure or system of values, was the greatest, and where emotional safety valves for bleeding off social tensions were the least.

In Europe, a common site of demonic assault were in convents, almost always winding up in the accusation that some priest—the unfortunate object of repressed sexual desire—was, in reality, an incubus. In 1491, a convent of nuns at Cambrai was attacked by demons; in

1551, the cloister of Saint Brigitte became possessed; in 1590, 30 nuns were seized near Milan; in 1609, the convent at Aix came under siege by Satan and his allies; in 1632, the famous epidemic at the convent in Loudon was reported; and as late as 1881, there was an epidemic at Jaca, Spain.

The Salem possessions, a psychological rejection of authority, fell into the niche provided for it by the harsh realities of Puritan society. For the first time in their lives, these girls found themselves to be powerful, significant beings, establishing their own realm of authority. When they spoke, all of Salem stopped to listen, for their shrill cries became law. This dramatic escape route for them was a sort of luxury but for many, it soon became a nightmare. By the beginning of the eighteenth century, most of the possessed and many of the convicting jurors had broken down under the weight of conscience, admitting publicly their error and asking forgiveness from God and their peers.

Many historians have argued that the Satanism at Salem was only the product of the demented minds of the confessors and the zealous dispositions of the judges. They are quite right in one respect—Satanism did not exist in Salem. However, there was something quite real in all the series of accusations and counteraccusations of the witnesses and the possessed—some definitely evil driving force that led humans to turn against one another like mad dogs lusting for the smell of blood. Satanism at Salem was a desperate projection of the Puritans' own social evils.

The assumption that the existence of Satanism was not real in New England is demonstrable from several points. The confessions of the accused were invalid, many of them having been extracted under the most severe conditions. Large numbers of the so-called witches were hounded day and night by their friends and relatives to confess their guilt. Exhausted by lack of sleep, seeing themselves alone and isolated, with no one believing in their innocence, they broke down and admitted to whatever was suggested to them by their interrogators.

One such woman, Deliverance Hobbs, after having been accused by her children of being a witch, became such a

malleable confessor that many of her own stories con-
tradicted each other. Although torture was not officially
sanctioned, the method of questioning involved tying the
accused "heels to head," in which position he remained
until a confession was extracted.

A second reason to disregard parts of the confessions
was that the confessors, in contrast to European practice,
were not being executed. The tolerant attitude toward
confessors was summed up by Cotton Mather when he
stated during the panic, "If any guilty creatures will
accordingly to so good purpose confess their crime to any
Minister of God . . . so I believe none in the Authority
will press him to discover it; but rejoyc'd in a Soul sav'd
from Death."[1] At such a time, when those protesting
innocence were being sent to the gallows and those
confessing to the practices of witchcraft and Devil worship were being spared by the tribunals, it is a wonder
that not more confessions poured in than, in fact, did.

Besides all the obvious procedural flaws, too much was
missing from the confessions themselves. Many *were* the
products of deluded minds. Mercy Lewis, for example,
claimed that the Reverend Burroughs had taken her to a
mountaintop and showed her the "mighty and glorious
kingdoms," offering them to her if only she would sign his
book. This was obviously an extraction straight from the
Book of Matthew.

The pattern of the Sabbat as it was reported to have
occurred in the pasture in Salem left much out of the
picture if Satan was to have presided over the meetings.
For instance, many of the witches stated they had flown to
the meeting on brooms or on animals. Similar confessions
were obtained from the witches of Europe, except there
the explanation of the phenomenon was tenable. On the
Continent, the participants said that, before they flew,
they rubbed on "flying ointment," a salve that contained
such ingredients as aconite, belladonna, and henbane,
powerful narcotics that, when applied to certain parts of
the body, would produce unconsciousness and sometimes
dreams of flight. There was no mention of this ointment in
the Salem accounts.

[1]Mather, Cotton, *Wonders of the Invisible World*, New York, 1950, p. 52.

The symbolism of the goat was not present, either. The Devil manifested himself in many forms to the confessors—as a horse, a fox, a dog, a cat, a pig, and as a black man, but never as a goat. At the Sabbats, the Devil was always present in the form of the Reverend Burroughs, apparently making no attempt to disguise his identity in any way. Neither was the all-important bloodletting present in the ceremonies, either in the form of a sacrifice or in the signing of the pact. There was no defiling of sacred objects nor mention of the administering of the witches' mark, a painful ceremony that was quite vivid in the minds of the European witches. The Sabbats, all in all, seemed to have been rather staid affairs, involving little wild ritual or debauchery.

As for the supposed purpose of the assembly—that is, to pay homage to Satan—the ritual adulation present in the European gatherings, the prostration before the deity, was not practiced at Salem. The purposes of the meetings were primarily political, not religious, for the action that was advocated was *human* action.

William Barker confessed that the plan of the group was to destroy the Church of God in Salem, to set up Satan's kingdom on earth. The Devil offered not immediate wealth or riches, but a new system of government, where all men would be equal, each man being free to "live bravely." He promised an end to beliefs. Whoever the Devil was at those meetings, he obviously did not seek adulation, but rather he sought to establish a more equal and suitable social order among men.

Taken in this context, the entire episode begins to sound like a huge projection, a gigantic wish fulfillment on the part of the disgruntled citizens, who were expressing disdain for the system that, in their eyes, had become oppressive. The figure chosen by the confessors as the Devil presiding over the midnight Sabbats, George Burroughs, was a likely symbol of this resentment, for he had been a minister in the Salem parish but had left on account of petty squabbles with the clergy there. It is not at all unlikely, due to the dissension he had introduced into the Church, that he bore animosity toward some members of the clergy and that he had himself become somewhat disillusioned by the system.

The principle of congregationalism—giving independence to the church congregations within certain bounds—had caused the Puritans much grief and had provided fertile soil for the growth of heretical splinter movements. Since 1635, with the Roger Williams heresy, Puritanism had been plagued with such schisms within its ranks.

Perhaps Burroughs actually had been holding nocturnal meetings in a pasture, preaching doctrines violently antithetical to the creed of the Church. But if this was so, why didn't he confess to his heresy and thereby save his life? Perhaps because he was aware that the mania had gone too far and that he wouldn't be believed anyway.

Why did the confessors call themselves witches instead of heretics? Perhaps driven by their feelings of guilt at having held heretical beliefs and desires, they felt a certain relief in shrieking out their blasphemous confessions as a way of "cleansing the soul."

At any rate, whether the meetings were real, which is doubtful, or whether they were imaginary, they were what the people wanted them to be—a revolt against the system. The inherent conflict between human nature and Puritanical harshness found a necessary psychological safety valve in the minds of the people: Certainly, since one definition of anti-sociability at that time could be summed up in the powerful word "witchcraft," the revolutionaries naturally thought in those terms. As Cotton Mather so aptly put it, "Rebellion is like witchcraft."[2]

In the rest of America, the witch craze was not as widespread. Virginia had a few cases, although some of these backfired on the accusers, ending up with slander suits being slapped on the plaintiffs. As late as 1706, however, trials were still being conducted there. A woman by the name of Grace Sherwood was accused and searched for witches' marks; she was convicted and sent to prison, but no record exists as to her fate. In 1712, in South Carolina, a mob seized and badly burned several persons suspected of working witchcraft; when the assaulted parties tried to press charges against the mob, their case was thrown out of court.

Apart from these isolated instances, there was little

[2] Mather, ibid, p 23.

REPRESENTATIVE DEVILS

TOP LEFT:
The Egyptian god Set, called Typhon by the Greeks, was symbolized as a snake or a crocodile.

TOP RIGHT:
Scaled and feathered Babylonian god of chaos, Tiamat.

BOTTOM RIGHT:
The famous print by magician Eliphas Levi of the Sabbatic Goat, or the Goat of Mendes. Note the hermaphroditic traits exhibited here by the Devil, namely the caduceuslike phallus and the female breasts.

ELIPHAS LEVI DEL

THE SABBAT

These seventeenth-century engravings show some popular beliefs about the proceedings of the Sabbat.

Initiates exchange a Bible for a book of black magic.

The administering of the "devil's mark."

The rebaptism in the name of Satan.

The *osculum infame*, or "kiss of shame."

A seventeenth-century Black Mass. The Abbé Guibourg performs an infant sacrifice over the body of Madame Montespan so that she might retain the favors of the King.

BLACK MAGIC AND PACTS

Symbols play a vital role in infernal conjuration. LEFT: the Goetic Circle of Pacts, drawn by Eliphas Levi in the nineteenth century, is supposed to be used when the sorcerer is to make a pact with the Descending Hierarchy. The three circles in the center are the standing positions of the sorcerer and his apprentices. The skull must be from a parricide, the horns from a goat, the bat must have been drowned in blood, and the black cat, whose head is placed opposite the skull, must have been fed on human flesh. RIGHT: The seal and characters of Lucifer, from the *Grimorium Verum,* sixteenth-century book of demonic magic. The characters are supposed to be written on parchment with the blood of the sorcerer, and worn by him at all times during the conjuration.

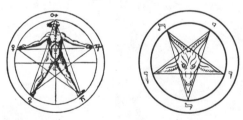

LEFT: The pentagram is an ancient Magical symbol which in its upright form was employed by "white" magicians for the purposes of good, perhaps because it corresponded to the general anatomical proportions of man. This representation was from *De Occulta Philosophia,* a magical book by Agrippa of Nettesheim (1486 - 1535).

RIGHT: Since the pentagram was a traditional symbol used in "white" magic, it is natural in the magical world of opposites that the inverted pentagram should be a symbol of Evil. The two points jutting upward affirm the universal duality, Good and Evil, while the bottom point is directed toward Hell. The goat's head superimposed within the star is recognition of Satan as the symbol of Lust.

The Beast 666.
Aleister Crowley
at the age of 37.

Underground filmmaker,
author (*Hollywood Babylon*),
Crowley disciple, and founding
member of the Church of Satan,
Kenneth Anger.

An ominous scowl by the High Priest of the Church of Satan. The object on his finger is a trapezoidal quartz crystal held in the gold talons of a bird of prey.

A 1968 recruiting poster for the Church of Satan, with Satan the Accuser replacing a scowling Uncle Sam.

An early ritual at the Church of Satan (1966). The phallic object in the hand of the woman on the right is an aspergillum, or holy water sprinkler.
The man holding the skull, Forrest Satterfield, was the *first* man to be wed by the Church of Satan in 1966, before the publicized wedding of Judith Case and John Raymond.

A bevy of witches surrounds LaVey at one of his witches' workshops. The young brunette at the far right is Susan Atkins, who three years later would confess to licking the blood off the knife that she had plunged repeatedly into a pregnant Sharon Tate. At the time of this picture, she was part of LaVey's "Witches' Sabbath" topless show, fittingly playing a vampire.

The High Priest performs a private ritual for priestess Jayne Mansfield at her Pink Palace home in Hollywood. The skull and chalice were owned by Jayne and used by her in the Satanic rites she regularly practiced during the year preceding her tragic death.

The Church of Satan High Priest in the company of a onetime follower, Sammy Davis, Jr.

Actors John Travolta and Tom Skerritt, part of the cast of *The Devil's Rain,* take time from the day's shooting schedule to pose with Anton LaVey and his wife High Priestess, Diane. LaVey acted as a technical advisor on the film, which was about a group of Devil worshippers who inhabit a ghost town.

Anton LaVey today, on a return trip to the midway with daughters Karla (center) and Zeena.

The Kerk du Satan, Amsterdam, Netherlands.

INSET: Martin Lamers, High Priest of the Kerk du Satan in Amsterdam, Netherlands, flashing the "sign of the horns."

The Walburga Abbey, Amsterdam's Satanic sex club.

One of the few existing photographs of Robert DeGrimston, founder of The Process.
This photo was taken after DeGrimston had decided he was Jesus, as can be seen by the carefully cultivated likeness.

THE PROCESS
CHURCH OF THE FINAL JUDGEMENT

Ipsissimus Michael A. Aquino and
his wife High Priestess Lilith
Sinclair, founders and inspirational
leaders of the Temple of Set, at their
home in San Francisco.
CREDIT: MICHAEL LANG

Paul Douglas Valentine. Potentate,
Church of Satanic Liberation.
Copyright © Paul Douglas
Valentine

A smattering of
heavy metal rock
albums featuring
Satanic themes.
CREDIT:
BOB KIERAN

Black Sabbath.

Ozzy Ozbourne.
CREDIT:
FIN COSTELLO

Kiss.

Mötley Crüe.
CREDIT:
GARY LEONARD

Teenagers give the "sign of the horns" at a Slayer concert.

Ray Buckey and his mother, Peggy McMartin Buckey, discuss
legal strategy at their trial for over one hundred counts of ritualistic
child molestation at the McMartin Pre-school, in Los Angeles.
CREDIT: AP/WIDE WORLD PHOTO.

Satanic cannibal Stanley Dean Baker (with beard) at his arraignment for
murder in Livinston, Montana, in 1970. Seated with Baker is Harry A.
Stroop, who was arrested in California with Baker. Although both
defendants denied Stroop's participation in the grisly crime, he was also
convicted. CREDIT: RUSS WELLS

At his arraignment for murder, Richard Ramirez, the so-called Night Stalker killer, holds up the Satanic pentagram he drew in his hand.
CREDIT: AP/WIDE WORLD PHOTO

Satanic activity, real or imaginary, in frontier America. Too busy fighting the physical environment, the American pioneers found little time to carry on a fight against the ephemeral dangers of a nebulous spirit world. Reports of witchcraft and Satanism became stilled and the memory of Salem grew dim in the minds of Americans until the latter part of the nineteenth century.

CHAPTER VI

From Freemasonry to Crowleyanity

"Teach us Your real secret, Master! how to become
    invisible, how to acquire love, and oh! beyond all,
    how to make gold.
But how much gold will you give me for the Secret
    of Infinite Riches?
Then said the foremost and most foolish: Master, it
    is nothing; but here is an hundred thousand
    pounds.
This did I deign to accept, and whispered in his ear
    this secret:
A SUCKER IS BORN EVERY MINUTE."
          —Aleister Crowley, *The Book of Lies*

In 1892, a book entitled *The Devil in the 19th Century*,
written by a mysterious Dr. Bataille, took France by
storm. In it, the author "exposed" the diabolic rites of
Freemasonry, arguing that the Freemasons were in reality
devout Satanists, carrying out blasphemous and hideous
rituals beneath their sinister cloak of secrecy.

The headquarters of the movement, under the leadership of Albert Pike, Gallatin Mackey, and others, was,
Bataille claimed, located in Charleston, South Carolina,
with celebrants of their horrible Black Masses spread all
over the world. Their rites supposedly involved the sacrificial slaying of a white lamb, the partaking of a sacrament, and the saying of a Satanic paternoster, among
other more odious practices. Dr. Bataille went so far as to
state that the lodge in Charleston had an infernal telephone hooked up to Hell, through which the leaders spoke
to Lucifer.

The stories recounted by Dr. Bataille were backed up by another mysterious figure, one Diana Vaughan, in her book published in 1895 entitled *Memoirs of an Ex-Palladist*, in which she gave a detailed account of her experiences with the "Satanists" in Charleston. She had been, according to her own admission, Grand Mistress of the Temple and Grand Inspectress of the Palladium, a diabolic Masonic order, allegedly founded in Paris in 1737. She claimed to have been descended from Thomas Vaughan, a seventeenth-century alchemist, and due to her hellish origin was chosen to be High Priestess of Lucifer and the bride of Asmodeus. The book went on to describe the orgiastic Black Masses that were taking place at that very minute in South Carolina under the guise of Freemasonry.

As incredible as all this may sound, it found a large reading audience in France and elsewhere in Europe, where tales of a Masonic-Satanic conspiracy had been widely circulated since the early 1700s. In 1738, Pope Clement XII issued a papal bull forbidding Catholics to join or support Freemasonry on threat of excommunication, saying that Masons were "depraved and perverted . . . most suspect of heresy," and that "if they were not doing evil, they would not have so great a hatred for the light."

Belief in the infernal core of Masonry was so strong, in fact, that even after a French journalist, Gabriel Jogand, publicly confessed in 1897 that he was the mysterious "Dr. Bataille" and had authored the *Confessions* as a practical joke, many Masonic detractors refused to relinquish their belief in them claiming that Jogand had been bought off by the forces of darkness.

Freemasonry is a nonsectarian fraternity claiming to teach a system of morality veiled in the allegory and symbols passed down from the caste of stonemasons who built the original Temple of Solomon. It allegedly binds its members by an oath of secrecy that imposes death on the betrayer, uses secret passwords and signs, and performs rituals purporting to relate to the history of its origins. Its organization is hierophantic, the members receiving the "secrets" of the order as they pass through the higher degrees. In reality, its "secrets" can be purchased in any used-book store, its functions have always been more social than mystical, and, despite the claims of some of its members, its antiquity can be documented no further back than the latter part of the seventeenth century.

The movement really seems to have gotten its start with the establishment of the Grand Lodge in England, in 1717. From there, it spread to France and Germany, and it did not take long for serious-minded students of the occult, attracted by its ritualistic and secretive trappings, to find their way into its ranks.

The famous alchemist and mystic Count Allesandro di Cagliostro dominated the Lyon Lodge in France, created his own brand of Egyptian Masonry, and taught that he could make gold, heal the sick, and raise the dead. In England, there were many ties to the mystical Rosicrucians, while the Royal Order of Scotland claimed to practice secret rites handed down from the Knights Templar. In Germany, the Stricte Observance claimed to be under the tutelage of the "Unknown Superiors," a race of godlike spiritual guides.

A great part of the Church's fear of Freemasonry stemmed not only from the heretical beliefs and practices of the order but from suspicions that the lodges were covers for political conspiracy. The Devil, being a rebel against heaven, has always been portrayed by the powers-that-be as the chief insurrectionist against the existing political and religious order. The enemy cannot be God, for God is on the side of the ruler. Therefore, the enemy of the ruler must be Satan.

It is true that many of the Masonic lodges were supranational in outlook and espoused democratic values. It is also true that some of the groups were infiltrated and used for purposes of political intrigue. The Illuminati incident was one such episode.

In 1776, Adam Weishaupt, professor of law at Ingolstadt, Bavaria, founded a secret society dedicated to the scientific and political enlightenment of mankind. To achieve this goal, the group intended secretly to work toward the abolition of all monarchies and the establishment of a one-world government, to be run by those few presently Enlightened, or Illuminati. Since professing such republican ideas could be dangerous, Weishaupt disguised the group's aims by wrapping them in a cloak of occultism. He adopted the grades of Freemasonry and promised initiates that the magical secrets of the universe would be revealed to them only when they reached the upper levels.

The cult rapidly spread through Germany and in 1780 found a convert in Baron von Knigge, who happened also to be an influential Freemason. Through his efforts, the Illuminati became linked with the older Masonic group. The union was short-lived, however, and after squabbling broke out between Weishaupt and von Knigge, the latter withdrew from the Illuminati. Not long after that, some Illuminati initiates, disgruntled over finding the cult's mysticism just a smoke screen, blew the whistle. Weishaupt fled, and in 1785, the Illuminati and Freemasonry were outlawed in Bavaria.

Though no longer in existence, the Illuminati had its legend secured in 1797. It was then that French Jesuit Abbé Barruel wrote a five-volume treatise claiming that the French Revolution had, in reality, been the result of an ancient conspiracy tracing back to the Knights Templar, as well as to the Assassins, a mystical Moslem sect whose members carried out political assassinations while crazed on hashish. The Templars, Barruel asserted, had not been stamped out in 1314, but had gone underground and survived in a network of secret societies, two of which were the Freemasons and the Illuminati. This secret network was in league with the "Sons of Satan"—international Jewry—and was presided over by a Grand Master who ordered assassinations and fomented revolutions in order to establish the one-world government of the Antichrist. Barruel's paranoid visions found a receptive audience in right-wing political and occultist circles in Europe, eventually becoming embodied in the mystical anti-Semitic mythology of the Nazi state.

Although the links between diabolism and Freemasonry were the product of fevered imaginations and literary fraud, the Masonic teaching continued to exert an influence on the thought of certain mystical thinkers and practitioners of ceremonial magic. One such was Aleister Crowley, an English author, poet, adventurer, and mountain climber, whose scandalous reputation endures to this day.

Often mislabeled a Satanist by the press, an identity Crowley himself fostered by referring to himself as "the

Great Beast 666" and "Baphomet," Crowley actually practiced a complex system of magic that was a synthesis of Eastern and Western mystical traditions. Although the rituals he performed were often debauched, liberally dosed with sex and an occasional animal sacrifice, and although he had a fascination for the diabolic that dated from a childhood reaction against his puritanical Christian upbringing, Crowley considered himself too refined a sorcerer to dabble with such crude ceremonies as the Black Mass. Yet, though not a Satanist himself, Crowley's writings and legend were later to exert a great influence on the development of contemporary Satanism.

Crowley's system, which he dubbed "MAGICK," was a sophisticated mixture of Kabbalistic, Egyptian, and hermetic magic, injected with Tantric yoga, but it differed from all of those disciplines in certain important respects.

In the teachings of the Kabbala, man is viewed as being a microcosm, an exact duplicate on a small scale of the larger physical and spiritual universe, the macrocosm. Since the universe and man are indissolubly linked by this relationship, an act performed by man under certain conditions may affect the universe at large, just as an occurrence in the outer universe may affect man.

This interaction between similarities is the underlying basis of all magic, black and white both, and is not limited to the Kabbala. Sex was a sacred act for the Hebrew mystics, for it was the earthly counterpart of God's creative force, the symbolic energy by which he created the universe. Coitus, if properly executed, enabled man, the Kabbalist felt, to form a direct link with divinity, for, by partaking in a sacred act, man inevitably becomes sacred.

Tantrism, on the other hand, is an intentional indulgence in physical excess in order to overcome physical being entirely. Sex is linked to the carnal in order to transcend the carnal. Pleasure in any form is not sought and it may indeed be disastrous to the performer if pleasure is derived from such an act, for that is detrimental to the karma. The object of Tantrism is to have such a complete mastery over the senses as to be able to rise above every pleasure and achieve total identification with natural energy.

Crowley's conceptions of the sexual act were more

empirical than either of these views, for in sex he saw a means of harnessing internal and external power. Unleashing sexual inhibitions, in Crowley's view, releases vast amounts of energy, both physical and psychological, and sets up "vibrations" in the surrounding atmosphere, which, when under stringent control, can be directed and used for whatever purpose the magician desires. Kabbalistic sex magic stipulates that only in a holy bond between a female and male—that is, marriage—could spiritual elevation be achieved, while Crowley seems to have been more open-minded when choosing a sex partner for his rituals.

In Tantrism, the purpose of sex is to transcend excitement altogether, the main objective being the retention of semen, but in Crowley's system of magick the outpouring of energy through orgasm is necessary to achieve power. Crowley thus bastardized both these forms of sexual magic, but in so doing formed a much broader base of appeal for those having occult leanings.

One point essential to an understanding of Crowley's view of magic is the distinction between what he called evocation and invocation. Evocation was a calling *forth*, while invocation was a calling *in*. The old methods of evocation practiced by traditional sorcerers in Crowley's view, were clumsy and inferior. In such rituals, the magician summoned the demon or deity while standing within the protection of a magical circle drawn on the floor, the object of the sorcerer being to control and direct the entity to do his bidding. Crowley's aim, however, was spiritual enlightenment. He sought to achieve total identification with the godhead, to *invoke* the god so that it actually took possession of his consciousness. The resulting state experienced by the magician was a type of *samadhi*, or temporary loss of ego, but just to make sure of his change in consciousness, he ingested every kind of known hallucinogen, from hashish to belladonna to opium.

Crowley's magical education began in 1898, when he was inducted into the Hermetic Order of the Golden Dawn, a magical fraternity that boasted such illustrious members as William Butler Yeats, Algernon Blackwood, Sax Rohmer, and Bram Stoker. The Golden Dawn practiced a mixed-bag form of magic based on the Jewish

Kabbala and the Rosicrucian belief that there existed somewhere in the East a brotherhood of "Secret Chiefs," god-men with superhuman intelligence controlling the fate of mankind. This Buddhist bodhisattva concept had already been popularized in the Western world by Madame Helena Blavatsky, the founder of the Theosophical Society, who in the 1870s in her best-selling *Isis Unveiled* had written about a society of "Ascended Masters" who, from its residence in Tibet, guided the course of human history.

As in Freemasonry and Rosicrucianism, initiates into the Golden Dawn rose through a hierarchy of degrees as they achieved enlightenment—the top three degrees being Magister Templi, Magus, and Ipsissimus. The last of those titles was held only by the dictatorial leader of the group, S. L. MacGregor Mathers, who claimed to be the personal contact with the Secret Chiefs.

It didn't take long for personal rivalries to erupt between Mathers and the strong-willed Crowley. This feud ended in a magical duel in which Mathers—according to Crowley—was slain by a vampire Mathers conjured up to kill Crowley.

The Golden Dawn broke up shortly thereafter, but Crowley continued his magical pursuits. In 1904, in Cairo, he achieved a major breakthrough when, while in a trance, he was contacted by his holy guardian angel, Aiwass, who told him he was the harbinger of a new age, the "aeon of Horus," and proceeded to dictate to him the "gospel," *The Book of the Law*.

The basis of the new Aeon was to be the "Law of Thelema," *thelema* being the Greek word for "will." Its axioms were "Do what thou wilt shall be the whole of the law," "Love is the law, love under will," and "Every man and woman is a star," credos that precipitated a Crowley revival amid the 1960s counterculturists.

Crowley began to search for a vehicle to spread his gospel, and in 1912 found it in a German secret society called the Ordo Templi Orientis, or O.T.O.

The O.T.O. had been founded at the beginning of the century by Karl Kellner, a rich German occultist and Freemason, who claimed to be following secret teachings dating back to the ubiquitous Templars. An early tract of the group proclaimed: "Our Order possesses the KEY which opens up all Masonic and Hermetic secrets, namely, the teaching of sexual magic, and this teaching explains, without exception, all the secrets of Freemasonry and all systems of religion."[1]

The "sexual magic" Kellner espoused was the invocation of various deities through intense mental imagery while engaging in sexual intercourse. After Kellner's death in 1905, leadership of the group was assumed by one Theodor Reuss, and chapters were started up in Denmark, France, and England.

The O.T.O.'s emphasis on sex in its rituals suited Crowley's personal tastes, and after an eventful meeting with Reuss, it was agreed that Crowley should take over as head of the British chapter.

Crowley's brilliance, his penchant for poetry, and his unbounded lechery—both homo- and heterosexual—soon expanded the vistas of the O.T.O. rituals.

In 1920, with a small band of his followers, Crowley moved into a farmhouse near Cefalu, Sicily, and founded his Abbey of Thelema, from which he hoped to see his gospel spread. It was here, away from the prying eyes of society, that he began to revive barbaric rites that had not been practiced since the time of the Dionysian cults in ancient Greece. During one ritual in 1921, he induced a he-goat to copulate with his constant female companion and "Scarlet Woman," Leah Hirsig, then slit the animal's throat at the moment of orgasm.

The new "religion" failed to sweep the world, and the gospel of Crowleyanity suffered a further setback when Mussolini expelled the group from Italy, after one of the abbey's male members died following a ritual in which he drank the blood of a distempered cat.

Crowley died in 1947, a poverty-stricken drug addict, but several O.T.O. chapters survived him. One was the Church of Thelema in Pasadena, California, under the leadership of rocket-propulsion scientist Jack Parsons, who had helped develop JATO (jet-assisted takeoff) during World War II.

The church was a legacy of the Agape Lodge, started up in Hollywood by Wilfred Smith in the 1930s and frequented by a thrill-seeking movie-studio crowd. Squabbles within

---

[1] King, Francis, *Sexuality, Magic, and Perversion*, Seacaucus, N.J.: Citadel, 1972, p 97.

the lodge forced Smith to hand over stewardship of the group to his disciple, Parsons, who rechristened the lodge and moved it to his own estate on Pasadena's Millionaire Row in the early 1940s.

It did not take long for rumors to begin to circulate around the neighborhood of crazed sexual orgies and nightly processions of hooded, candle-bearing figures around the Parsons grounds. The brilliant but eccentric Parsons encountered his downfall, however, in the personage of red-headed L. Ron Hubbard, science-fiction writer and future founder of the pseudo-scientific Scientology movement.[2]

It seems to have been Parsons's friendship with Hubbard that spurred him to undertake what he considered his greatest magical feat—the attempt to bring the "Whore of Babalon" down from the Astral Plane and incarnate it in the womb of a living woman. On the first three days of March 1946, Parsons performed various incantations and had repeated sexual intercourse with a willing devotee while Hubbard acted as a scribe.

Upon hearing of Parsons' project, a mystified Crowley wrote to the head of his U. S. O.T.O. operation: "Apparently Parsons or Hubbard or somebody is producing a Moonchild. I get fairly frantic when I contemplate the idiocy of these louts."

Crowley did not have to worry, however. Parsons' "great experiment" bombed after the sexually exhausted scientist failed to impregnate his earthly choice for Whore. To add insult to infertility, Hubbard shortly thereafter absconded with both Parsons' girlfriend and $10,000 of his money. Parsons managed to catch up with Hubbard and recover at least part of the loot.

Embittered by the betrayal, but undaunted, Parsons continued in his magical Grail. In 1948, he undertook the "Black Pilgrimage," changed his name to Belarian Armiluss Al Dajjaj Antichrist, and wrote in his notebooks: "I am pledged that the work of the Beast 666 shall be fulfilled, and the way for the coming of BABALON be

[2]Scientology teaches that all personal limitations and aberrations are the result of "engrams," or moments of unconsciousness caused by painful experiences, and that once purged of these engrams through a program of analysis, one may become an "Operating Thetan"—a godlike being possessing superhuman powers.

made open and I shall not cease until these things are accomplished."

What the thirty-seven-year-old Parsons accomplished, in 1952, was to blow himself to smithereens while conducting a strange chemical experiment in his basement workshop. Hours later, the scientist's mother, who lived on the estate, committed suicide with an overdose of sleeping pills.

It was thirteen years later, the period of human maturation, that twins were born in San Francisco—the counter-culture and the Church of Satan.

Chapter VII

The Counterculture Club

"These children that come at you with knives, they are your children. You taught them. I didn't teach them. . . . I am whoever you make me, but what you want is a fiend; you want a sadistic fiend, because that is what you are."

—Charles Manson, at his trial

In June 1968, while researching contemporary Satanism, I looked up an old girlfriend who had been living in Haight-Ashbury, on the off chance she had run into some demonic practitioners there. I found the girl, D., staying with two young female friends at a ranch outside Victorville, in the California desert. D. knew nothing about Satanism or Satanists, but invited me to spend the night, an offer I declined. Nothing about her two girlfriends was to stand out in my mind, except that they were high on acid and giggled a lot. It would be a year and a half before I found out that one of those nondescript females was Leslie Van Houten, an eighteen-year-old high school dropout who was soon to be a member of the Manson Family murderers. The day after I'd left, Bobby Beausoleil, also a future murderer, had shown up at the ranch to pick up Leslie and take her to join Charles Manson and the rest of the Family. After practicing his bowie knife-throwing act on the living room walls, and unsuccessfully trying to talk D. into coming with them to meet "Jesus Christ," the pair stole D.'s Volkswagen and drove it to North Beach in San Francisco, where it was later found, gutted.

The fact that D. had not known anything about "Satanism," or whom she was living with, was apropos for the time. Aside from drugs, nobody knew what he was into in those days, not even Charles Manson. It was also appropriate that the Bethlehem the murderous pair chose to slouch toward was San Francisco. That city was where it all began.

By the summer of 1965, the Haight-Ashbury district of San Francisco had become a mecca for disenchanted dropouts from all over the country who converged to partake in their own great social experiment. They were alienated by the sterility of a technological society that elevated scientific materialism and rational planning as its ultimate ideals, yet could not solve basic problems such as poverty and economic injustice. They were frustrated by the hypocrisy and failures of religious and political institutions that preached Christian tolerance, yet supported the ecology-raping practices of big business, racial intolerance, and the horrors of Vietnam. They sought solace in an atavistic romanticism. En masse, they "tuned in, turned on, and dropped out."

This "counterculture," according to social historian Theodore Roszak, was a full-fledged revolt against the American technocracy, "that social form in which an industrial society reaches the peak of its organizational integration."[1] In an attempt to blot out the vision of a "brave new world," in which corporate profits supersede all other goals, these youths came together in an attempt at a utopian tribal society, in which man was in harmony with the environment, and in which the needs of all members of the tribe would be taken care of willingly, without government coercion.

Just as children or primitives believe they can change the universe at large by performing magical rituals, they sought to transform society by transforming themselves. They flaunted their separateness from mainstream society by letting their hair grow long and donning buckskin and beads. They exorcised the Christian demon—sex—by advocating and practicing "free love" and communal living. They shook off the fetters of Western religion by dabbling in arcane schools of thought and Eastern religions. They revolted against the Western emphasis on rationality by rejecting objective consciousness as the only method of gaining access to reality. In one fell swoop, three hundred years of science were thrown out the window, and magic,

[1]Roszak, Theodore, *The Making of a Counterculture*, New York: Anchor, 1969, p. 5.

paganism, and witchcraft were revived as viable worldly outlooks. Roszak observed at the time:

> Western society has, over the past two centuries, incorporated a number of minorities whose antagonism toward the scientific world view has been irreconcilable, and who have held out against the easy assimilation to which the major religious congregations have yielded in their growing desire to seem progressive. Theosophists and fundamentalists, spiritualists and flat-earthers, occultists and satanists . . . it is nothing new that there should exist anti-rationalist elements in our midst. What *is* new is that a radical rejection of science and technological values should appear so close to the center of society, rather than on the negligible margins.[2]

Much of the interest in the occult was a by-product of the psychedelic revolution. LSD achieved the status of a religion, with advocates like Timothy Leary and his League for Spiritual Discovery urging people to "go on to 'the next stage'" by dropping acid and getting "in touch with the ancient reincarnation thing we always carry inside."[3]

In a society historically impatient with long-term solutions and advocating drugs as a standard way of dealing with anxiety, it is not surprising that psychedelics should become a shortcut to *samadhi*, the state in Eastern religious disciplines in which man achieves union with the Infinite. But Eastern mystics have always professed that shortcuts to *nirvana* can be dangerous. Once the doors of consciousness are thrown open, those without the proper discipline cannot control what gets in. Along with the Bhagavad Gita, kids discovered the works of Aleister Crowley.

Narcotics have always played a role in Western ceremonial magic. Hemlock, henbane, opium, and belladonna were traditional sorcerer's drugs, and in the traditional Black Mass, hashish was often burned instead of incense. It is much easier to materialize a demon from the depths

---

[2]Roszak, Ibid., p. 51.
[3]Roszak, Ibid., p. 167.

of one's own mind than all the way from Hell. People began to believe in the Devil again because they could *see* him.

By 1967, the population of the Haight had swelled from 50,000 to 200,000, and the vibes had begun to change. Magical spells hadn't ended Vietnam, drugs had turned a lot of minds to mush, and free love had spread the clap. Stoners had begun to fall from third-floor windows, methedrine and heroin had replaced acid as the most-trafficked drugs, and dope dealers had started to turn up murdered. Kids still came to San Francisco, but not all of them wore flowers in their hair. Some, like Charles Manson and his Family, came in black buses.

San Francisco was fertile recruiting ground for Manson. The young, says social philosopher Eric Hoffer, are susceptible to religious and political proselytizing movements because they are "temporary misfits" who have not yet found their place in life but are impatiently searching. Manson sought them out, and through drugs, fear, love, sex, music, hate, and manipulative skills he'd learned during his many years in prison, he turned them into "permanent misfits." It was no accident he called his band of nomads "the Family." He opened his arms to those who felt depersonalized, small, and expendable, those who had been battered or neglected as children, who felt helpless and expendable.

It is a psychological fact that frustration can lead to aggression and that the more a person is frustrated from achieving a goal, the more aggressive he will become. If not able to vent that aggression against the cause of his frustration, he will readily deflect it to a less deserving object. Cult leaders and political demagogues have traditionally channeled and used those aggressive feelings by teaching their followers that they are the elect, and the rest of the world (Catholics, Jews, blacks, etc.) is inferior.

Manson, who called himself Christ and Satan, taught his Family that the Apocalypse, in the form of a black-white race war, was at hand, and that he, "the Beast of the bottomless pit," would lead them to salvation. The Family would trigger these cosmic events by murdering rich, white "piggies" and blaming it on the blacks, a reign of terror he called Helter Skelter, after a song from the Beatles' *White* album. According to Manson, after a white backlash, the blacks would rise up and defeat "whitey," but being inferior and not capable of intelligent rule, they would be forced to ask Charlie, who would be waiting things out with his Family in the desert, to take over as world leader.

As bizarre as these ideas may sound, the Haight for a few brief years in the sixties was a place out of time and space, and Manson had little trouble finding minds receptive to his acid-activated rap. He found Susan Atkins, a topless dancer who had briefly been a member of the Church of Satan and had prophetically played a blood-sucking vampire in LaVey's "Witches' Sabbath" stage show at Gigi's nightclub in North Beach. He also found Beausoleil, guitar player for a Digger band called the Orkustra and former protégé of underground filmmaker and later author of *Hollywood Babylon*, Kenneth Anger, a Crowley disciple and one of the original members of LaVey's Magic Circle, out of which the Church of Satan evolved.

Beausoleil, who was also called Cupid because of his boyish good looks, had played the part of Lucifer in Anger's *Invocation of My Demon Brother*, but the two had had a falling-out after the film's 1967 autumnal equinox debut at San Francisco's Straight Theatre. Anger had held a Black Mass on the stage of the theatre in honor of the occasion, but Beausoleil spoiled things by ripping off some camera equipment and Anger's copy of the film. Anger put a curse on his pretty protégé and took to wearing a locket with Beausoleil's picture on one side and a toad on the other, along with the inscription "Bobby Beausoleil—who was turned into a toad by Kenneth Anger." It took two years for the transformation to be complete, but by July 1969, Beausoleil was arrested, and later received a life sentence for the torture-murder of musician Gary Hinman.

Although not strictly a Satanist, Manson seemed to have picked up at least some of his ideas from a cult that definitely was Satanic. In the summer of 1967, long-haired, black-caped members of The Process, or the Church of the Final Judgment, appeared in the Haight, walking attack-trained white Alsatian dogs and handing out their literature proclaiming the end of the world. The Process recruiting headquarters was on Cole Street, two blocks from where Manson was crashing. Later, when

Manson was in jail in Los Angeles awaiting trial for the murders of Sharon Tate and others, he would be visited by some of The Process "brothers" and would contribute an article for the "Death" issue of the group's magazine.

The Process was a British import, the child of a union between Shanghai-born architectural student Robert De-Grimston More and his ex-prostitute wife, Mary Anne. (They would later drop the More and just use the name DeGrimston.) The two had met while taking a course at the Scientology Institute in London. In 1963, the DeGrimstons decided to form their own variety of engram therapy, called Compulsions Analysis, and began to attract a core of white, middle-class, young people dissatisfied with their lives. Within a year, the group had changed its name to The Process, and had taken on a religious aura. Its symbol was a swastika-like mandala composed of four P's coming together.

Disenchanted with the urban bustle of London, the DeGrimstons in 1966 bought a piece of land on the coast of Yucatán, Mexico, and with thirty members founded a community, XTUL. It was there that DeGrimston began to realize he was Jesus Christ and reveal the divine word. According to DeGrimston, there were three gods, or operating principles, in the universe: Jehovah, full of rectitude, abstinent, unforgiving; Lucifer, fun-loving, sensual, mystical, and material; and Satan, cruel, rapacious, and lustful. At the end of time, which was coming soon, "the Lamb and the Goat must come together—pure Love descended from the pinnacle of Heaven, united with pure hatred raised from the depths of Hell,"[4] and the three gods would be reconciled. Anyone committing himself to any of the three paths—self-denial, pleasure, or violence—would achieve salvation; the rest, the fence-straddlers, would be swallowed up by the "Grey Forces," the Establishment forces of mediocrity and middle-of-the-roadism.

"Three paths and a quagmire," an issue of the group's magazine later stated. "Where do you belong? Are you Jehovah's man, taking the stringent road of purity and rejoicing in the harsh strength of self-denial? Do you follow Lucifer, pursuing the ideal of perfect human love in a blissful atmosphere of self-indulgence? Is Satan your

[4]*Process*, No. 4, "Sex."

Master, leading you into dark paths of lust and licentiousness, and all the intricate pleasures of the flesh? Or do you take the road to nowhere, half-in, half-out, half-up, half-down, your instincts and ideals buried in a deep morass of hypocritical compromise and respectable mediocrity? Three paths and a quagmire. Time is running out."[5]

After a hurricane decimated the XTUL commune, DeGrimston and company returned to London and set up shop in a mansion in the Mayfair district. By 1967 they had packed up their bags and moved to New Orleans, where they officially incorporated as The Process, the Church of the Final Judgment. Sensing San Francisco was ripe for proselytizing, they soon showed up in the Bay City wearing their black capes embroidered with red Goats of Mendes and silver crosses. Their stay there was short and unfruitful, and after unsuccessfully trying to form a union with the Church of Satan—Anton LaVey dismissed them as "kooks"—they departed for Los Angeles, where their efforts to gather converts reaped similar results.

In 1968, they tried New York, but results there, too, were disappointing. Boston, Chicago, and Toronto, however, proved fertile ground. In Boston, the cult recruited through its soup kitchen and through several rock bands started up by members, and it even had a rock show on a local radio station. At its height in 1972, The Process claimed to have 100,000 members, although that is highly unlikely, as the largest chapter, Chicago, reportedly numbered only 250.

By 1974, the cult had begun to experience problems. The publicity generated by the Manson connection had backfired, and to appear less fearsome to the public, Process members had forsaken their ominous black robes for gray leisure suits. They themselves had succumbed to the Grey Forces. The group had begun to attract misfits, and internal squabbling was rife. Robert DeGrimston, who had retired from public view, and whose godlike pronouncements were handed down like commandments from Heaven, was ousted from his divine throne by his ex-hooker wife and returned to England. Mary Anne, in an effort to save the church, changed its name, dropped all

[5]*Ibid.*

the gods but Jehovah, and allegedly laid plans to settle in a rural area and regroup. Shortly thereafter, she, too, dropped out of sight, and that officially ended the cult's existence.

Some, however, like retired Captain Dale Griffis, of the Tiffin, Ohio, Police Department, believe that Mary Anne is still around, and only went underground to achieve her goals. He is convinced that she was the mysterious "Circe" (Mary Anne had used that name at times) who had surfaced in Toledo, Ohio, in the mid-1970s and opened an occult shop, and the same woman who bought a nearby chunk of rural real estate adjacent to a location reputed by informants as being a site of Satanic rituals involving human sacrifice. In 1985, law enforcement officials dug up the site, and although some ritualistic paraphernalia was found, no evidence of murder was unearthed. Shortly before the police raid on the property, the occult shop in Toledo closed and Circe disappeared.

Just what The Process was into is a matter of debate. Some, like William Bainbridge, who studied the group, say it was a peace-abiding, Armageddon cult whose Satanic cosmology was just an outgrowth of its counter-culture-sixties evolution. Others, like Ed Sanders, author of *The Family*, think it was a bloodthirsty, orgiastic, mind-bending cult under the direction of a Manson-like leader, only much more frightening than Manson could ever be in that it was able to successfully maintain a facade of eccentric legitimacy while secretly conducting vicious human sacrifices to its gods. He intimates a connection between one of the group and a cult rumored to have been conducting cannibalistic rites in the Santa Cruz Mountains in 1969, called the Four Pi movement.

The internal structure of The Process was hierarchical, and the "mysteries" and rites were strictly withheld from neophytes. Sanders claims that those rites were bloody and orgiastic, a claim denied by Bainbridge. But the image Bainbridge tries to portray of a peaceable counter-culture religion is hard to reconcile with some of the group's literature. The cult's slick and glossy magazine was filled with shrieking, winged skeletons, swastikas, Nazi-helmeted bikers, and Holocaust photos of bulldozed bodies. In the "Sex" issue, Satan's advocate, Mendez Castle, adjures followers to partake in necrophilia and graveyard desecrations or whatever other sexual act is required to "throw off the needless coverings that for society's squeamish sake you wear in public . . . Satan, your God, is among you, black and lowering, reeking of evil and the pit. You stand transfixed before Him, knowing you've only just begun to taste the divine degradation that He offers for your pleasure." In *Satan On War*, Robert DeGrimston exhorted those members choosing the Devil's path to "release the fiend that lies dormant within you, for he is strong and ruthless and his power is far beyond the bounds of human frailty."

The cult's literature repeated the theme of a union between the group and violent biker groups. Process leaders reputedly envisioned those groups as future shock troops in the coming Armageddon. A concerted effort was made by The Process to recruit members of the Hell's Angels and Gypsy Jokers and other radical biker clubs, who were seen as the "forces of Satan." It is perhaps no coincidence that Charles Manson had much the same idea, and used the sexual favors of his girls to attract biker clubs like the Straight Satans and Satan's Slaves to the Spahn Ranch.

Investigative reporter Maury Terry, in his 1987 book, *The Ultimate Evil*, flatly states that the cult was into murder and mayhem, teaching its members that by spreading violence and chaos, they would be helping to fulfill the prophecies of Armageddon and speed up the coming of the Final Judgment. Terry claims that David Berkowitz, the "Son of Sam" killer, who killed six and wounded seven others in New York in 1977, was not the "lone gunman" portrayed by New York City police, and had been part of a Satanic cult that trafficked in drugs and pornography, whose aims were to spread panic and destruction.

The cult, Terry claims, was a "Process offshoot with O.T.O. crossovers," and continues to operate secretly in six major U.S. cities. He blames the cult for dozens of murders before, during, and after the Son of Sam reign of terror, including the brutal 1974 murder of Arlis Perry in the chapel of Stanford University and at least two 1985 murders in New York, one a sadomasochistic homosexual killing in which a man's heart was cut out.

Berkowitz, who when caught claimed his killings were directed by the "Devil's henchmen," seemed to have some knowledge of the killing of Perry in California. Later, however, he recanted that part of his story, saying that the killings were "stupid" and random, and that the "Satan" stories were "baloney," made up to bolster an insanity plea.

Although Terry has amassed a considerable amount of evidence pointing to the possibility that Berkowitz had not, in fact, acted alone, his contentions that he had been part of a surviving splinter of The Process are considerably less compelling. His "proof" consists of items such as the fact that in taunting letters written by the Son of Sam to the police and columnist Jimmy Breslin during the murder spree, the British spelling of the word "colour" was used. The Process, as well as Aleister Crowley, was from Britain. He also cites other "Process-like terms" in the letters, such as the word "messenger," which was a Process rank. Messengers also deliver mail. He finds remarkable coincidences in the fact that the Process used to walk white Alsatian dogs and that German shepherds were being found mysteriously slaughtered—presumably as part of some terrible ritual sacrifice—and that Berkowitz was caught by police on August 10, Robert De-Grimston's birthdate!

Terry's bringing the O.T.O. into the picture also strains credibility. At one point, Terry states that The Process "incorporated the ideas of a number of its ancestors and current occupants of the occult landscape, including the O.T.O. Accordingly, there was an intermingling of philosophy, membership, and networking among the groups . . . Charles Manson, for example, was exposed to the practices of a renegade O.T.O. lodge in Southern California as well as having been influenced by the Process."[6]

Although there is ample evidence that Manson had been influenced by The Process, there is no evidence whatsoever that The Process and the O.T.O. had overlapping membership or ideas, or that Manson ever had any contact with the O.T.O. The "renegade lodge" Terry is referring to was the Solar Lodge, a secret magical society run by one Jean Brayton and her philosophy teacher husband, Richard. The Brayton cult operated a boardinghouse near the University of Southern California campus in Los Angeles in the late sixties and recruited members from the

[6]Terry, Maury, *The Ultimate Evil*, New York Doubleday, 1987, p. 181.

student body there. It also operated a commune and occult shop near the desert community of Blythe.

The Brayton cult held Crowley-like rituals involving drug use and animal sacrifice, but it was not sanctioned by the authorized O.T.O. headquartered in Livermore, California. In fact, the group may have been responsible for the theft of valuable Crowley books and ceremonial robes from the elderly widow of Karl Germer, a Crowley disciple.

The cult was broken up in the summer of 1969, when Riverside County sheriffs raided the Blythe commune and found a six-year-old boy chained in a packing crate. The boy was alledgedly being punished for setting fire to one of the commune's buildings, and had been kept in the crate for fifty-seven days during 110-degree temperatures. The Braytons, along with the boy's father, James Gibbons, an English teacher and Brayton disciple, fled when felony child-abuse warrants for their arrest were issued.

I aided Riverside County Deputy District Attorney Gary Scherotter in the investigation of the case and talked to informants from the cult, as well as the Braytons and the elder Gibbons, after they turned themselves in to the FBI a year after the commune incident. There was absolutely no evidence that Manson or any of his followers had any contact with the Solar Lodge, or that there was ever any crossover of ideas or membership between The Process and that, or any other, O.T.O. group. The source of those ideas seems to have been Ed Sanders, who in his book *The Family* postulated a Manson-Brayton link, and who seemed to be willing to swallow any unsubstantiated rumor he was fed and regurgitate it as fact.

Terry's claims of a "Sons of Sam" conspiracy are intriguing and deserve investigation. But his laying it on the doorstep of The Process is less so. Despite its literature, no hard evidence linking The Process to violence has been made, and there is no evidence that the cult survived after its breakup in 1974.

The incorporation of violence in magical ritual has had several historical rationales. It has been claimed by some, such as Aleister Crowley, that the biological energy released at the moment of death of an animal or human, combined with the emotional frenzy induced in the magician by the sight of blood, can be focused through the working of the ritual and sent psychically to do its work.

Second, in conjurations, the blood of a sacrificed animal can allegedly be used by the demon being summoned to form a physical manifestation in this plane.

On a psychological level, ritual murder and other barbaric acts have functioned as the identification with what Mircea Eliade terms the "Sacred Time" of the primitive, a time beyond the banality of the material world and the moral strictures of society. But the role of violence has played an even more important sociological role in the history of secret societies, as a centripetal force holding groups together. By forcing members of the group to partake in illegal, socially deviant, and violent acts, the leader further alienates those members from the outside world, fosters feelings of paranoia, and increases psychological and emotional dependence on the group.

Psychiatrists have increasingly turned from the Oedipus complex to the theories of Alfred Adler and others, who postulate the "striving for superiority" as the primary human motivation. People who feel a lack of control over their affairs experience hopelessness, depression, and feelings of low self-worth. One way to feel control, if one cannot feel it in his day-to-day affairs, is to exert it over others. The ultimate form of that control would be the control over another's life or death. The murderer then becomes God, the ultimate high. The trouble is that getting high can be addictive, and when that happens, the tolerance level keeps getting higher. Bigger dosages are needed to get the same effect.

By the end of 1969, the ceremony of innocence was drowned, the great social experiment was over, and all that remained in the Haight were the burned-out dregs and hard-core heroin addicts. But the Age of Aquarius had left a legacy. Hundreds of thousands had come to drink at the fount and departed. The Diaspora had begun.

A natural stopover for emigrants was the heavily wooded mountains around Santa Cruz, a hundred miles south of San Francisco. By late 1969, police in that area had begun to hear about orgiastic, drugged-out nocturnal rituals involving fire dancing, animal sacrifices, blood drinking, and infanticide. By 1970, Santa Cruz was dubbed the "murder capital of the world," after it was swept by a wave of brutal and bizarre killings. John Linley Frazier, a long-haired, bearded auto mechanic who was into Tarot cards, executed wealthy ophthalmologist Victor

Ohta and his family and left a note in the windshield of the doctor's Rolls-Royce warning "death to all those who defile the environment," and signed it the "Knight of Wands, the Knight of Cups, the Knight of Swords, and the Knight of Pentacles."

Then there was the case of Herbert Mullin, who killed nine people, including a priest whom he kicked to death in a confessional, as human sacrifices to the Earthquake God to stave off the Big One. The Psychedelic Revolution had spawned a new ecological outlook, and it spread like AIDS.

In May 1970, eighteen-year-old Patricia Hall, aka Inca Angelique, was arrested with three male drifters for the rape and cat-o'-nine-tails flogging of a teenage girl in a Hall of Horrors Wax Museum on Bourbon Street in New Orleans. Hall, described by police as a "hippie-type with tattoos," threatened to turn the arresting officers into frogs and claimed to have been baptized by the "Black Pope" in San Francisco. (Anton LaVey denies that Hall was ever one of his members.) She was later extradited to Florida, where she was convicted of the stabbing murder of a sixty-six-year-old man.

In June 1970, Steven Hurd, twenty, a barbiturate addict and self-proclaimed Satanist, was arrested, along with four friends, for the cannibal slaying of an Orange County, California, schoolteacher. The Hurd group, a Manson-type family of trolls, who, when they did not have the money to spend for motel rooms lived under bridges and in fields, had forced their way into the unfortunate teacher's car and driven her to a nearby orange grove, where they stabbed her to death and cannibalized her after offering up the body parts to Satan. The night before, the group had murdered a gas station attendant with a hatchet for twenty dollars and a can of STP. After being diagnosed as a paranoid schizophrenic, Hurd was sent to Atascadero State Hospital for the criminally insane, where he claims to be visited by his "father, Satan," whom he describes as a "man wearing a gold helmet, with the skin of a pinecone."

Less than a week after Hurd's arrest, Stanley Dean Baker, a twenty-two-year-old Wyoming lumberjack, along with a companion, Harry A. Stroop, were stopped by the California Highway Patrol near Big Sur, for suspicion of hit-and-run driving. After the registration of the vehicle they were driving failed to check out, the officers searched the pair and came up with a small bone Baker was carrying in his pocket. When asked what it was, Baker responded with a classic of understatement: "I have a problem. I'm a cannibal." He then proceeded to lay out to the astounded cops a tale from a modern horror movie.

The former owner of the car *and* the finger, it seemed— ill-fated Montana social worker James Schlosser—had picked up Baker hitchhiking outside Livingston, Montana. While camping that night on the Yellowstone River, at the foot of an area appropriately named Devil's Slide, Baker had awakened to a sky flashing with lightning. Baker claimed that he had experienced cannibalistic compulsions ever since he had suffered severe electrocution burns during an automobile accident as a teenager. Maybe the lightning triggered those compulsions, maybe it was the acid he had dropped earlier. Whatever incited him, Baker shot, dismembered, and beheaded the sleeping Schlosser, then cut out his heart and ate it and, knowing it was going to be a long ride to California, took one of Schlosser's fingers to snack on.

Despite the fact that both Baker and Stroop denied the latter's participation in the crime (they both claimed they had split up their hitchhiking efforts before Baker was picked up by Schlosser, then rejoined in California), and despite the fact that no real evidence was presented that implicated Stroop, he was also charged, and later convicted, of the murder.

Aside from being a cannibal, Baker, who had an IQ of 130, claimed to be a practicing Satanist and to have belonged to a blood-drinking cult in Wyoming. Investigation failed to turn up the cult, however, and the picture that emerged of the Satanic cannibal was that of a psychotic loner, too weird for even the hardened inmates of Deer Lodge Prison, where Baker was sentenced to life. After a few "werewolf" episodes, during which Baker would crouch in his cell and "growl like an animal," he was transferred to a maximum security prison in Illinois. There, Baker's behavior took a marked change and he became a model prisoner, and later gave lectures on Transactional Analysis to inmates with drug problems. His Satanic ideals did not wane, however, and in 1976, while still in prison, Baker unsuccessfully applied for membership in the Church of Satan.

During his trial, Baker was also linked by San Francisco police to an earlier slaying in that city of a nationally known lamp designer. The killer had slit the victim's throat, cut off his ear, and written "Satan Saves" in blood on the apartment wall. Baker was never tried for the crime, but San Francisco detectives working the case considered it closed with Baker's conviction in Montana.

A year later, in June 1971, a Vineland, New Jersey, teenager, Mike Newell, was found drowned in a sandy wash, his hands and feet bound with adhesive tape. A subsequent investigation turned up that Newell had been a leader of a group of about thirty high school students who practiced Devil-worship ceremonies, which included shaking up hamsters in a nail-studded box.

Newell, who believed that Satan would put him in command of "forty leagues of demons" if he died violently, enlisted the aid of two male members of the group, telling them that if they didn't help him commit suicide and thereby keep his "Satanic appointment," he would kill someone else. The two teenagers accompanied Newell to the wash, bound him, and pushed him into the water. Later investigation revealed that part of Newell's suicidal wishes may have been precipitated by an unrequited homosexual love affair.

Not all such cults formed in the late sixties indulged in ritualized violence. Some ceremonies, like those of the Brotherhood of the Ram, bordered on low comedy. Headed by Don R. Blythe, a man in his mid-forties who claimed to be the reincarnation of Aleister Crowley, as well as the earthly incarnation of Satan, the Brotherhood held its weekly meeting in a black-walled room on the second floor of a dilapidated Hollywood Boulevard office building. Blythe, who also ran a nearby disco called Satan's A Go-Go, worked for a Los Angeles pathology lab, and had presumably used that position to secure an assortment of decorative accessories for the Brotherhood's ritual chamber, such as a mummified human hand, the mummified remains of a human body in a sarcophagus (wrapped in strips of new linen bedsheet for authenticity), and the bottom half of a human skull mounted on a pedestal. The "kicker," though, which he saved for "adepts," he kept in a glass altar, covered with a black drapecloth. It was a "pickled punk"—carnie terminology for a dead baby in a jar of formaldehyde—which Blythe claimed was his son, Adrian. (Adrian was the name of Satan's child in *Rosemary's Baby*.)

About twenty were present at the ritual I attended, for the most part teenaged, long-haired, white, unemployed drug users. A reading of Baudelaire's "Litany to Satan" was followed by an invocation of Satan by two followers, after which four new initiates were sworn into the group by Blythe, who was dressed in a cowled black robe. The initiation consisted of each person reciting a prayer to Satan and smearing blood from a pinpricked finger on a piece of paper on which his or her name had been written.

Following the completion of the blood pact, the initiates were required to drink a liquid reputed by Blythe to be formaldehyde, thus "proving" Satan's protective powers, after which candles were extinguished and mysterious Day-Glo green eyes began to float around the room, indicating a "demonic" presence. Other carnie tricks equally as ludicrous were employed and eagerly swallowed by the gullible congregation. At one point in the "ceremony," Blythe commanded a fifteen-year-old girl to bare her breasts to the mummy, perhaps indicating another, more primal reason for the Brotherhood's weekly meetings.

The rituals of another group I investigated in the late sixties came awfully close to a traditional Black Mass, but I was assured by the participants that the resemblance was superficial. "The Black Mass is only being performed by sexual perverts and people over fifty," the High Priestess of the coven, a girl named Bobbi, told me. This group did believe in the magical efficacy of the Catholic Mass, so elements of it were employed, but the rituals were not intended as blasphemy. Although Satan was invoked during the ceremony, there were no inverted crosses, and the sexuality of the traditional Satanic Mass was absent.

The coven met in the candlelit living room of Bobbi's apartment. On a plain cinder-block altar, beneath a wire goat's head hanging from the ceiling, were a bell, black candles, an inverted pentagram, and a vial of wine consecrated by the long-haired and bearded High Priest, Bobbi's husband. Dressed in a black, hooded robe, he began the ritual by ringing the bell and lighting the candles while offering a prayer to Satan.

The Clarification was then performed, Bobbi stating formally the reasons for the meeting—the acquisition of money, for example—followed by the Purification, the blessing of the congregation by the sprinkling of a mixture of consecrated water and semen. During the Invocation, the word "Lucifer" was substituted for "Christ," and then the Catholic Latin missal was read, back to front. After the priest drank the wine and allegedly was possessed by Satan, the magical purpose of the evening was consummated and the ritual closed out.

Though this group may appear to have been anti-Christian, it was not. Its theology, like that of other cults flourishing in the late sixties, was an untraditional mishmash of Eastern mysticism, Kabbala, astrology, hermetic magic, and the *I Ching*. Its members believed that the Christian angels were once powerful magicians who had ascended into the Astral Plane, that spaceless and timeless middle ground between pure spirit and matter. While God was transcendent and ruled the upper part of the Plane, Satan and his group of elemental spirits ruled the lower levels. The composition of the membership was typical of the time—long-haired, disaffected, Caucasian dropouts, ranging in age from nineteen to thirty. Several had been part of the hippie movement in Berkeley and had drifted south, finding their way to Bobbi's coven through contacts at the Compleat Enchanter, an occult supply shop in Hollywood.

Also typical of such groups was the incorporation of drug use in their theology and rituals. Hallucinogens were the recommended method for communicating with the elemental spirits. One semicomical evening, I accompanied members of the coven as they drove all over L.A. in a quest for lard, a primary ingredient in a hallucinogenic "flying ointment" to be used in a midnight ritual. Although nothing else about this group was traditional, Bobbi insisted on adhering to the old witch's formula she had dug out of a *grimoire* (Crisco was not around in the seventeenth century), and the search continued until some lard was finally located at a Mexican market. All of the efforts to make kosher ointment turned out to be for naught, however, when Bobbi's husband broke the blades of his industrial blender trying to grind up a foul-smelling tannis root, a sure "magical sign" to the group that that evening was not propitious for a ritual.

By the early 1970s, the decline of the counterculture and the use of hallucinogens led to a waning popular interest in the occult. Spiritual realization and wicca groups lost membership as people once more became fixated on material goals. The "me" generation, forerunners of the yuppies, came into prominence. For a while, groups like the Church of Satan, which exhorted egotism and a pragmatic, selfish brand of ritual magic, thrived, but by 1975, interest in all magical groups dropped as the economy took an upturn and people got what they wanted through more practical means.

Aside from the occasional surfacing of an adolescent outlaw group, such as the Black Magic Cult in Northglenn, or a similar cult of high schoolers in Lake County, Illinois, in 1972, and a flurry of rumors of Satanic cattle sacrifices in the Midwest, all was quiet on the Satanic front.

The early 1980s, however, saw a revival of Satanic-related activity across the United States and Canada. Many of the reports have proven to be spurious, but some have had a basis in fact. In July 1983, a dozen churches in Portland, Maine, were defaced with Satanic slogans. In that same month, two teenagers were charged in Surrey, British Columbia, with grave robbing and the theft of religious objects from an Anglican church. In January 1984, bodies were snatched from a Tampa, Florida, cemetery, apparently for ritualistic use, and two months later, authorities in Hopkinsville, Kentucky, reported a similar incident, blaming "Satan-cultists."

Much media attention has focused in particular on marauding outlaw gangs of nihilistic adolescents who have adopted the name "stoners" and who are reputedly into dope, heavy metal music, and Satanic rituals involving grave robbings, vandalism, blood drinking, and animal sacrifice.

The "Satanism" of these "stoners," like that found in

most adolescent diabolist groups, seems to be more a way of venting aggressive, antisocial feelings than for the purposes of trying to raise demons in any literal sense. From all available evidence, their "rituals," whether involving the desecration of a church or graveyard, the ritualistic disembowling of a cat, self-mutilation or blood drinking, are made-up-as-you-go affairs, inspired more by the use of narcotics or the deviant attraction of the acts themselves than by any real commitment to or knowledge of Satanism.

According to juvenile authorities, the youths involved in stoner gangs are poor students or high school dropouts who have emotional problems at home and difficulty socializing with peers. Their nihilistic outlook, as well as their adoption of Satan as a hero, is a symbolic assault on parental authority and the citadel of social acceptability.

Sociologist Orrin Klapp sees all forms of cultism as a response to an identity crisis brought on by: (1) emotional impoverishment, (2) banality, and (3) stylessness. In a wider social context the impromptu gatherings of most Satanic stoners would clearly fill the bill on all three levels. When the activities of such a group become socially deviant and illegal, however, participation reaches a level of seriousness that indicates pathological desperation.

"There is no reason to assume that only those who finally commit a deviant act actually have the impulse to do so," says another sociologist, Howard Becker, who has made a study of deviant behavior. "It is much more likely that most people experience deviant impulses frequently. At least in fantasy, people are much more deviant than they might appear. Instead of asking why deviants want to do things that are disapproved of, we might better ask why conventional people do not follow through on deviant impulses they have."[7] Becker concludes they don't because they have a stake in society, and therefore a vested interest in conformity.

As Becker points out, the less stake someone has in society, the less he would have to lose by freeing his inner demons. Manson, Ramirez, Kasso, Hurd, and other Satanic outlaws fit that pattern. They came from broken homes, were abandoned and physically abused as children, alien-

[7]Becker, Howard, op. cit., p. 26–7.

ated as adolescents, and showed early propensities for violence. They were outcasts, shunned by their peers and tormented by their own failures and visions of others' success. Put that kind of hostility into a cauldron, mix in the eye of a newt and the blood of a bat, stir in a little LSD and a few Reds, maybe a pinch of Angel Dust, and you have a recipe for murder, whether the murderer calls himself a Satanist, a Nazi, a Klansman, a Yahweh, a Black Muslim, or a Jesus freak.

In the 1930s, horror writer H. P. Lovecraft penned a series of stories about a prehistoric race of god-men who, by practicing black magic, had lost their foothold on the world and been expelled into another dimension. There they wait, just beyond the realm of time and space, ready to be summoned to take back the earth. In all of Lovecraft's tales, the reader is constantly reminded that man is just a short step away from insanity and the most depraved forms of bestiality.

Some consider Lovecraft's gods to be an insightful metaphor for the irrational elements in man's psyche and believe that all that is needed is a slight tear in the fabric of objective consciousness for man to be overwhelmed by the gods of Cthulhu. Some of us may be forgiven if we believe that that tear was made in 1966, and that the gods are already here, having entered through the gaping hole left by the dying Age of Aquarius.

CHAPTER VIII

The Church of Satan

> The Devil does not exist. It is a false name invented by the Black Brothers to imply a Unity in their ignorant muddle of dispersions. A devil who had unity would be a God.
> —Aleister Crowley, *Magick in Theory and Practice*

> "P. T. Barnum said, 'A sucker is born every minute.' With the population explosion, by now there must be five."
> —Anton Szandor LaVey, conversation, 1986

From the outside, it is an unlikely looking Vatican. Apart from the electronically controlled, barbed-wire-topped gate barring uninvited visitors, the three-story gray Victorian house from the outside appears little different from its neighbors. The interior, however, is a different story.

The living room contains such arcane bits of furniture as an Egyptian sarcophagus, a sled-chair once owned by Rasputin, and a coffee table made from a yogi's bed of nails. In the den, a wall of shelves lined with books on every esoteric subject imaginable—from the carnival to cannibalism—is, in reality, a secret passage that opens into an adjoining sleeping chamber decorated with ceremonial masks. The entire house, in fact, is honeycombed with secret passages, left over from its days as a bordello and speakeasy. The fortunate visitor might even be taken down the staircase behind the fireplace and into the old speak, now the Den of Iniquity, a private saloon created by the master of the house, the so-called Black Pope—Anton Szandor LaVey.

Glowing against one wall, an old Rockola jukebox faces

a drum set and Hammond organ with red- and blue-lit keys. A disheveled woman is passed out in one corner, her dress hiked up above the tops of her garter-secured nylons, a puddle of urine spreading between her splayed legs. At the bar, a sailor in uniform has his fist raised menacingly to a glassy-eyed slattern wearing a ratty-looking fur boa.

But there will be no violence there tonight or on any other night. These patrons are regulars at the Den of Iniquity, and although they begin to look real after a time, and even *feel* real, they are polyurethane mannikins fashioned by LaVey himself. The Satanic High Priest often comes down in the middle of the night to serenade them with songs from the 1940s, the period that the Den of Iniquity was set up to evoke.

"This place is a time warp," the Black Pope proclaims as he plunks out a rendition of "Devil Moon." "It is more Satanic than a Black Mass because it is more stimulating to the imagination. You wait. After a while, those manni-kins will start to *move*."

And they do.

The fact that it is merely an illusion makes no differ-ence, LaVey insists, for that is the purpose of any magical ritual, to blur the lines of subjective and objective reality. The basis of all magical thinking, from primitive to modern, is that by altering the subjective the practitioner can alter the objective.

Sixteen years ago, a passerby, hurrying through an evening fog, might have heard strange chants coming from inside the then-black house. But in 1970, LaVey stopped holding Satanic rituals at this home, now using it solely as an administrative headquarters for his church. Today, all one might hear would be one faint strain of "Honolulu Baby" or "I'm Heading for the Last Roundup" from either the Den of Iniquity or the mass of synthesizer keyboards occupying most of the upstairs kitchen.

LaVey, whose working day, like that of a vampire, is from dusk to dawn, plays almost every night in those hours when most people are asleep and at their peak of psychic receptivity. His music is a form of ritual magic, he asserts, and its vibratory frequencies are setting in motion forces that will result in a worldwide takeover of the ideals of a new Satanic Romanticism.

"Certain frequencies transmitted on the ether effect the

human subconscious and control behavior, much in the same way elephants can be made to march by the playing of certain circus tunes," LaVey explains. However, the effects can be more than psychological: LaVey believes things like the weather can be affected, and blames his angry banging on the keyboards one night for the disastrous 1986 earthquake in Mexico.

Is the man serious, or merely suffering from a major ego problem? It is often difficult to know when LaVey is kidding; he has the irreverent, cynical sense of humor of a true carnie, and like a carnie, will try to get away with whatever the rubes will allow. "LaVey is a junkyard intellectual," wrote *Washington Post* reporter Walt Harrington after interviewing him, "a philosopher of the sordid, a savant, an ingratiating and funny man. He's a man who could find no faith, until he discovered magic. But Anton LaVey worships only Anton LaVey. His religion is egotism, and that, as LaVey would say, is truly Satanic."[1]

At the age of sixteen, LaVey ran away from his Oakland home to join the Clyde Beatty Circus as a cage boy, later becoming assistant lion tamer, which he credits with having taught him force of will. At eighteen, he left the circus to work in a carnival. There he became a stage hypnotist and mentalist and also learned to play the organ, a skill he transferred a few years later to burlesque houses. It was at one of those clubs, the Mayan, in Los Angeles, that he played bump-and-grind—both on and off stage—for a young stripper named Marilyn Monroe, who LaVey described as a willing, but not very imaginative, sex partner.

Inspired by his first wife to live a more sedate life, LaVey entered San Francisco City College as a criminology major and soon landed a job as a photographer for the San Francisco Police Department. That job only reinforced his growing cynicism, for it exposed him to the degraded and aggressive side of human nature. Man was much worse than the four-legged variety of animal, he decided. So if there was a God and this was his crowning achievement, then he must be terribly flawed.

Disgusted with the senseless violence he witnessed, LaVey returned to playing the organ for his livelihood,

[1]Harrington, Walt, "The Devil in Anton LaVey," Washington Post Magazine, Feb 23, 1986, p. 7.

and on the side resumed a serious study of the occult teaching and practices of ceremonial magic, which had always fascinated him. He became so proficient in esoteric subjects that he began to hold Friday night lectures in his house, and for a small fee the public would pack the front living room to learn about werewolves, vampires, sex magic, and witchcraft. During one such lecture on cannibalism, a severed human leg was brought from East San Francisco Bay Hospital by a physician-member, basted in Triple Sec, and served to the less queasy in the group.

The lectures, the strange black house, and LaVey's own colorful background and character made perfect fodder for local columnists like Herb Caen, who began to write about LaVey's midnight investigations of haunted houses and other alleged examples of psychic phenomena. Another favorite subject of Caen's was LaVey's odd choice of pets—a black leopard and a housebroken 400-pound Nubian lion named Togare—which lived with LaVey and his second wife, Diane. (The leopard escaped and was killed by a car and LaVey was eventually forced to give away Togare after neighbors repeatedly complained to the police about the animal's nocturnal roaring.)

A core of serious students of the arcane began to find their way to the house, like filmmaker Kenneth Anger and novelist Steven Schneck, and with them LaVey formed the Magic Circle, whose weekly rituals were *not* open to the public. The thought soon struck LaVey that the energy the group was being squandered trying to move a teacup by psychic means and might be better put to use spreading the philosophy he had developed throughout his eclectic evolution. Thus, on Walpurgisnacht 1966, the Magic Circle became the Church of Satan, with LaVey as its High Priest, and his pretty blond wife, Diane, as High Priestess.

In 1967, the Church received national press coverage when LaVey performed a Satanic wedding of socialite Judith Case and radical journalist John Raymond. In May of that year, it made news again when LaVey performed a Satanic baptism of the LaVeys' three-year-old daughter, Zeena, and in December, he created another media event when he performed Satanic last rites for a sailor member, complete with a full naval color guard. With the publicity came a flood of would-be initiates to the church.

Among the curious seeking entrance to the "Devil house" were celebrities like Sammy Davis, Jr., singer Barbara McNair, and veteran actor Keenan Wynn, upon whom LaVey later bestowed an honorary priesthood. Davis was such a fervent member that, for a time, he wore a Satanic Baphomet medallion on stage and actively proselytized the cause, setting up dinner meetings at his Los Angeles home between LaVey and various movie and entertainment personalities. While most of the more famous Hollywood figures requested their affiliation with the church be kept secret for fear of harming their careers, one who didn't mind was buxom sex symbol Jayne Mansfield.

Mansfield showed up at the church in 1966 with a request that the High Priest put a curse on her second husband, Matt Cimber, with whom she was engaged in a child custody battle. After she won a favorable court ruling, she became an ardent Devil's disciple. When her young son, Zoltan, was later critically mauled by a lion at Jungleland Wild Animal Park, the actress called LaVey for help. The High Priest drove to the top of Mount Tamalpais, near San Francisco, and in the middle of a torrential rainstorm summoned all his magical powers while bellowing out a soliloquy to Satan. Mansfield credited the boy's miraculous recovery to Satanic intervention and swore her undying loyalty to LaVey and the Prince of Darkness.

Unfortunately, the relationship with LaVey inspired the jealousy of Mansfield's boyfriend, Sam Brody, who threatened to expose LaVey as a charlatan unless he stayed away from Jayne. LaVey responded by putting a curse on Brody, who shortly thereafter smashed up his Maserati and broke his leg. Undeterred, Brody continued his threats and LaVey retaliated with yet another cursing ritual, this one more serious.

LaVey claims that he called Jayne and warned her to stay away from Brody, but she did not, and on June 29, 1967, the car in which she and Brody were traveling rear-ended a truck outside New Orleans. Brody and the driver were killed instantly and Mansfield was decapitated in the crash. LaVey blamed himself for Jayne's death. It seems that while clipping some newspaper articles, he noticed that on the back of one was a photograph of Mansfield and

that he had cut off her head. It was then he received the
phone call saying she had been killed. To this day, LaVey
claims to be shaken up by the "coincidence."

Mansfield's tragic death and the subsequent revelations
about the "curse" proved to be a media bonanza for the
Church of Satan, and membership mushroomed. LaVey's
The Satanic Bible, expounding his philosophy, became an
immediate occult best-seller upon its publication in 1969,
its sales soon topping the half-million mark. There was
even a poster parodying the Army's image of Uncle Sam: a
horned, pointing LaVey announcing, "Satan Wants You."

Applicants with emotional disorders could generally be
spotted from their corespondence, as was the case with a
female executive in a large East Coast cosmetic firm, who
was coming to California on a two-week vacation and
wanted to pay LaVey five hundred dollars to crucify her in
the woods. The woman had her own "gold spikes" and
wanted to be up "at least five days, not twenty-four hours,
like that wimp, Jesus Christ."

The ones harder to weed out were the numerous early
male recruits who believed the more lurid publicity and
joined the church ready to dedicate themselves to Satan in
the Friday night orgies. Generally, these fellows were
disappointed, for, although a naked woman was used as
an altar, there were no orgies.

Not only were there no orgies, there was not even a
Devil on or near the premises. Satan was not a literal
deity, LaVey told his followers, but merely a *symbol*, as
defined in his nine Satanic statements:

1. Satan represents indulgence, instead of absti-
   nence!
2. Satan represents vital existence, instead of
   spiritual pipedreams!
3. Satan represents undefiled wisdom, instead of
   hypocritical self-deceit!
4. Satan represents kindness to those who deserve it, instead of love wasted on ingrates!
5. Satan represents vengeance, instead of turning the other cheek!
6. Satan represents responsibility to the responsible, instead of concern for psychic vampires!

7. Satan represents a man as just another animal, sometimes better, more often worse than those that walk on all fours, who because of his divine spiritual and intellectual development has become the most vicious animal of all!
8. Satan represents all of the so-called sins, as they lead to physical or mental gratification!
9. Satan has been the best friend the church has ever had, as he has kept it in business all these years![2]

Social psychologist Marcello Truzzi, who has studied the Church from its inception, says:

> The Church of Satan's philosophical world view is really more accurately designed as an ideological than a religious one. The name "Satanism" and its other seeming relations to Christianity are actually somewhat misleading, for these are mainly used in a symbolic sense (thus, Satan is simply the symbol of the Adversary, in this case to the dominant belief system of Christianity). Thus, the Church of Satan is not really a sect of Christianity in the same sense as are most present and past Satanic groups."[3]

His brand of Satanism, explains LaVey, was designed to fill the void between religion and psychiatry, meeting man's need for ritual, fantasy, and enchantment while at the same time providing a rational set of beliefs on which to base his life. The other major religions are outmoded, he asserts, because they are trying to keep superstition alive in a technological age. Christianity preaches the virtues of altruism and asceticism, LaVey acknowledges, but for political, not world, reasons.

"What are the Seven Deadly Sins?" he is fond of asking. "Gluttony, avarice, lust, sloth—they are urges every man feels at least once a day. How would you set yourself up as the most powerful institution on earth? You first find out

---

[2]LaVey, *The Satanic Bible,* New York: Avon, 1969, p. 26.
[3]Truzzi, Marcello, "Towards a Sociology of the Occult: Notes on Modern Witchcraft," in Irving I. Zaretsky and Mark P. Leone, ed., Religious Movements in Contemporary America," Princeton: Princeton University Press, 1974, p. 645.

what every man feels at least once a day, establish that as a sin, and set yourself up as the only institution capable of pardoning that sin."

For LaVey, it is the guilt that makes people sick, not their urges. If an individual is law-abiding and causes harm to no other creature, then he or she should be able to indulge in whatever activity, sexual or otherwise, that he or she finds pleasurable. Distinguishing self-indulgence from compulsion, however, LaVey cautions, "If a person has no proper release for his desires, they rapidly build up and become compulsions."

In reality, it might not be so easy to tell when the line between the two has been crossed. Like a drug addict or alcoholic who insists he can stop anytime he wants, a person may try to present a sexual compulsion simply as a preference. Yet, as long as the compulsions weren't alarmingly overt, LaVey, in the early days of the Church of Satan, was not strict in applying the distinction. He recognized that many of those applying for membership did indeed have emotional and psychological problems and were attracted to his church *because* of their feelings of alienation from the rest of society. In fact, many of the rituals held at midnight on Fridays at the black house took that fact into account with accommodating calculation.

For those former Catholics still emotionally involved with their old religion, a blasphemous Black Mass was performed, minus any horrific elements. Other rituals bordered on psychodrama, such as the Shibboleth, its purpose to reduce certain fears by confronting them and acting them out.

During a performance, Shibboleth participants would dress up and behave like someone they considered hateful and intimidating. A man who feared his authoritarian employer might stomp around the room, for example, threatening to fire everyone for incompetence, or a woman who was afraid of her domineering husband might shout at the female members in the room to get dinner. After the role-playing, a kangaroo court would be held at which the Satanic priest for the evening would take the part of the accuser and through a penetrating cross-examination, expose each "actor's" defense mechanisms.

While, admittedly, it's difficult for participants in a psychodrama not to appear foolish and while many of the early rituals were designed to grab the attention of the media, some ceremonies—far from being frightening or even dramatic—were so silly they appeared to be an orchestrated mockery by LaVey of his own members. Like a nightclub singer handing a microphone to a drunk, LaVey often seemed to be turning his members loose for his own amusement.

"Das Tierdrama," a ritual authored by LaVey as a paean to man's animal nature, was an exception, for it had a dramatic impact that stood in great contrast to those daffy moments when men and women climbed into coffins together, with onlookers shouting, "Hail, Satan!"

This solemn rite begins in total darkness. After a preliminary invocation, the four cardinal points are invoked, symbolically opening the "gates of Hell." Then the circle of light reveals the scarlet-robed priest seated on a throne, wearing the mask and hairy hands of a werewolf. A lictor stands beside the throne, holding a bull whip in his black-gloved hand. Next the priest summons the "beasts" by banging a wooden staff on the floor; one by one, they emerge into the light, wearing the papier-mâché heads of various animals.

The litany used in this ceremony had its origins in the combination of an obscure 1930s occult tract called *The Emerald Book of Thoth* and H. G. Wells's *The Island of Dr. Moreau*. First the priest:

> I am the Sayer of the Law. Here come all
> that be new, to learn the Law . . .
> Say the words! Learn the law.
> Say the words! Say the words!
>
> Not to go on all fours: this is the law
> Are we not men?

Then the beasts:

> Not to go on all fours: that is the law.
> Are we not men?

Invocator:

> Not to show our fangs in anger.
> Are we not men?
> (Repeated by beasts)

Invocator:

> Not to snarl or roar. That is
> the law.
> Are we not men?

Invocator:

> Man is God. (Repeated)
> We are men. (Repeated)
> We are gods. (Repeated)
> God is man. (Repeated)

After this is ended, the red-robed invocator, representing half man, half beast, drinks from a chalice, containing any liquid *but* blood. Finally, a live mouse in a cage is produced and turned loose. The "beasts" crouch down, as if tempted to chase it and kill it, then restrain themselves and slouch out of the light. The ceremony is concluded in the standard way, with the priest "closing the gates to Hell" by ringing a bell while turning counterclockwise in a circle.

The purpose of the ritual, according to LaVey, was for the celebrants to willingly regress into "an animal state of honesty, purity, and increased sensory perception."

"Das Tierdrama" was just one of the nontraditional Satanic ceremonies authored by LaVey. Another, "Die Elektrischen Vorspiele," inspired by pre–World War II German expressionistic films like *Metropolis*, employed Van de Graaff generators, neon tubing, and strobe lights in an effort to "charge" the ritual chamber with energy.

LaVey even commissioned one of his members, Michael Aquino (who later broke away and formed his own Satanic group), to author a set of rituals based on the works of horror writer H. P. Lovecraft. Some traditionalists have scoffed at his "Cthulhu" rituals, saying that they invoke gods that do not exist. But LaVey says these critics miss the point: all gods are fictitious. The purpose of his ritual, he says, is to evoke emotion, because "there are virtually no Satanic rites over one hundred years old that elicit sufficient emotional response from today's practitioner, if the rites are presented in their original form.

. . . In short, one no longer reads a Victorian romance for sexual titillation."[4]

Emotion, or "adrenal energy," as LaVey calls it, is the cornerstone of his system of magic. His rituals, he has explained, were designed to induce in the celebrant a subjective state through which he or she might be able to summon and direct his or her own psychic powers to achieve external goals. This is not "magic," in the classic sense of invoking demonic entities and sending them out to do one's bidding, but the harnessing of one's own extrasensory biological powers—what LaVey calls "applied psychology multiplied tenfold."

There is nothing supernatural about his magic, the High Priest insists. It is merely tapping into and exploiting a system of causal relationships always operational in the universe but presently unknown to modern science. As he puts it:

> I don't believe that magic is supernatural, only that it is supernormal. That is, it works for reasons science cannot yet understand. As a shaman or magician, I am concerned with obtaining recipes. As a scientist, you seek formulas. When I make a soup, I don't care about the chemical reactions between the potatoes and the carrots. I only care about how to get the flavor of the soup I seek. In the same way, when I want to hex someone, I don't care about the scientific mechanisms involved whether they be psychosomatic, psychological, or what-not. My concern is with how to best hex someone. As a magician, my concern is with effectively doing the thing— not with the scientist's job of explaining it.[5]

That LaVey's magical ideas were strongly influenced by the writings of Aleister Crowley can be seen in the distinction he makes between "greater" and "lesser" magic. Crowley defined "MAGICK" as the science of effecting environmental change in conformity with one's will that could be manifested in mundane forms of physical and mental control, such as banking or farming.

[4]LaVey, Anton Szandor, *The Satanic Rituals*, New York: Avon, 1972, p. 25
[5]Truzzi, Marcello, ibid., p. 645.

Similarly, LaVey's "lesser magic" is that lower order of "magic" which man uses to manipulate his everyday environment—moving the right way, saying the right thing, using appearance and demeanor to accomplish one's goals. In this sense, the use of sex is a basic tool of lesser magic, and in 1970, LaVey put out a sexually oriented how-to-manipulate manual for females called *The Compleat Witch, or What to Do When Virtue Fails.* "Greater magic," on the other hand, is regarded as the accomplishment of changes in the objective universe through those "great subjective outpourings of the will" summoned during a ritual. This is how curses work, LaVey says, although he is quick to point out that even if a curse doesn't work objectively, it doesn't matter, because it is cathartically beneficial to the curser.

Throughout the early 1970s, LaVey's Church of Satan continued to grow. By 1973, grottos, as the local chapters were called, were flourishing in New York, Boston, Detroit, Dayton, Phoenix, Denver, Los Angeles, Seattle, St. Petersburg, Louisville, Las Vegas, Indianapolis, and Chicago, as well as in Vancouver and Edmonton in Canada. Estimates for membership at that peak time range from 300 (a figure given by disgruntled former Church of Satan Members) to 10,000 (by COS spokesmen at the time), with a more accurate number probably being closer to 5,000. Members were disaffected refugees from disbanded wicca, or "white" witchcraft groups, fed up with self-effacement and attracted by the Church of Satan's values of ego-aggrandizement and personal gain.

Some sought the Church as a reaction against their strict fundamentalist upbringing. Still others, notably homosexuals, were attracted by Satanic attitudes of sexual tolerance. The occupational spectrum of the proselytes was wide, ranging from doctors, lawyers, computer programmers, and FBI agents to plumbers, electricians, and bartenders.

As previously noted, quite a few of those seeking admittance also shared another trait—dissatisfaction with their lives. Many seemed to be underachievers who expressed bitterness about their economic plight or lack of social status, or who complained about the boring nature of their jobs. A common lament was the lack of control these people felt over their own lives. Often, feelings of inadequacy were turned inside out, and at social gatherings the Satanists would sneer disdainfully at "outsiders." "Normal" people were chumps, moronic conformists; they, the Satanists, were different.

In joining the Church of Satan, these people not only managed to inject a little mystery and exoticism into their otherwise banal lives, they achieved a satisfying sense of mastery over their own fates by the practice of ritual magic. By becoming masters of arcane powers they became unique. As Edward Moody, an anthropologist who observed the church, noted, many Satanists were seeking "successes denied them—money, fame, recognition, power—and with all avenues apparently blocked, with no apparent means by which legitimate effort will bring reward, they turn to Satanism and witchcraft."[5]

But when insecure, frustrated initiates began to rely more on the grottos for their feelings of internal worth, and less on the mundane world, problems began to surface. Rapid expansion and the competition for titles within the hierarchical system LaVey had set up accentuated personal jealousies between some members, and San Francisco headquarters was soon bogged down by requests from grottos all over the country for arbitration of rivalrous disputes.

One particular source of complaints was the Babylon Grotto in Detroit. There Wayne West, a lame, defrocked Catholic priest from Britain and head of the grotto, was accused by some members of taking unauthorized fees and infecting the group's rituals with his personal sexual preferences for bondage and homosexuality. West was excommunicated but had enough loyal followers to found his own Universal Church of Man, described as "Satanism without Satan." It never really got off the ground, and West eventually faded from sight.

Detroit was not the only grotto to experience trouble. In February 1973, in Dayton, Ohio, the charter of the Stygian Grotto was revoked for "violation of the law" and administrative irregularities, after allegations were made that certain leaders had been dealing in stolen property. Stygian John DeHaven, along with members Joseph

---

[5]Moody, Edward, "Magical Therapy: An Anthropological Investigation of Contemporary Satanism," in. Irvine I. Zaretsky and Mark P. Leone, ed., *Religious Movements in Contemporary America*, Princeton: Princeton University Press, 1974, p. 358.

Daniels, Harry Booth, a 300-pound ex-biker named Ron Lanting, and two dozen other disgruntled members from Dayton, Detroit, and Indianapolis, responded by forming a rival organization, the Church of Satanic Brotherhood. While the beliefs of the Brotherhood remained philosophically akin to the teachings of *The Satanic Bible*, the sentiment within the group was definitely anti-LaVey, and a new set of rituals was performed. Without the charisma of a LaVey to hold it together, however, the group disintegrated within a year.

Another short-lived splinter, the Ordo Templi Santanas, was formed by Joseph Daniels in 1974 but lasted only long enough to perform a "memorial service" for DeHaven. That ex–High Priest had moved to St. Petersburg, Florida, and while working as a disc jockey at a radio station there, had announced on the air his conversion to Christianity.

In the meantime, two former Detroit members still affiliated with the Church of Satan, Michael Grumbowski and John Amend, aka Seth-Klippoth, aka Seth-Typhon, founded yet two more groups: the Order of the Black Ram (OBR) and the Shrine of the Little Mother, both of which combined Satanism with quasi-mystical ideas of Aryan racial superiority. As espoused in its newsletter, *Grimorium Verum*, the OBR's beliefs were a hodgepodge of Satanism, paganism, astral projection, geomancy, and the cult of the Little Mother. The "Shrine" departed radically from Church of Satan doctrine in that it performed chicken sacrifices during its rituals, and both groups had a definite neo-Nazi flavor. Amend, a paramilitary type, attempted to establish close ties between the OBR, James Madole's small but violent neo-Nazi National Renaissance Party, and Canada's Odinist Movement, a right-wing, anti-Semitic, Wagnerian nature religion founded in Australia in the 1920s.

Madole, a rabid anti-Semite, had been trying to forge an alliance between his NRP and the Church of Satan for some time. Not only did he have a huge Satanic altar in the living room of the walk-up New York City apartment where he lived with his mother, he listed Church of Satan works for sale in his Party *Bulletin*, established occult study units to work alongside his brown-shirted goon squads, and at political rallies played side two of LaVey's "Satanic Mass" record.

From the strong influence of magical secret societies on the development of National Socialism in Germany, to the close links in America between groups like the bizarre I AM cult and William Dudley Pelley's fascistic Silver Shirts in the 1930s, the historical affinity between occultism and the radical right has been well documented. Both believe and adhere to the conspiracy theory of history—that is, that events are shaped by the workings of small, elite, but concealed groups—and both believe in the ability of one man, whether it be a Magus or a Hitler, to alter global events through the sheer force of his will. Thus, a 1971 *Newsweek* article expressed concern about LaVey's political intentions: "If there is anything fundamentally diabolic about LaVey, it stems more from the echoes of Nazism in his theories than from the horror-comic trappings of his cult."[6]

Radical-right groups besides Madole's had sought to ally themselves with the Church of Satan, including the American Nazi Party and Robert Shelton's United Klans of America, but LaVey had always rejected the overtures, just as he rejected Madole's.

That the Klan, allegedly the last bastion of white Christianity holding back the "Commie-Jew-atheist hordes of Satan," would seek to align itself with the dark forces it professes to abhor is not as strange as it might first appear. According to sociologists Charles Glock and Rodney Stark, religious cults and radical political movements spring from the same source—deprivation. When a person is economically, socially, or psychologically shut out of the mainstream of society, he will seek solace in extreme solutions. Whether by joining a cult or putting on a sheet, the individual becomes part of an extended family, which in turn gives him a feeling of power and prestige and thus eliminates his feelings of deprivation.

Radical rightists saw an ally in LaVey presumably because of his Machiavellian, power-oriented philosophy and because of public statements he'd made advocating establishment of a "benign police state," not to mention the strong Germanic flavor of some of his rituals. But although LaVey was willing to use the sympathies of these groups when possible to his benefit, he kept them at arm's

[6]"Evil, Anyone?" *Newsweek*, Aug. 16, 1971.

length and privately expressed contempt for their anti-Semitic, racist ideas.

In 1974, LaVey wrote:

> The N.R.P. is enamored with the Church of Satan. Their racist ideals are also worn on their sleeves, and, I believe, are as removable as their armbands. . . . The C/S must be O.K., like the Hell's Angels. The colors are similar. The Angels, the Nazis, and the C/S. All together. Even the Klan. Night Riders all. Now the enemy is the weakling. All my life I've been the weakling, but with my swastika, I'm strong. My Satanic amulet gives me power. I'm not the misfit anymore, with pimples and a heart murmur and flat feet. What does it matter anymore that I can't play baseball or don't spell too good? So what if I can't get a girl? I got my armband. You see, we are dealing with intelligence levels on which imagery and ideals are easily interchangeable.[7]

In 1975, Aquino, the editor of the Church of Satan's newsletter, accused LaVey of selling priesthoods. Aquino contended that such degrees should be conferred solely on the basis of personal magical achievement, but LaVey dismissed the complaints, saying that members who contributed monetarily or with services to the Church often helped the cause more than "theologians." LaVey considered the degrees as symbols reflective of the members' status in the outside world, and reserved the right, as High Priest, to confer them as he saw fit.

In protest, Aquino resigned his priesthood and with Lilith Sinclair (aka Pat Wise), head of the New York Lilith Grotto, announced the formation of the Temple of Set. Other resignations followed.

LaVey claims the defections were part of his own master plan to dismantle the problem-plagued grotto system and purge the church of the "dependent, parasitic personality types" it had bred. "These people were groupies, not Satanists," he explained. "They were the kind of people who would attend a ritual, then put on their Baphomets and go out to the nearest Denny's. Big deal."

[7]Anton LaVey, personal papers.

The various grottoes were phased out. The San Francisco headquarters continued to process individual membership applications, but no more group charters were issued. LaVey, disenchanted by the fickleness of his flock and sick of the huckster image consistently foisted on him by the media, slammed the doors of the church shut. He refused to give interviews and became increasingly reclusive, leading observers to conclude that the Church of Satan was moribund.

LaVey, however, depressed by his inability to get the general public to take him and his ideas seriously, was going through a period of introspective reevaluation. Behind closed doors, Diane LaVey continued to handle most of the day-to-day administrative work and correspondence. In the meantime, LaVey's older daughter, Karla, had followed in her father's footsteps. After earning a degree in criminology, she acted as a roving church ambassador, delivering lectures on Satanic beliefs and practices to college audiences across the country. In the face of the disappointing turn of events with his church, LaVey decided to utilize Karla's talents elsewhere, sending her to evaluate the European scene and investigate the feasibility of making the Magistralis Grotto, located in Amsterdam, the new international headquarters of the Church of Satan.

The Magistralis Grotto had been established in the Netherlands in 1972, under the supervision of Martin Lamers. Lamers, a former actor who had bankrolled a Dutch version of the stage show *Oh! Calcutta!* had been first exposed to Satanism while vacationing in New York the year before. After picking up a copy of *The Satanic Bible*, he felt as if he had to talk to LaVey, and flew to San Francisco. A meeting of the two resulted in Lamers' returning to the Netherlands shortly thereafter with a charter for what was to be the Grotto Magistralis.

The first location of the Dutch Kerk du Satan was in Etersheim in one of the oldest Protestant churches in Holland, but after operating there for three years Lamers decided in 1976 to move the operation to Amsterdam. He bought a pair of back-to-back buildings in the heart of the city's red-light district, directly across a garbage-littered canal from Oude Kerk, Amsterdam's oldest church. He installed the kerk in one, and in the other opened Walburga Abbey, a club where patrons paid by the minute to watch the "monastic sisters" masturbate on stage.

Despite a Dutch tradition of moral liberalism, Lamers encountered difficulties with authorities from the outset—not because of what he preached, but because of money. In declaring tax-exempt status not only for the church operation but also for the Abbey, Lamers drew fire from government officials who scoffed at the contention that the Abbey's stage was really an "altar" on which the "sisters" performed "acts of symbolic communion with Shaitan," and that the money spent by patrons was "religious donations."

Lamers took the issue to court and although he won the first round, the decision caused a rift between him and the LaVeys, who sided with the Dutch government in the debate. Precisely to avoid such problems with the IRS, the LaVeys had never applied for tax-exempt status for the Church of Satan in the United States, as evidence of his feelings that *all* churches should be taxed, and they regarded Lamers's actions as damaging to the church's credibility. Karla returned to the States, and for a time the LaVeys considered pulling the Amsterdam charter and moving the international headquarters to London. That plan was scrapped after an uneasy reconciliation.

Although the attention brought on by his court battles made the young and dapper Lamers a local celebrity, he blames the focusing of the media on sex and taxes for his inability to get the public to take him and his followers seriously. "We're treated as a student's joke," he lamented in 1986.

The increased publicity has not resulted in a substantial increase in membership, which has remained at a constant "forty to fifty full-time active members"—that is, members who regularly attend the kerk's Sabbaths, which are held every nine days. On special holidays like Walpurgisnacht, however, attendance is in the "hundreds," with members coming from as far away as Austria, Germany, and Norway. Despite having large numbers of sympathizers in such countries, Lamers considers Holland to be a Satanic island in a sea of European repression. "There are groups that should be part of the Church, but they don't dare affiliate because they are afraid," Lamers says.

A case in point is Belgium, where a large Satanic

following has to stay underground because of an old witchcraft law still on the books. European souls were obviously not ripe for conversion, and when bickering broke out, the experiment in Amsterdam only confirmed LaVey's conviction that the grotto system did not work and that the church had gotten away from its philosophical essence—egotism. The cell concept was good, he decided, but its purpose was defeated when socialization became an end in itself—what LaVey terms the "Moose Lodge Syndrome." The word "occult," the High Priest points up, merely means "hidden," or "secret," which was the antithesis of what his grottoes had been practicing.

LaVey decided to create a network of "true" occultists—"underground men," in the Dostoyevskian sense of the term. The mind of Western man, as he saw it, was being anesthetized and controlled through the manipulation of the electronic media; in particular, television. It is the ultimate goal of the political powers that be, LaVey believes, to create through television the uniform society in which individualism is stifled and the masses are preprogrammed to march to whatever tune is played.

Satanists pose a threat to such a vision, LaVey asserts, but not in the way claimed by religious alarmists. It is his contention that true Satanists do not meet in groups in dimly lit basements plotting ritual murders. Rather, they are the truly dangerous individuals who have turned off their television sets and sit by themselves, thinking. Thought, according to LaVey, is the biggest enemy of the uniform society.

Instead of his previous play on the old army slogan "Satan Wants You," LaVey decided to give his recruitment procedures a Marine-like slant: "We're looking for a few good men." To find those men, LaVey has essentially cut off all communication to members from the San Francisco headquarters, except for the monthly *Cloven Hoof* newsletter. Larry Raybourne, a New Orleans astrological columnist and longtime Church of Satan member, expressed surprise recently upon being told that LaVey had named him as the Church of Satan's principal contact in that city, saying that he had not heard from San Francisco in almost two years. What's more, Raybourne avoids attending group rituals or being in contact with other Satanists.

"Frankly, as a whole," he said, "I can't stand Satanists. Most of them are nut cases."

Ronald Adams, a London electronics engineer and also a church member for many years, has expressed similar sentiments, calling Satanists the "lunatic fringe of the occult." Adams told me he needs no group to practice his Satanism, which to him is more of a philosophy than a religion. "The essence of Satanism is material success," he said. "Your own positive outlook gives you success, and that outlook comes from Satanic doctrine."

When told about both men's feelings about their fellow members, LaVey, rather than expressing disapproval, said emphatically, "*Those* are the kind of members I want—people who can stand on their own without a bunch of slobbering idiots propping them up!" LaVey claims that this is what differentiates his cult from others. Unlike other cult leaders, he does not seek to impose his "truth" on his members. He does not even profess to know the truth. "The truth never set anyone free," he wrote in 1969. "It is only DOUBT which will bring mental emancipation."[8] True Satanists, he says, now need no hierarchy to tell them how to think. And once that bulwark of Satanists is formed, the old order will fall.

It is difficult to say how much of this LaVey actually believes, and how much of it is rationalization to compensate for his unwillingness to deal with the inevitable personality conflicts that would accompany the building up of another organization. But at the present time, the fifty-seven-year-old High Priest seems more interested in compiling his essays for publication, transferring obscure pieces of celluloid to videotape, and playing his keyboards than committing himself to administering the day-to-day needs of his flock.

Although he is purposely vague when discussing membership figures, saying that the positions of the players carry greater importance than mere numbers, LaVey will assert that subscribers to *The Cloven Hoof* the church newsletter, stand at about two thousand. More significant, perhaps, is the *increase* reported by LaVey in membership applications since 1982. LaVey attributes the rise to the new public visibility of the church in response to the recent wave of allegations of Satanic child abuse, and

[8]LaVey, *The Satanic Bible*, New York: Avon, 1969, p. 39.

ARTHUR LYONS

theorizes that the current hysteria has perhaps generated a perverse result.

But will the new recruits understand that LaVey's "brand of Satanism is the ultimate conscious alternative to herd mentality and institutionalized thought"? Proclaims the High Priest: "It is a studied, contrived set of principles and exercises, designed to prevent and liberate from the contagion of mindlessness which destroys innovation. Here are some reasons why it is called 'Satanism': It is most stimulating under that name, and self-discipine and motivation are easier under stimulating conditions. It means 'the opposition,' and epitomizes all symbols of nonconformity. It represents the strongest ability to turn a liability into an advantage—to turn alienation into exclusivity. In other words, the reason it's called 'Satanism' is because it's fun, it's accurate, and it's productive."[9]

Some of the "few good men" attracted to LaVey's free thinking, egotistic philosophy might be able to utilize it and turn it into a source of strength. But for the weaker-minded, turning "alienation into exclusivity" might only promote further alienation and exacerbate already existing psychological and emotional problems. Yet LaVey is optimistic that those people he seeks—his underground men—will seek him out, and that when they do, society will be transformed.

All that went before—the grottos, the striptease acts, the carnie jive—was part of the Master Plan, LaVey insists, like the trial-and-error procedure of programming one of his musical sequencers. "Eventually, you get the entire tune by pressing one note," he says with a diabolical glint in his eye. "It's like painting by the numbers. People can't see the picture until it's finished."

With LaVey, it is difficult to gauge just how serious he is in making such proclamations, but Walt Harrington summed up the man when he wrote: "Anton LaVey is not a cartoon Satan. He's far less frightening than you might imagine, because he is admittedly a carnival hustler. Yet he is still terrifying, because he touches, if not the mystical darkness, then the psychological darkness—the hate and fear—in us all. And because he, sadly, knows a haunting truth: Everybody wants to feel better than somebody."[10]

[9]*The Cloven Hoof*, Vol. 19, No. 3.
[10]Harrington, op. cit., p. 7.

CHAPTER IX

The Temple of Set, et Al.

Comrades, no we will not conquer the heavens.
Enough to have the power. War engenders war, and
victory defeat. God conquered, will become Satan;
Satan, conquering, will become God. . . . As to ourselves, we have destroyed Ialdaboath [God] our Ty-
rant, if in ourselves we have destroyed Ignorance and
Fear. . . . We were conquered because we failed to
understand that Victory is a Spirit, and that it is in
ourselves and in ourselves alone that we must attack
and destroy Ialdoboath.
— Anatole France, *The Revolt of the Angels*

The most vociferous split from the Church of Satan was
the Temple of Set. Led by Dr. Michael A. Aquino and his
wife, Lilith Sinclair, its headquarters was in San Francisco.

Aquino first encountered LaVey in 1968, when he attended one of LaVey's lectures. Then a lieutenant in Army
Intelligence, specializing in psychological warfare,
Aquino found himself immediately drawn to the Machiavellian orientation of Satanic philosophy. Soon after that
first visit, both he and his first wife joined the Church of
Satan.

In 1970, after returning from a stint in Vietnam, Aquino
was ordained into the Satanic priesthood and organized a
grotto in Kentucky, where he was stationed. He gave
lectures on Satanism at the University of Louisville and
eventually built up a small group of a dozen or so
members who attended rituals at the Aquino house.

An indefatigable writer, Aquino began to contribute
heavily to *The Cloven Hoof*. Diane LaVey, burdened with
paperwork, soon was willing to let his penchant for letter

writing ease the load of church correspondence. Meanwhile, Anton LaVey saw another use for the young priest. A former national commander of the Eagle Scouts Honor Society, Aquino presented the kind of upright American image LaVey could adroitly milk for public relations purposes. It didn't take long for Aquino to acquire the status of Magister IV, one grade below LaVey's rank. Magus LaVey further honored Aquino by commissioning him to author the "Call to Cthulhu" ritual, based on the works of H. P. Lovecraft.

It was while in Kentucky, fundamentalist territory, that Aquino saw his true mission and that of the Church of Satan: "to destroy the influence of conventional religion in human affairs. I understand that to mean not so much that we want everyone to be converted to Satanism as an *institutional religion*, but that we want to unravel the web of fear and superstition that has perpetuated all formal beliefs. Satanism should not be just another religion, it should be an unreligion."[1]

By 1972, a personal and philosophical rift had grown between LaVey and Aquino. LaVey was disaffected with Aquino's attitude, which he thought to be ego-motivated and overintellectual. Aquino, in turn, had grown impatient with the High Priest's refusal to relinquish administrative power and had become increasingly dissatisfied with the church's professed atheism, which he thought to be sterile. Aquino formalized his dissatisfaction by announcing his resignation. He was soon followed by Lilith Sinclair, head of the Church of Satan's Lilith Grotto in New York, and a handful of members from the New York, Washington, D.C., and Los Angeles grottos.

Due to the strength of LaVey's charisma and the fact that he held a trademark on the Church of Satan name, Aquino knew that any attempt to start up another Church of Satan would be futile, so he decided to summon up the Prince of Darkness and ask him what to do.

On the eve of the north solstice, June 21, 1975, Aquino performed a magical "Working" and Satan purportedly appeared to him in the image of Set—the oryx-headed god of death and destruction that Aquino claims is the earliest manifestation of the Christian Devil, dating back to 3400

[1]Correspondence with the author, 1971

B.C. The result was a document, *The Book of Coming Forth by Night*, in which Set declared the dawning of the "Aeon of Set." According to the document, the origins of the new era could be traced back to 1904, when Set appeared to Aleister Crowley in Cairo in the guise of his guardian angel, Aiwass, and declared Crowley the herald for the dawning "Aeon of Horus." In 1966, LaVey ushered in the Aeon of Satan, an intermediary phase that symbolized indulgence and that was to prepare the way for the Aeon of Set, which would bring forth enlightenment.

Not only was Aquino "anointed" worldwide leader for the new age, but he was also consecrated by Set as the Second Beast (prophesied by Crowley in *The Book of the Law*, as well as the Great Beast of Revelation), following not only in Crowley's footsteps but also in those of his ill-fated disciple, Jack Parsons. "*The Book of Coming Forth by Night* was thus for me a veritable Pandora's box," wrote Aquino, "promising marvels to come, yet forecasting a personal doom which only a fool or a child would envy. Yes, continue, it said, but only if you dare to take upon yourself a degree, an office, and an image which may well subject you to even greater disbelief, fear, and antagonism than those endured by Anton LaVey. Your comfortable days as a Magister are over; you must accept or reject the Mandate itself."[2]

Aquino accepted the Mandate and the image. Instead of shaving his head, he cut his hair in a widow's peak, plucked his eyebrows, and had a 666, the symbol of the Antichrist, tattooed under his scalp. As the goat's-head Baphomet symbol was also trademarked by LaVey, Aquino decided to take a plain inverted pentagram as the temple's symbol. Grottos became "pylons," Lilith Sinclair was designated Magistra, and Aquino assumed Crowley's Golden Dawn degree of Ipsissimus. Administrative decisions, including the advancement of initiates to a higher degree, issued from an inner committee of leaders called the Council of Nine, a name taken from the original officiating body of the Church of Satan.

All of the initial members of Aquino's Council of Nine, in fact, were ex-priests of the Church of Satan. But while much of the structure of the Temple of Set was taken from

---

[2]"Temple of Set Information Papers," 1986, p. 24.

LaVey's *The Satanic Bible*, the temple teachings differed from those of the Church of Satan in several ways, most important of which was the acceptance of Set, or Satan, as a literal reality.

Another main difference between the two groups was that whereas the Church of Satan exalts "egotism without tears" as the cornerstone of its philosophy, the main goal of Setians is the expansion of consciousness through a process known as "Xeper" (pronounced keffer). Xeper, which means "becoming," is the process through which an initiate strives to evolve into a "higher man" in quest of objective and subjective knowledge.

Setians believe that human intelligence was not an accident of evolution but a Promethean gift from Set, who bestowed it to enable man to manipulate nature and become a godlike being. However, to do this, man must first shake off that "sleeping state" which is his normal functioning condition, and achieve "self-consciousness," as outlined by P. D. Ouspensky in *The Psychology of Man's Possible Evolution*. After that he may move on to a state of "objective consciousness," in which he will be able to control all states of consciousness, know the truth about the universe, and become an immortal superbeing. This state may be achieved by dedicating oneself to reading, absorbing knowledge, and practicing rituals.

Although pylon meetings are usually held once a month, the emphasis in the Temple of Set is on individual, not group, rituals. Setian rituals are geared to concentrate the will of the practitioner in order to "break down the objective and subjective worlds" and reveal the reality behind the material veil. All initiates are required to adopt a "magical name" which they feel corresponds to their "true nature." During rituals, which may vary in purpose and content, he or she strives to become this other *persona*, or *ka*, a concept taken from Egyptian theology. Once the identification is achieved, the *ka*, or magical "double," is dispatched to the astral plane to execute the Setian's will, whatever that may be.

Rituals are held in a black room in front of an altar above which is a silver pentagram. On the altar are a goblet, a bell, a central flame source, and magical paraphernalia. Setians forgo naked human altars, and the ceremonial robes of the magician, while preferably black, may be of any color. He or she begins by ringing the bell nine times while turning counterclockwise. The flame is then lit, thus "opening the Gate" of communication between the magician and the Powers of Darkness. The invocation to Set is then read: "In the name of Set, the Prince of Darkness, I enter into the Realm of Creation to work my Will upon the universe. . . ." The celebrant then picks up the goblet or grail, which symbolizes truth and contains any beverage (*except* blood), and drinks. Following this, the magician performs the appropriate ritual for the occasion. The content is left pretty much up to the celebrant, including whatever deity he wishes to invoke. After the ritual, he or she closes the ceremony, reversing the opening procedure.

As the Workings are supposedly magical in nature and not for the purposes of worship, the emotional response is more important than the procedure one uses summoning it. "Gods exist as they are evoked to meaningful existence by the individual psyche."[3] Thus, Lovecraft's Cthulhu gods, for example, although fictitious, may have more emotional meaning for the practitioner. The only thing that is strictly prohibited by Aquino during the performance of any ritual—following the lead of LaVey, not Crowley—is the injury or sacrifice of any life-form.

Aside from its initial renegade Church of Satan converts, Temple of Set membership has been recruited primarily through ads in the San Francisco Yellow Pages and computer bulletin boards. Initiates must be eighteen or older, and applications must be approved by the Council of Nine. Once accepted, a fifty-dollar fee (twenty-five-dollar annual renewal) will put the applicant in touch with other members. They are then sent a comprehensive reading list and a bimonthly copy of *The Scroll of Set*, the temple newsletter.

Many Setians claim to have had an interest in the occult before finding their way to the temple, and quite a few are former "white lighter," or wicca, devotees. Most come from a Christian background, and while some may have joined as a reaction against their upbringing, the sentiments and philosophy of the temple, while being un-Christian, do not appear to be virulently *anti*-Christian.

[3]Ibid, p. 31.

For example, one former Jesuit found the Temple of Set after searching for a "civilized avenue for exploring the forbidden side of life." He and his wife teach at a Catholic school, say they have no problem with their religious past, playing down their conversion to the Temple of Set as "just something bound to happen."

There are members of all ages, although the average racial and economic profile is firmly Caucasian, white-collar, and middle-class. Considering Aquino's intellectual emphasis and his extensive required reading lists, it is not surprising that the educational level of the cult is fairly high. Typical occupations include college student, teacher, accountant, computer programmer, secretary.

Yet, according to Gini Graham Scott, who studied the cult in the early 1980s, "outside occupational status doesn't count for much within the group." This, she notes, is because the members consider their mundane jobs a hindrance to their magical development, and because they often feel that the jobs they have are boring, unsatisfying, and economically unrewarding. The group's emphasis on magical over worldly power, she found, enabled members to feel they were powerful beings, despite experiences outside the group which belied that. "Over and over again at meetings," Scott writes, "I heard [Setians] describe their everyday frustrations, which led them to want power—such as problems with jobs and relationships. Then, once they joined the group, they often used the practices they learned to counter these problems or vent their frustrations and anger. These practices in turn provided them with a socially channeled form to express these feelings."[4]

Scott's observations seem to be borne out, at least in part, by the evolution of the temple since its birth in 1975. At its zenith at the end of the 1970s, the cult had a membership of about one hundred, with pylons in Detroit, Los Angeles, Washington, D.C., New York, and San Jose. But by 1981 Aquino and his flock had begun to be plagued by the same problems that disrupted the Church of Satan. The same elitism that had attracted initiates in the first place led to frequent ego clashes as members competed for godlike status, resulting in increased dropouts and purges by the leadership.

[4]Scott, Gini Graham, *The Magicians*, Oakland: Creative Communications, 1984, p. 182.

In 1985, a female member, Lynn Johnson (later Butch), fiancee of William T. Butch, Aquino's brother-in-law and one of the Temple's higher-ups, left the group after becoming disenchanted with what she perceived to be the cult's authoritarian, anti-feminine bias, as well as its increasing emphasis on Nazi occultism. (Aquino had long been fascinated by Nazi mysticism and Hitler's political theories of crowd control). In 1986, she and William Butch incorporated the Temple of Nepthys as a non-profit church, and set up headquarters in Mill Valley, near San Francisco. The group's philosophical tenets are similar to those of the Temple of Set, with a feminist accent. (Nepthys is the female counterpart of Set). Members study the "Red Arts" (as opposed to black or white), which Lynn Butch claims to be a more individualistic method by which "the psychecentric consciousness can evolve towards its own divinity."

From nine founding members, the Temple of Nepthys soon grew to 23 full-time and 65 corresponding members. Membership is overwhelmingly female, with an average age between 18 and 34. By 1988, however, the group was experiencing financial difficulties as the $25 membership fees failed to cover expenses. Although the Temple of Nepthys has sought to form a loose affiliation with the Church of Satan, its future seems shaky.

Aquino and his Temple received another setback in October, 1987, when it was revealed by the San Francisco Police Department that it was investigating Aquino in connection with a child molestation case at the U. S. Army Presidio daycare center. Indicted in the case was a 34-year-old daycare center worker and Southern Baptist minister, Gary Hambright, who had no known connection with the Temple of Set or Aquino. Although no charges were filed against Aquino at the time of this writing, and although a police raid on Aquino's Russian Hill home failed to turn up evidence that Aquino or his cult had been involved in ritualistic child abuse, SFPD spokesmen maintain that the case against Aquino is still "open." Aquino, in the meantime, has sued the city of San Francisco for defamation of character, terming the entire affair a "modern witchhunt in the most classical sense."[5]

[5]San Francisco *Chronicle*, October 31, 1987, p. A14

Whether or not Aquino himself weathers the storm, the future of the Temple of Set, now in a state of organizational disarray, seems doubtful.

The newest church to emerge on the Satanic scene, not surprisingly, also owes its inspiration to Anton LaVey. Founded on January 8, 1986, in New Haven, Connecticut, by Paul Douglas Valentine, a thirty-one-year-old English teacher, the Church of Satanic Liberation claims over one thousand dues-paying members worldwide. Most are recruited through magazine ads and through the Magickal Childe occult shop in New York City. According to Valentine, the majority of the membership is female and well educated, many from upper-middle-class to upper-class backgrounds. The New Haven headquarters is the only chapter where rituals are held, but Valentine intends to expand the operations soon to accommodate the widespread membership. (States with the highest concentrations are California, New York, Maine, New Hampshire, Texas, Pennsylvania, and Nevada.) Before starting the Church of Satanic Liberation, Valentine, who holds a B.S. in primate paleontology as well as an M.A. in English, was involved in the occult for fifteen years, primarily in various aspects of wicca. His epiphany came when he picked up a copy of *The Satanic Bible* and realized "Satanism is a viable religion quite unlike what the movies and the Christers made it out to be."[6]

Although he adopted both LaVey's Satanic calendar and his trademarked Baphomet as the new church's symbol and freely borrows from *The Satanic Bible* and *The Satanic Rituals* (both in his ceremonies and his irregular newsletter, *The Devil's Advocate*), Valentine sees his organization as "taking up where LaVey's Church of Satan seems to be slacking off—educating those people of like mind who realize there is something better, something more honest, than what the major religions are offering."

Another distinction he perceives between the two organizations is his belief in the "importance of traditional Satanic pageantry and blasphemy as part of ritual," although much of the content of his rituals nonetheless seems to come directly from the LaVey *Rituals*.

However, one way of Valentine's group does seem to

[6]Correspondence with the author

differ markedly from LaVey's is in the emphasis on sex and its incorporation into magical ritual. Valentine, in fact, goes so far as to dub himself the "Roman Polanski of the Satanic world" and freely admits that he cares little for the age of the women he uses in his sexual rituals, "as long as they coincide with any individual state's 'age of consent.'"

Valentine, despite his flippancy, vigorously condemns child abuse and animal sacrifice, declaring that people who practice such acts "should be shown no mercy." He has no intention, he says, of letting the Church of Satanic Liberation "become a halfway house for misanthropes and social pariahs."

Two Satanic cults that illustrate the wide range of Satanic beliefs, although no longer in existence, are the Lady of Endor Coven of the Ophite Cultus Satanus, and the Orthodox Satanic Church of Nethilum Rite.

The Lady of Endor Coven was started in 1948 by a Toledo, Ohio, barber turned fortune-teller, Herbert A. Sloane, and ceased with his death in the 1980s. Sloane's creed, based heavily on gnosticism, taught that Satan was not evil, but the bringer of wisdom and the messenger of God. The Christian God was identified with the Demiurge, whose spirit was trapped in the material world, with Satan sent to earth to give man occult knowledge, or gnosis, so that the divine aspect within humanity could be returned to God.

The Orthodox Satanic Church, in existence from 1971 to 1974 in Chicago, which at its height claimed more than five hundred members, taught a similar system of beliefs. The group's anti-LaVey philosophy taught that God the Creator created Satan, who, in turn, became the teacher of all knowledge. Through ritual, prayer, and songs, held every Saturday night at Chicago's Occult Book Shop, members were exhorted to absorb as much of Satan's wisdom as they could.

In 1974, this group broke up after its leader, Terry Taylor, owner of the Occult Book Shop, was taken to court by his ex-wife to keep him from bringing his daughter to the cult's rituals. Taylor, she claimed, not only drove the girl to the shop in a hearse but also slept in a coffin. A splinter sect, Thee Satanic Church, was started by Dr. Evelyn Paglini, of the International Psychic Center, but it folded shortly thereafter.

For all their differences, all of the neo-Satanic churches share several structural and psychological traits, not only with themselves but with other occult sects. With hero worship often a large factor in the success of these groups their existence has been dependent on the charisma and continued life of the leader. As he or she goes, so goes the cult—which has resulted in a short life span for a majority of occult and virtually all Satanic organizations.

As seen, most Satanists are frustrated people reacting against the banality and powerlessness of their lives. Feeling like insignificant cogs in a machine, bewildered by the complexities of various bureaucracies, these people seek out a group that will accept them, in which they can vent their feelings of hostile alienation without being censured. Through the practice of "magic" and the achievement of "adept" levels they can feel that they are unique and powerful.

But becoming part of an elect elite can have side effects. While aiding the individual in feeling more powerful, it can make relating to others outside the group even more difficult. A Satanist who formerly felt out of sync with society suddenly realized why: *he* was the one who was really *in* sync all the time; it is the rest of the world who are the "chumps." Socializing with others of like mind only reinforces the process; an inferiority complex is transformed into a superiority complex. Weird becomes weirder.

Once that happens, the need to believe becomes even stronger. Freud likened the belief in magic to a stage found in primitives and obsessional neurotics in which the thought processes themselves become overvalued compared to reality. He called this the "omnipotence of thought" and noted that patients who exemplified this would go to extreme lengths of self-deception in order to protect their belief system.

Any accidental connection can reinforce the neurotic's belief in his own powers: think of someone, and if that person appears, the thought *made* him appear. The several thousand other times that the person *didn't* appear are conveniently forgotten.

One can often see this phenomenon at work among Satanists, from the claim that the sudden appearance of a parking space was "proof" that it had been magically conjured up, to the attribution of survival of an automobile accident to "protection" by infernal powers. Seldom will a Satanist blame the Powers of Darkness for letting him get into the accident in the first place; if he did, he would be an ex-Satanist, perhaps a born-again Christian.

One advantage of magical thinking is that the results do not have to be definite and are subject to misinterpretation. Flexibility is built into the system and a ritual does not have to achieve its total purpose in order to be deemed successful. If a magician puts a death curse on an enemy, for example, and three days later the would-be victim burns his finger, the magician is able to interpret that as proof that his ritual just wasn't strong enough.

The danger in such groups is that as the members come to rely more on this mode of thought, they can become totally emotionally dependent on the group as their alienation from society increases.

Psychologist Erich Fromm divided religions into two principal categories: humanitarian and authoritarian. Humanitarian religions, according to Fromm, concern themselves with the goals of self-realization, while authoritarian religions emphasize the importance of their own power. "The essential element in authoritarian religion," he wrote, "is the surrender to a power transcending man. The main virtue of this type of religion is obedience, the cardinal sin, disobedience."[7]

Most Satanic cults are authoritarian in nature. The members join the group to remedy feelings of powerlessness and inadequacy by submitting to cult leaders in order to be taught the "occult secrets of magic." Thus, they feel themselves as part of an elite group, in possession of exclusive powers, superior to the rest of humanity. Paul Valentine unabashedly states that one of the reasons he started a Satanic religion was the feeling of power it gives him.

While teaching that the ultimate goal of the Setian is self-realization, Michael Aquino states that the governing principle of magic is the ability to "control people without their realizing how or why they are being controlled."

[7]Fromm, Erich, *Psychoanalysis and Religion*, New Haven: Yale University Press, 1950, p. 35.

Gini Graham Scott's experience with the Temple of Set echoes my own observations of other Satanic and occult groups: "The power of the High Priest increases the power group members feel. He derives much of his power from the members' belief that he is better able to communicate and manifest (Set) through his being. Also, when members honor him with salutes and hails, he appears that much more powerful. His power, in turn, reflects back on the group."[8]

But although the orientation of both the leadership and the laity of most of neo-Satanic churches such as the Temple of Set and the Church of Satan is authoritarian, and stresses control, there is no evidence that any so-called "brainwashing" techniques are employed within these groups to program the thoughts of their members—as has been alleged in contemporary cults such as the Moonies or the Hare Krishnas.

James T. Richardson, Mary Harder, and Robert Simmonds, in their paper, "Thought Reform and the Jesus Movement,"[9] equate the conversion processes used in some cults in the modern "Jesus Movement" with those employed by the Chinese on Western prisoners of war in Korea in the early 1950s. Such comparisons have also been made by psychiatrist Robert J. Lifton,[10] who related such "thought-reform" to religion with his concept of "religious totalism," which he broke down into eight separate elements: (1) milieu control, or the control of human communication, (2) mystical manipulation, or the installation of a sense of higher purpose by which members are taught they have been "chosen" by forces outside themselves to carry on some mystical imperative, (3) the demand for purity, or the adoption by believers of a black or white picture of the world, (4) the cult of confession for past sins, (5) the "sacred science," which teaches that the group's dogma is completely true, (6) the loading of language, or the language of "non-thought," (7) the subordination of human experience to the claims of doctrine, and (8) the severance of ties with those not doctrinally pure (family, friends, etc.)

[8]Scott, op. cit., p. 190.
[9]In *Youth and Society*, Vol. 4, No. 2, Dec. 1972.
[10]Lifton, R.J., *Thought Reform and the Psychology of Totalism*, N.Y.: W.I.W. Norton, 1963

Lifton suggests that the more those eight components combine in a group situation, the more likely is the possibility of altering a member's behavior and thoughts. That would be true in religious cults or radical political movements, and the dynamics have been clearly observed to be in operation in such cults as the Jim Jones cult in Guyana, the Moonies, and the Yahwehs, as well as the Manson Family. The more communication from the outside is cut, and the more dependence upon the group is fostered, the more likely group behavior will be infected by the beliefs and commands of a charismatic leader. If the beliefs of the leader are violent, the group can turn violent.

With the possible exception of The Process in the early 1970s, no organized Satanic church has attempted to attain that kind of control of its membership. The Church of Satan, the Temple of Set, and the Church of Satanic Liberation, although displaying some of Lifton's eight components—assuming at times a fascistic, authoritarian tone—have not attempted to break down the thoughts of their members. In fact, their stress on egotism, individualistic thought, and nonconformity—although within their groups, their members have simply arrived at another kind of conformity—has been a barrier to the implantation of any cohesive system of thought. This, perhaps, has been a source of failure of such groups as LaVey's and Aquino's to consolidate and add to the gains in membership they made in the early 1970s.

Back in 1971, before he became certain that Set was a real entity, Michael Aquino seemed to anticipate this built-in program for failure in his own temple when he wrote that "a large percentage of letters to *The Cloven Hoof* portray Satan as a *de facto* God to be served, worshipped and adored—not as an anti-god. For such persons, the distinction between Christianity and Satanism is principally semantic. The long-term influence of such a trend could be disastrous and I suspect the question may be called shortly. Some people, I suppose, cannot exist without a master to serve. Erich Fromm is alive and lurking in the ritual chamber."[11]

[11]Correspondence with the author.

CHAPTER X

Dead Cattle, Satanic Child Abuse, and Other Urban Legends

"For some reason, in the 1980s, children are being sexually abused and possibly even murdered during what appears to be Satanic-type rituals."
—Sandra Gallant,
quoted in the *San Francisco Examiner*, 1986

"It's too bad stupidity isn't painful. Then maybe some of these people would go get some help."
—Anton LaVey, interview, 1986

As the 1960s faded into the more staid 1970s, lurid media accounts of Satanic activity and ritualistic murders became sporadic. But in 1975, the wire services began to pick up stories that cattle ranchers in Colorado and other western states were increasingly concerned about the safety of their herds, large numbers of animals having been bizarrely slaughtered. The cattle were apparently not being killed for food, as little of the meat had been touched, but, in many cases, the blood had apparently been drained and the sexual organs and lips had been surgically removed. To add to the mystery, no footprints, animal or human, were found around the carcasses.

Speculation about the identity of the culprits ranged from UFOs to secret government experiments. A movie, *Endangered Species*, was even produced, postulating the latter theory. Then in Arkansas, several head of cattle were found dead near sites that exhibited evidence of ritualistic activity—and Satanic cultists, who from the beginning were suspected villains, supplanted extraterrestrials and Uncle Sam as the most popular explanation for the rash of killings.

As reports of the number of mutilations increased and

alarm among ranchers spread, animal pathologists were called in to investigate. Not only did they find the cattle mortality rate no higher than normal, but autopsies on the animals determined that in almost all cases the cattle had died from natural causes, or by predatory attack, and that the mutilation had been the postmortem work of scavengers, not cultists. Teeth, not knives, had been used to remove the sex organs and lips, those parts being attacked because they were the softest and most accessible.

Then, amid hundreds of similarly discredited reports, several mutilations in Idaho and Montana were determined to have indeed been the work of a knife-wielder. There, evidence gathered by law enforcement officials implicated several Satanic cults operating in those states. The cults, which up to that time had allegedly preferred dogs and cats as sacrifical victims, had read about the mutilations in the papers and decided to add cattle to their ritual list.

The work of the copycat cultists turned out to be truly a case of life imitating art. An astrologer named Dan Fry, host of a Minneapolis radio program called *Cosmic Age*, admitted on a Texas talk show that he had made up the cattle mutilation rumor as a joke, but things had snowballed when the story was repeated as fact by the *Houston Post* and picked up from there by the wire services. Thus had Fry created an "urban legend."

An "urban legend" is a term coined by contemporary folklorists to describe a popular story that spreads swiftly by word of mouth and is soon accepted as truth. These folk tales are always reported as having actually happened, often to the friend of a friend, which is what keeps them "immediate."

When the media picks up such stories and prints them as fact, as it did with the cattle mutilation stories, they acquire a further stamp of truth. A recent study by *Psychology Today* of reported "trick or treat" poisonings on Halloween failed to turn up one serious injury and found that, in almost every case, the tamperings were the work of the child victim himself, in an attempt to get attention from parents and friends. Yet every Halloween, newspapers print warnings about tampered treats. And, in the mid-1980s, tales of Satanic animal mutilations have begun to resurface from California to Alabama, despite the protests of investigating game and animal control officials who have said that, in almost all the cases, the animal deaths were the work of predators or poachers.

The Devil, after all, has been an old favorite subject of urban legends. In 1977, for instance, the rumor was widely circulated in fundamentalist circles that the secret of McDonald's success was that the chain donated a portion of its profits each year to the Church of Satan. Corroboration of the Satanic tithing allegedly came from no less a personage than McDonald's owner, Ray Kroc, who was reputed to have admitted to the diabolic connection while appearing on the Phil Donahue show. In fact, Kroc had been a guest on the Donahue show in May of 1977, but his most startling admission had been his intention to introduce the McDonald's "Filet o' Fish" in Cincinnati.

The idea of a Satanic "pact"—trading one's soul for earthly wealth—is an ancient one, and it cropped up again in 1980 when rumors surfaced that the Procter & Gamble moon-and-stars trademark was in reality a Satanic symbol, and that the company was run by Satanists. The story went that the owners of Procter & Gamble long ago made a pact with the Devil that ensured the company's success in exchange for putting Satan's logo on all its products. "Proof" cited for this ludicrous claim was that a company executive had revealed the demonic truth on *Donahue* or *60 Minutes*, depending on the version. It mattered little that Donahue and spokesmen for *60 Minutes* denied any such interview ever took place. Neighbors told neighbors that they had talked to someone who saw the show, or heard it from someone who heard it from someone, etc. By mid-1982, Procter's consumer services department was getting 15,000 calls a month from people wanting to know about the company's Satanic connections. Eventually, a counter-publicity campaign was launched, but in the end, the company wound up changing its logo.

It was also in 1980 that a new twist was giving to Satanic paranoia with the publication of *Michelle Remembers*, a book by Michelle Smith and Dr. Lawrence Pazder, a psychiatrist. It seems that, while undergoing intense psychotherapy with Dr. Pazder for an assortment of emotional disorders, Smith began to recall repressed childhood memories, which Pazder concluded were the source of her problems. What she revealed to him was that, as a five-year-old in Vancouver, she had been offered up by her mother to a Satanic cult and forced to participate in unspeakable rites.

During a three-month ceremony called the Feast of the Beast, she had been forced to recite childish rhymes while closed in a coffin within a grave and been put naked in a cage, the floor of which was alive with slithering snakes. She had seen robed men and women tear apart kittens with their teeth. She had been sexually assaulted by both male and female initiates, including the cult's leader, Malachi, and most loathsome of all, she had seen babies ritualistically slaughtered and eaten.

In the end, however, through prayer, all the cult's efforts to convert her were thwarted.

As Smith's mother was long dead, it proved impossible to verify her story. Despite problems with the horror-filled narrative—namely, why the group would allow her to live to tell the tale—and despite the fact that such nightmares as Michelle's are not uncommon in emotionally disturbed cases, Pazder said he believed Michelle's story to be literally true and helped her spill out her fantasy in book form.

Shortly after the publication of *Michelle Remembers*, the *National Enquirer* carried a story by a "Samantha Smith" (admittedly a fictitious name), who purported that she, too, had been the victim of child abuse by a Satanic cult that practiced infanticide. It didn't take long for the other tabloids to get into the act, and soon newsstands everywhere were carrying the gruesome accounts of other horror-haunted cult victims.

Then in August 1983, the tabloid accounts made national news as Los Angeles District Attorney Robert Philobosian announced that criminal charges were being filed against teachers and administrators of the McMartin Preschool in Manhattan Beach, a small coastal town south of Los Angeles. His office was responding to complaints by parents that their children were being sexually molested. On the basis of taped interviews with pupils, conducted by therapists at Children's Institute International, seven adults were indicted on 208 counts of felony child molestation, oral copulation, and sodomy.

But the story did not end there.

Out of the legal proceedings, stories soon began to emerge of Satanic rituals at the school involving robed adults, chanting, and animal sacrifices. Some of the children claimed to have had their faces smeared with feces, urine, and blood, and to have witnessed babies cooked and eaten. Others said they had been forced to perform in kiddie-porn movies.

In what was to become the most costly legal proceeding in California history, investigators searched in vain for any evidence to corroborate the children's stories. Prosecutor Lael Rubin told the press that the finding of "toy rabbit ears, a cape, and a candle" proved the "Satanic" aspect of the case, but those three items were the most ominous pieces of evidence investigators were ever to turn up.

The children's revelations became more and more bizarre. Several of them claimed to have been flown to a different city to attend rituals, one said he had been put naked in a cage with a live lion, and another identified a city attorney who had questioned him (as well as movie star Chuck Norris) among his molesters.

Some prosecutors began to express doubts about the integrity of the case, one going so far as to resign from the D.A.'s office. Matters became even more complicated when it was revealed that the mother whose initial complaint had launched the entire investigation had a history of mental problems. Newly elected D.A. Ira Reiner promptly dropped all charges against five of the defendants, terming the evidence against them "incredibly weak." He contended that the accusations of the children had been improperly elicited by interviewers at Children's Institute International. He let stand, however, over one-hundred charges against Ray Buckey, twenty-seven, and his sixty-year-old mother, Peggy McMartin Buckey.

Twenty-three of the McMartin parents, expressing outrage at Reiner's decision, filed a civil suit against the McMartin school and waged an unsuccessful campaign to get the dropped charges reinstated. They held press conferences, did interviews on TV talk shows, put up a $10,000 reward to locate pornographic pictures of children in the case, and hired a backhoe to dig up a vacant lot next to the school. There they found some turtle shells and a few animal bones, which they claimed proved the children's allegations, but which police asserted proved nothing.

Meanwhile, the media had jumped, inevitably, on the sensational Satanic aspects of the case, and parental alarm spread as children around the country began to come up with stories shockingly similar to the McMartin accounts:

August 1983, Concord, California. A mechanic is accused by his stepdaughter of being part of a Satanic cult that made her kill an infant and eat feces as part of its rituals. *Hung jury, no plans for retrial.*

August 1983, Antelope Valley, California. A child-abuse case turns bizarre when a foster mother reported that three children in her care confided in her tales of Satanic rites involving murder and the eating of human flesh. Although sheriffs conduct an extensive dig in the area, no bodies are ever found. *The childrens' father is convicted of felony physical child abuse, but no other charges are filed.*

September 1983, Jordan, Minnesota. Twenty-four adults out of a population of 2,663 residents are charged with molesting hundreds of children during rituals that include murder and animal sacrifice. *Although one adult is convicted of straight child abuse, charges against all the others are dropped after a prolonged investigation by the FBI and state attorney general's office conclude the stories of torture and murder to be fantasy.*

October 1983, Parker, Arizona. Four children tell police they were kidnaped by a Satanic cult, drugged, and sexually abused. *No evidence is found, no charges filed.*

June 1984, Bakersfield, California. Sheriff Larry Kleier announces an investigation of charges that as many as seventy-seven adults participated in cannibalism, blood drinking, sexual child abuse, and the murders of as many as twenty-nine children during Satanic rites at a local church. Despite the facts that the church is quickly cleared, that no bodies could be found after a massive search, and that several of the children later admit they had made up the stories, Sheriff Kleier insisted that he believes the stories of ritual abuse. *Five of seventeen defendants are convicted of child molestation, but no murder charges are ever filed, and all charges against the other defendants are dismissed as the grand jury chastises the sheriff's department for using interrogation techniques tantamount to "brainwashing" on the children.*

June 1984, Memphis, Tennessee. Three teachers and the Reverend Paul Shell are accused of molesting, torturing, and baptizing twenty-six children "in the devil's name." An FBI memo terms the charges "irrational and unbelievable," but the case was filed. *The first trial ends indecisively with a hung jury. A second trial is pending at the writing of this book.*

October 1984. A special sheriff's task force is set up to look into charges brought by parents of children attending preschools in Torrance, Pico Rivera, Whittier, and Covina, California, that the children had been forced to participate in sexual Satanic rituals involving human and animal sacrifices. *After a year-long, million-dollar investigation the task force is disbanded without having found any hard physical evidence.*

A month earlier, the first child-abuse conviction in the nation having ritualistic overtones is obtained in Miami, Florida. Cuban ex-convict Francisco Fuster, whose wife testifies he raped her with a crucifix and sexually assaulted children procured through his baby-sitting service, received a 165-year sentence. Animal sacrifices, chanting, and the eating of excrement are among other bizarre elements mentioned at the trial.

June 1985, Toledo, Ohio. On the basis of information obtained from several informants who claimed they had attended human sacrifices by a Satanic cult at a nearby rural site, lawmen spend ten hours digging up a field, searching for the remains of up to eighty victims allegedly sacrificed over the past sixteen years. Some animal but no human bones are found, along with body paints, a headless doll with nails driven through its feet and a pentagram tied to its wrist, a pile of sixty male children's left shoes, a pick, a hatchet, and a knife, plastic sacks containing cleaned and pressed children's clothing, and a nine-foot wooden cross with ligatures attached. Drawings of a goat's head and pentagrams along with an anatomy dissection book are found in a house adjoining the property. *No charges are filed, no arrests made.*

1985, Hamilton, Ontario. Two young sisters are turned over by their mother to a local Children's Aid Society after she decides she could not adequately care for them and cope with her own personal problems at the same time. Before she changes her mind and sought to take them back, however, the girls began to tell their foster mother horrifying tales of cannibalism, Satanic rites, murder, and sexual perversion performed by their mother, her estranged husband, and her former boyfriend. An investigation results in no criminal charges being filed, but it does create a two-year wardship hearing. *Two years after the first allegations, the same foster mother reports to authorities a similar set of tales from a new set of children in her care.*

The "epidemic" continued to spread through 1986. Cases were filed in Kings County, Texas; Richmond, Virginia; Maplewood, New Jersey; Cornelius, Oregon; Port Angeles, Washington; West Point, New York; and Reno, Nevada. A network of parents formed to share information and combat Satanic child abuse, which was linked to the disappearance of thousands of children every year. Members appeared on national television to warn the public of the danger.

Almost overnight, an entire new industry was born. Special police anti-occult task forces were formed to cope with the new menace. Child psychologists, social workers, probation officers, and born-again Christians were asked to speak to concerned parent groups, and seminars were conducted for law enforcement personnel by self-proclaimed "experts on Satanic crime." Ritualistic child molestation had suddenly become, as Mills College psychologist Aline Kidd put it, "the pop art of the child abuse field."[1]

By the early 1980s, child abuse in general had become a subject of national concern. Figures from the National Resource Center for Child Abuse show documented reports increasing from 669,000 in 1976 to 1,928,000 in 1985. Although a large majority of the reported cases were physical rather than sexual child abuse, the Resource Center confirms a seventeen-fold increase in reports of sexual molestation between 1976 and 1984.

Katy Bond, of the National Child Abuse Hotline, attributes much of the increase not to the fact that more child abuse is going on, but that people today are more willing to report it—and that children in many states are receiving education in school about what they should be aware of and report. "Sex has come out of the closet," she told me during a telephone interview. "There is now widespread knowledge about child abuse."

Bond also admitted that there has been a marked increase of false accusations in child custody cases and that in some instances child protective services are being used for the purposes of revenge by disgruntled spouses or emotionally unbalanced neighbors. This is a result mainly of a 1974 federal law which establishes that an accuser is no longer required to identify himself in reporting a suspected incident.

If child abuse has always been more prevalent than previously thought, the new set of reports differed markedly from what investigators were used to dealing with in cases of straight physical or sexual abuse. The idea of an underground conspiracy of child-molesting, blood-drink-

[1]"A Presumption of Guilt," *San Francisco Examiner*, Sept. 28, 1986, p. A–7.

ing, cannibalistic Satanists, kidnaping and killing children as part of unspeakable religious rites, added an even more horrifying dimension to an already horrifying subject. As bizarre as some of the tales sounded, police investigators did not take them lightly.

Concern in law enforcement circles was fueled by the knowledge that an underground communication network of people sharing pedophiliac tendencies actually did exist. In 1973, the arrest and indictment of seven men, including Christopher Lewis, son of movie star Loretta Young, for sexual misconduct with minors and pornography, precipitated an investigation that turned up an international network of male homosexuals who were recruiting young male runaways from as far as away as Houston and flying them to Los Angeles to take part in kiddie-porn flicks. One of the defendants in the case, Guy Strait, owner of D.O.M. Films, was found to have a mailing list of 50,000 clients. As the ripples of the investigation spread, other organizations were unearthed with similar mailing lists, such as the Children's Sensuality Circle, based in San Diego, and the Rene Guyon Society, based in Beverly Hills, whose motto was "Sex Before Eight, Before It's Too Late."

Hints of acts even more nefarious came when investigators connected several suspects in the case to Dean Allen Corll, a Houston utility worker who, with two teenage accomplices, had been convicted of the torture-murders of twenty-seven young boys in that Texas city. But in the end, detectives failed to uncover "any evidence of violence or more than a loosely-knit group of homosexuals."[2]

What they had found was a network of pen pals with similar tastes, which distributed literature and acted as a channel through which members could contact one another. Nothing was unearthed of ritualistic significance and nothing to indicate that children were being molested as part of religious rites.

Still, the fact that such a large underground existed undetected until the early seventies, along with the growing case files of nearly identical "Satanic abuse" reports, was enough to set investigators seriously search-

[2]Interdepartmental memo from the Los Angeles County Sheriff's Sex Crime Unit, Sept. 7, 1973.

ing for a similar network of Satanists. To combat this, specially formed task forces logged thousands of police man-hours investigating reports all over the country. But despite the heavy commitment of personnel and a tremendous amount of media attention, only a handful of adults was convicted of misdemeanor and felony child abuse, and not one piece of concrete evidence was ever turned up to corroborate a Satanic conspiracy.

As one case after another fell apart, explanations by the conspiracy buffs became more and more fantastic to accommodate the lack of evidence. The use of portable crematoriums and "altar babies"—that is, babies without birth certificates born secretly to cult members at home for the specific purpose of sacrifice—were offered as reasons why no infant bodies had been found. After all, the stories *had* to be true: they were too consistent and too detailed to be lies or fantasies, especially since the children, separated in some cases by thousands of miles, had no contact with each other.

An investigation by the FBI Behavioral Research Unit, however, came to different conclusions. It found a "cross-contamination of ideas" taking place between parent and law enforcement groups, and between the children and the social workers interrogating them. A prosecutor in one recent case, for example, admitted that he had used *Michelle Remembers* as a guidebook in preparing his case, despite the fact that no evidence has ever been offered to support the book's allegations or determine whether they were anything more than a sick woman's fantasies.[3]
Another, it turned out, had sent his investigators to Ken Wooden, founder of the National Coalition for Children's Justice and coproducer of an ABC *20/20* segment called "The Devil Worshippers," which spotlighted the child-abuse issue, to be "debriefed" before conducting their investigation.

Darlyne Pettinichio, an Orange County, California, probation officer who conducts Satanism training seminars, during a recent television interview told of teenage cultists who used human fetuses to make ceremonial candles. In a later, off-camera interview, she admitted she had not personally interviewed the teenagers but had "heard the

---

[3]"A Presumption of Guilt," *San Francisco Examiner*, Sept. 28, 1986, p. A–7.

story from two counselors"—a case of the urban myth at work.

A memo widely circulated to police departments across the country, designed to serve as a Satanic primer for investigators, was authored by Sandi Gallant, an intelligence office with the San Francisco Police Department. In the memo, Gallant, who is often quoted as the "leading expert on Satanic crime," cites the 200-year-old Guibourg mass as a typical Satanic ritual, and lists, among other things, ceramic cats, stained glass, and drawings of any geometric shape (including stars, circles, and rectangles), as "Satanic" items of evidence for investigators to check for at a crime scene.

Another newsletter distributed nationally to law enforcement personnel for the purpose of monitoring criminal cult activity is *File 18*, originating out of Boise, Idaho. While purporting to be objective, an indication that the newsletter is slanted to reflect a religious, pro-conspiracy bias was the fact that, along with one 1986 issue, subscribers were sent an article called "America's Best Kept Secret," reprinted from a Christian magazine called *Passport*. The posed front-page photograph shows a cross section of white, middle-class America—doctors, nurses, housewives, businessmen, and happy-looking young children—all surreptitiously giving each other the "sign of the horns," clearly indicating exactly what America's "best-kept secret" is. The content of the article, in the meantime, is rife with unsubstantiated allegations, inaccurate statements, and biblical references.

However, at least some law enforcement officials subscribing to *File 18* apparently accept its allegations as fact. One San Bernardino County sheriff's detective who is currently investigating a case of ritualistic child abuse, when asked whether he could cite one piece of hard, physical evidence that corroborated his belief in the theory of a child-molesting Satanic conspiracy, replied, "There are the 'WICCA Letters.'"

The "WICCA Letters" refers to a document purportedly intercepted by law enforcement officials after a 1981 convention of the Witches International Coven Council in Mexico. The document, which reads like a rehash of the *Protocols of the Elders of Zion*, purports to be a political blueprint for an international takeover by Satanists. In fact, no such convention was ever held, no such organization as the Witches International Coven Council exists, and the document is a complete fabrication. The *Passport* article, nonetheless, cites it. Although the detective quoted the document as "proof" of the existence of a conspiracy, his knowledge of the "Letters" seemed to be limited to the information about it contained in the article.

One of the most vociferous advocates of the Satanic child-abuse connection is Ted Gunderson, retired head of the FBI's Los Angeles office. Gunderson seemed to be parodying Joe McCarthy during a recent taped interview when he claimed to have information on a cult that killed eighteen persons. The names of the cult members were allegedly sealed in twelve envelopes, and were to be "sent to authorities" in case something happened to him.[4]

Dale Griffis, who lectures law enforcement groups on criminal cult activities, reports that he has found among many cops today a predisposition to believe. "I try to tell them there aren't occultists hiding under every rock," he said. "They often don't like what I have to tell them. Their job is to enforce the laws, not their own religious beliefs."[5]

L.A. sheriff's homicide sergeant, Ray Verdugo, who investigated Satanic allegations in a 1983 Antelope Valley child-abuse case, says that the will to believe might not even stem from religious convictions, but from simple boredom. "You kind of find yourself wanting to believe it," he told me. "I mean, you go through crime reports day in and day out, and you come across a statement like that, and it jumps off the page at you. It's something new and exciting."

In some cases, however, the search for excitement has led to a waste of police manpower, the harassment of innocent individuals, and the embarrassment of the police agencies themselves. On February 5, 1987, for example,

---

[4]Scream Greats II, "Satanism and Witchcraft," *Fangoria* Movie Series.

Mr. Gunderson must not realize that he is breaking the law by withholding evidence about murder. Is he waiting for this vicious cult to kill again before he does anything about it? The FBI assured me when I called that Mr. Gunderson was no longer with the FBI but merely his *ex*-connection with the Bureau ensures media attention and, in some minds, undoubtedly lends a measure of credibility to conspiracy tales.

[5]Telephone conversation with the author.

police in Tallahassee, Florida, announced at a press conference that they had arrested two well-dressed young men at a local playground in the company of six dirty, disheveled, insect-bitten children, ranging in age from two to seven. After a search of their van turned up photographs "consistent with a Satanic cult," including pictures of ritually mutilated animals, Tallahassee police charged the two men with aggravated child abuse and announced that they belonged to a "bizarre Satanic cult" called the Finders, headquartered in Washington, D.C.

The children, the police claimed, had been given up by their parents to the cult, which was part of an international child-pornography network. "As far as we're concerned," a spokesman told reporters, "this goes from coast to coast and from Canada to Mexico. . . . Adults are encouraged to join this group and one of the stipulations . . . is that they give up the rights to their children."[6]

On the basis of the arrests, Washington, D.C., police and the FBI searched the local headquarters of the Finders but came up with no evidence to back up the allegations of Satanism. After an anonymous tipster told police that they could find human remains on a Finders farm in Virginia, authorities spent a week digging but found nothing. Newspapers like the *New York Times*, which had played up the "Satanic cult" angle, began to work their follow-up stories more cautiously, labeling the Finders a " '60s-style commune." Within a matter of days the allegations began to fall apart. The Washington police issued a statement saying that they had turned up no evidence linking the Finders to any criminal activity.

Selective perception seemed to have played a role in their investigation when it was revealed that an ominous "gravestone" observed by one detective on the Finders' property turned out to be a statue of angels and a "Satanic circle of stones" was in a neighbor's field seventy yards away.

In Tallahassee, meanwhile, evidence of sexual child abuse had become "inconclusive," and charges against the two men were dropped to two counts of misdemeanor

[6]*New York Times*, Feb. 7, 1987.

child neglect. All mention of any photographs of cult rituals, as well as the accusations of pornography, ceased as the Finders were determined to be not followers of Satan, but of the Chinese philosopher Lao-tse. In the *Washington Post*, ombudsman Joseph Laitin blamed the news media for not being more skeptical of the original police speculations, saying, "There was an element of a witchhunt, of Salem, here."[7] Most of the newspapers that had trumpeted the Satanic accusations in bold type, however, merely dropped their coverage of the story as the sensational aspects of the case began to evaporate.

The possibility that tales of Satanic child abuse are the creation of a headline-minded media, misguided investigators, and overzealous parents has often been successfully argued by experts called in by defense attorneys in such cases. Dr. Lee Coleman, a Berkeley psychiatrist who testified at the McMartin pretrial and several similar cases in other states, has said: "I haven't seen a single case yet where the fantasy wasn't first stimulated by an adult."[8]

Prosecution witnesses like Michael Durfee, a child psychiatrist and medical coordinator for the Los Angeles County Department of Health Services child-abuse prevention program, disagrees. "The reason kids talk about rituals and chanting and wearing robes and killing babies is because it happened," he insists. "I don't want to believe that people are doing these things to children, but the stories are too patterned, too consistent, not to be true."[9]

But experts, like Dr. Coleman, argue that the bizarre nature of the stories is proof that they did not occur. "While you can manipulate the child, you can't control his fantasy, so you come up with some of the most wild things imaginable," Coleman says.[10]

At least part of the problem seems to be in the way the children are being questioned. Few are saying that an interviewer would purposely implant such horror stories in a child's mind, but according to Dr. Stan Katz, a psychiatrist formerly with Children's Hospital in Los Angeles, and a specialist in child abuse cases: "What

---

[7]*Detroit Free Press*, February 23, 1987, p. 12A.
[8]Quoted in Charles Rappleye, "Satanism and Child Abuse," *Fate*, Apr. 1987, p. 41.
[9]Ibid, p. 40.
[10]Ibid, p. 42.

seems to be happening is that the people who are interviewing and evaluating these cases want to help the children. But they come in with a bias, that whatever is said, happened. That isn't necessarily true."[11]

In fact, the idea that children always tell the truth has only recently become popular among child abuse experts, which was why, up to this time, the legal system has required independent corroboration of the childrens' accusations.

According to Bruno Bettelheim, "Far from being innocent, the mind of the young child is filled with anxious, angry, destructive imaginings."[12] In dreams and daydreams, which they often have difficulty separating from reality, children are constantly pursued by angry animals and giants—symbols of their own guilts and fears—threatening to devour them.

Fairy tales abound with cannibalism, murder, dismemberment. Children find them so satisfying because they embody childhold anxieties, particularly fears of being devoured—and at the same time offer comfort by reassuring the child that he can vanquish the enemy threatening him. Children around the age of four or five—the age of the McMartin Preschool students—are particularly fascinated by cannibalistic tales, says Bettelheim, because it is a time when children are plagued by anxieties of being separated from their parents. Such tales symbolize a regression to an oral-aggressive stage of childhood when the child lived symbiotically off his or her mother's breast. For example, let's look at "Hansel and Gretel."

In it the two kids, mistakenly thinking they are being rejected by their parents (enrolled in day care), leave home and find their way to the gingerbread house (the preschool) where they are befriended by the witch (teacher), who at first appears maternally benevolent, but is really a cannibal (the destructive aspect of orality) who intends to eat them. The children trick her, however, and cook her in her own oven, after which they return home to find out it was all a mistake and their parents really loved them all along. In the end, Hansel and Gretel, reunited with their parents, bask in the attention of which they had

---

[11]Conversation with the author.
[12]Bettelheim, Bruno, *The Uses of Enchantment*, New York: Vintage, 1977, p. 122.

been deprived, and reap praise for conquering (exposing) the witch.

"One has to remember what infantile hatred is like," writes historian Norman Cohn, "that where a small child hates, it wishes to kill, smash, utterly destroy the hated object. At the same time, it feels intensely guilty. This feeling of guilt is quickly repressed into the unconscious, but it finds an outlet nevertheless. . . . So it comes that the small boy constructs out of his own destructive impulses and his own sense of guilt a father-figure of queit monstrous cruelty and murderousness—a castrating, torturing, cannibalistic, all-powerful being beside whom even the harshest of real parents would appear harmless."[13]

Skeptics argue that the children in many of these cases are being rewarded for their fairy tale-like fantasies by the attention given to them by their parents, police, and clinical interviewers. But what about the adults' willingness to believe them? Former law enforcement personnel, before just run-of-the-mill cops, attain prestige as "experts" on Satanic crime, while some parents, unconsciously overreacting, are attempting to alleviate feelings of guilt and responsibility for having ignored their children. There is also the fact that myths, like fairy tales, externalize psychological needs, even for adults. As Cohn states: "The trouble is that many men who never cease to be small boys in their emotional lives continue to see these monsters around them, incarnated in other human beings."[14]

"The essential facts about monsters," writes Shirley Park Lowry, "is that they come from beyond the wall. . . . Monsters are everything uncontrollable that we fear. We fear angry parents . . . large animals, noisy machines. We fear dark, narrow places, strangers in our yard, jobs we cannot handle, unresponsive bureaucracies. . . . We fear being defenseless and alone, bereft of love, choices. But attempts to describe realistically the people and events we fear seldom raise the hair on other people's head. Even our friends shrug."[15]

[13]Cohn, Norman, *Warrant for Genocide*, New York: Harper & Row, 1967, p. 258.
[14]Cohn, Norman, Ibid., p. 258.
[15]Lowry, Shirley Park, *Familiar Mysteries*, New York: Oxford University Press, 1982, p. 179.

Accusations of cannibalism have been historically linked in many cultures with accusations of incest and other perverted sexual acts. These accusations are usually made by hostile neighboring groups for propaganda reasons—that is, for the purpose of creating an image of inhuman barbarity.

"Incest and cannibalism are probably the two most widespread taboos in the world," observes Pat Shipman, paleontologist at Johns Hopkins University School of Medicine, "and both are governed by interesting rules that dictate appropriate social distances between self and others. . . . Because both cannibalism and incest violate rules of accepted distances, the two are often believed to be practiced together. Thus to accuse a group of both cannibalism and incest is tantamount to denying their humanity."[16]

In his study of the seventeenth-century European witch craze, Cohn discovered that the myth of an underground secret society dedicated to evil and the destruction of civilization has been around since the second century. This secret society is alleged to indulge in the most perverse sexual acts and to kidnap babies for cannibalistic ritual sacrifices to its phallic god.

Ironically, Christians were the first to be accused, by the Romans. But as Christianity gained power, Jews took their place. The myth became formally institutionalized with the Inquisition and went on to survive the witch burnings—eventually Jews, gypsies, and Satanists all took their turns being portrayed as baby-stealing monsters.

Cohn points up the fact that well into the twentieth century, it was a widespread belief throughout eastern Europe that Jews used the blood of Christian babies to make Passover bread. More than one observer has noted the similarity of the accusations. "What we have going on here is similar to an outbreak of hysteria that happened in Lyon, France, in the 1970s," sociologist R. George Kirkpatrick explained in a recent interview. "It was widely rumored that Jews were kidnapping Christian girls and selling them into prostitution. In fact, there were no girls missing but people believed the rumors anyway."

If myths reflect the fears and anxieties of living, those

---

[16]"The Myths and Perturbing Realities of Cannibalism," *Discover*, Mar. 1987, p. 71.

that come with today's complex society are often too subtle to describe. Despite our technological sophistication, we still need the bogeyman to articulate those dark, irrational forces that threaten to overwhelm us. Vampires and werewolves have lost their commissions as generals of the armies of the night, replaced by Mansons and Ramirezes and Lucases, figures even more terrifying because of their ability to move among us in broad daylight without being detected.

In the face of the lack of physical evidence, the burden of truth has come to rest exclusively on the stories of the children, and as each story is disproven or recanted, the theory of a widespread Satanic conspiracy grows more and more dubious. Yet many parents remain unshaken in their belief that their children are telling the literal truth and vow to carry on the fight.

Vicky Meyers, who insists her three-year-old son was sexually molested and witnessed murders by a Satanic cult in Pico Rivera, despite the fact that a full police investigation there found no evidence of criminal activity, has led groups of parents to dig up empty lots, and has appeared on *Oprah Winfrey* and other television talk shows in an effort to convince the public of the truth.

"I'm kind of running on anger," she tells her audience. "You can't get emotional about it. You can't even think about it. Anger is what's saving me. I know that if I let myself get scared, I won't be able to keep it up."[17]

Robert Currie, father of one of the McMartin children, stated unequivocally at a press conference in Hollywood: "We are going to show that ritualistic abuse is happening all across the country. We have vowed to continue the fight to warn the public of the reality of the danger, and that these things are really happening."

Indeed, the dedication of these parents to the cause seems to be so complete that no amount of evidence (or lack thereof) can sway their belief in the truth of the Satanic conspiracy. I witnessed this firsthand when I was visited by several parents of alleged victims who came to me to ask about some of the ritualistic aspects of their cases.

One father told me that his son claimed he had been

[17]Rappeleye, op. cit., p. 42.

taken to a house and put naked in a cage with a live lion. What part did lions play traditionally in Satanic ritual, he wanted to know. I replied, none that I was aware of and asked why he believed the lion had been used.

"To instill fear in my boy," he replied.

I observed there had to be other, easier ways to instill fear in a child. Had he ever heard a lion roar? I told him I'd spent three months in Africa and during that time my tent had been literally shaken by a lion roaring three hundred yards away. The likelihood of a person being able to keep a lion in a cage in his house, undetected by neighbors, would be slight.

He persisted, "What if the lion's vocal cords were surgically removed?" So I posed the question, wouldn't it be easier to assume that the boy was fantasizing than that a Satanist would buy a four-hundred-pound lion, cage it and feed it thirty pounds of meat a day, clean up its excrement, and have its vocal cords removed, all for some ritualistic purpose?

Suddenly he became irritated: I was no longer a sympathetic listener but had become, instead, a challenge to his belief system.

In the 1950s, psychologist Leon Festinger and two colleagues infiltrated a flying-saucer cult that believed that the end of the world was approaching, in an effort to find out why the religious zeal of many doomsday groups increases when their predictions fail to come true. They coined the term "cognitive dissonance" to explain the phenomenon. According to Festinger, "Two opinions, or beliefs, or items of knowledge are dissonant with each other if they do not fit together—that is, if they are inconsistent, or if, considering only the particular two items, one does not follow from the other."[18]

Dissonance produces psychological discomfort, says Festinger, which, in turn, creates pressure to relieve or eliminate the discomfort. A creationist, for example, confronted with irrefutable evidence of the truth of the theory of evolution, might feel extremely uncomfortable and might take steps to accommodate the new information. There are several ways he might go about this, and thus alleviate the discomfort these two disturbing facts

[18]Festinger, Leon, Henry Riecken, and Stanley Schachter, *When Prophecy Fails*. New York: Harper & Row, 1956, p 25.

have brought. One, he may change his old views. Two, he may deny the validity of the new facts. Or three, he might proselytize—that is, try to persuade more and more people that his beliefs are correct. If the world shares his beliefs, they *have* to be true.

Whether or not cognitive dissonance is the principle that is keeping the conspiracy theory alive, the social costs of the crusade are mounting. The McMartin case became the most expensive trial in California history, with untold dollars to be spent on pending civil suits. Families have been broken up, never to be the same. Children have been traumatized by the inquiry while the adults forced to defend themselves against accusations have been financially and socially ruined. Six of the seven McMartin defendants have been declared legally indigent. Moreover, the social stigma often does not end with acquittal. In spite of the dismissal of the cases and the findings, a recent poll showed that eighty percent of the town of Jordan, Minnesota, still believed the allegations.

As belief in the rumors persist but remain unproven, frustrations can mount, raising the specter of vigilantism. Summers and Kagen, in their study of the cattle mutilation stories in the 1970s, found that several religious groups in Missouri were, as in the case of the Finders, singled out as "Satanic" and investigated by police agencies simply because of their unorthodox beliefs. In Houston, Texas, in 1987, the fundamentalist Houston-West Assembly of God Church was repeatedly vandalized and riddled with bullets after rumors began to circulate that the church was a front for Devil worshipers. The source of the story turned out to be a teenager who had spread it as a prank.

Giving unskeptical endorsement to the stories at the investigative level can have another undesirable side effect: as dubious cases fall apart, prosecutors could become reluctant to file cases in which the child abuse is real.

J. Gordon Melton, of the Institute for the Study of American Religion, has noted that the current spotlight on Satanism has blinded the public to the fact that most proven cases of religiously related child abuse are among fundamentalist Christian groups, which take the admonition of Hebrews 12:6 literally ("For whom the Lord loveth he chasteneth, and scourgeth every son whom he receiveth").

Among such groups recently charged are the Gideons in Ocala, Florida; the River of Life Tabernacle in Montana; Stonegate Christian Community in West Virginia; Northeast Kingdom Community in Vermont; the Covenant Community Fellowship in Indiana; and the Church of Bible Understanding in New York. Many of these groups believe in demonic possession and beat their children to drive out the devil. Says Melton:

> Religious people also inherit the violence transmitted by families from generation to generation. Given the high level of family violence in the United States (from child abuse to neglect), it is unlikely that cults will be able to exclude people who carry those deep-seated tendencies to violence from joining them and even to rising to positions of leadership, just as they do within mainline religious groups.[19]

That is not to say there are no Satan-worshiping child molesters out there. Unfortunately, it would not be particularly unusual for a personality so twisted that he would feel the compulsion to molest sexually or kill children to accept the Lord of Evil as his master.

In the early 1970s, reports surfaced that certain wife-swapping clubs were beginning to dress up their fantasies by holding orgiastic Satanic masses, a la the old Hellfire Club. It is not beyond possibility that certain elements of the pedophiliac community have gone a similar route. William Holmes, of Northeastern University's Center for Applied Social Research, in his study of the 1984 Malden, Massachusetts, case (in which Gerald Amirault was convicted of sexually molesting children in a "magic room," wearing a clown suit and white facial makeup), concluded: "The use of mystical elements like costumes and masks is not done just for the sexual pleasure, but for the domination of a helpless victim."[20] If a fetishist will don a clown suit, why not a cowled robe or a set of horns?

[19]Melton, J. Gordon, *Encyclopedia Handbook of Cults in America*, New York: Garland, 1986, p. 257.
[20]"A Presumption of Guilt," *San Francisco Examiner*, Sept. 28, 1986, p. A-8.

Psychopathic homicidal personalities, however, are generally loners and have trouble relating socially to others. Groups that kill, like the Manson Family, are rarities, and are only able to survive because they live on the fringes of society and are constantly on the move. Also, as homicide detective Ray Verdugo notes: "Those kinds of groups don't hold together long. Somebody always snitches."

Even the Church of Satan and the Temple of Set (the leaders of both of which vehemently deny that any "true" Satanist would molest a child) have not been able to keep the "normal" membership together. The likelihood that a widespread cult of child-molesting, murderous, cannibalistic Satanists could stay together over any period of time and maintain their secrecy is slight.

Catholic theologian Aidan Kelly has this to say: "Child molesting is evil in itself; dressing it in ritual trappings does not make it any more evil, or any less. On the other hand, it seems clear from the newspaper reports I have seen linking child molesting with 'Satanic Rituals,' that the phenomenology of the Salem witch trials is being created all over again; that is, innocent adults are being accused by hysterical children. It would seem important to bring this to the attention of the police officers specializing in these cases; but I don't know how to do that."[21]

[21]Kelly, Aidan, op. cit., p. 5.

Chapter XI

Sympathy for the Devil

[Rock music's] vitality and appeal stems from the fact that it . . . proselytized for an alternate religiousness. This makes it a much more potent threat to the established order than even its most vociferous opponents believe it to be. Here is the very essence of the cultural revolution taking place in America: the rejection of America's religious heritage and its replacement with something contrary. It is not the devil behind rock and roll—it's another god.
—Robert Pielke, *You Say You Want a Revolution*

Frequently cited as proof of the existence of a rapidly growing underground Satanic movement is the recent popular explosion of so-called heavy metal rock groups whose symbology and songs promote the demonic themes of death, doom, violence, and social nihilism. Since 1980, record sales of groups and solo artists like Iron Maiden, Black Sabbath, Venom, Mötley Crüe, Ozzy Osbourne, AC/DC, Ronnie James Dio, Mercyval Fate, and Slayer have skyrocketed, to the alarm of some parent and Christian groups.

Thousands of teenagers wearing T-shirts emblazoned with inverted pentagrams flash the "sign of the horns" and chant Satan's name at rock concerts. Spray-painted Satanic symbols and slogans, along with the names of various heavy metal groups, now regularly deface the walls of junior and senior high schools.

In Los Angeles the alleged murder spree of Richard Ramirez, the so-called Night Stalker, was reputed to have been inspired by the AC/DC song "Night Prowler" from that group's *Highway to Hell* album. Music critics and heavy metal fans protest that AC/DC cannot be held accountable for Ramirez's homicidal binge any more than the Beatles should be blamed because Charles Manson took his name for Armageddon from their song "Helter Skelter." Still, authorities continue to blame the synergistic combination of Satanism and heavy metal for an increasing number of bizarre and violent crimes.

In San Diego and Los Angeles, detectives have publicly blamed marauding gangs of "Satanic heavy metal rockers" for a rash of local crimes in 1986, ranging from vandalism to grave robbing and burglary. The California State Taskforce on Youth Gang Violence, in the same year, concluded that the phenomenon is not limited to those cities but is statewide. It claims that gangs of nihilistic adolescents, calling themselves "stoners," are engaged in Satanic worship, cemetery desecrations, and blood sacrifice. Unlike black and Latino gangs, which organize to defend a "turf," the report says that these new gangs are formed out of a common allegiance to certain rock groups and consist of mainly middle-class white youth.

Ominous musical influences were cited as a contributing cause in the February 2, 1986, shotgun slaying of a seventeen-year-old Monroe, Michigan, youth named Lloyd Gamble. At a press conference, sheriffs displayed an assortment of heavy metal LPs alongside ceremonial robes, an inverted crucifix, and other Satanic paraphernalia as evidence seized during the murder investigation. The killer, Gamble's younger brother, a self-styled Satanist and AC/DC fan, told detectives he had murdered his brother to "release him to a higher plane of consciousness." He had picked the February 2 date, he said, because it corresponded to Candlemas, a Satanic holiday. Although the younger Gamble was a loner and belonged to no cult, and police termed the killing an "isolated incident," certain investigators claimed to have identified groups at three Monroe County high schools involved in devil worship in conjunction with heavy metal music.

Parents of an Indio, California, teenager recently filed a multimillion-dollar suit against Ozzy Osbourne and CBS Records after their son, John McCollum, committed suicide in 1984 while listening to Osbourne's "Suicide Solution." Osbourne, who admits that he himself tried to commit suicide several times before he turned fourteen "just to see what it felt like," disclaims any responsibility for the death, saying that the song's message is really antisuicide. The "solution" referred to in the song, he says, is a liquid one—drugs—and his message is that anyone who takes drugs is committing suicide. As for the assertion that he is a practicing Satanist, Osbourne terms any such charge patently absurd.

Like Osbourne, most heavy metal performers flatly deny having any connection with Satanism (one exception is King Diamond, of Mercyval Fate, who openly claims to be a Satanist), and say they are merely trying to entertain their teenage audiences. But critics say that it does not matter what the artists themselves believe. Their music, by espousing sex, bloodlust, and Devil worship, is influencing many young people to get involved in the black arts, while also inciting them to violence. Yet some observers, like *Los Angeles Times* music critic Robert Hilburn, see nothing more ominous in such songs than a case of adolescent rebellion against parental and societal authority. "I don't think the kids take it more seriously than going to a movie on a Saturday night," he insists, and suggests that the "biggest danger is that parents will overract to this."[1]

Aidan Kelly agrees, attributing the current heavy metal rage to what he calls the "ooga booga factor."[2] Just as a primitive witch doctor tries to scare away evil spirits by shouting, "ooga booga" Kelly says, so teenagers are saying "ooga booga" to their parents by adopting the trappings of heavy metal. And where there is a market, there will always be someone around to cash in on it.

"Our music is for kids who have parents beating them down and telling them what they can and can't do,"[2] says Dee Snider, of Twisted Sister. That sentiment was echoed a bit disingenuously in an interview with Bruce Dickinson, of Iron Maiden, who called accusations that the group was into Satanism "rubbish." His explanation: "We never started out singing songs like that it was simply an unfortunate coincidence that we had that album *The Number of the Beast*. We got all that publicity, you know. And it's like, well, what do we do?"[3]

[1]*Los Angeles Times*, Sept. 2, 1985, p. A-3.
[2]*Hit Parader*, Oct. 1985, p. 35.
[3]*Rock Scene*, Oct. 1985, p. 22.

As Marcello Truzzi puts it: "What is there left to shock parents with? Sex isn't shocking anymore. Only the Devil is left."[4]

But not only is this shock-rock an expression of rebellion, it is also a means for its listeners to differentiate themselves from previous and coexisting generations of rockers. Just as punk rockers painstakingly declared themselves uniquely outside society by dying their spiked hair red and green, adopting barbaric and aggressive styles of dress and dance, and listening to a monotonic, robotic music, so the heavy metal enthusiasts announce their own uniqueness through their own music and dress.

"It's a fad," says San Diego State University sociology professor R. George Kirkpatrick, who has made a study of modern witchcraft and neo-pagan groups. "These kids pick up the trappings for a while, then drop it. It is a cultural phenomenon among working-class youth, rather than the work of any cult or group."[5]

Joseph Kranyak, a crime analyst for the San Bernardino Police Department and an expert on cult violence, says: "One hears about cases, but when you track them down, you find you're chasing mostly shadows. The vandalous nature of these things may not be organized and conspiratorial, but a response to stimuli, like rock music."[6]

Others, however, vehemently disagree, persisting in their belief in the existence of a centralized, demonically orchestrated conspiracy to brainwash and control youth through music. One such believer is Pastor Fletcher A. Brothers, whose New York–based Freedom Village distributes antirock literature to law enforcement groups across the country and regularly exchanges information with other antirock interest groups, such as Parents Music Resource Center, which has been lobbying for a rating system for LPs and concerts.

In its newsletter, *The Villager*, Freedom Village has accused many popular musicians—not just heavy metalists—of sexual perversions and Devil worship. Among the group's list of Satanic performers are Pat Benatar, the Beatles, Marvin Gaye, and Stevie Wonder (whose interest

[4]Conversation with the author.
[5]Conversation with the author.
[6]Conversation with the author.

in astrology has been condemned by Brothers). Freedom Village does not merely restrict its activities to the printed medium; it has sought to achieve its aims through more direct political methods. At the September 15, 1986, Senate hearings into so-called porn rock, for example, Pastor Brothers brought busloads of children to testify that they had been "abused" by rock music. The group also orchestrated demonstrations of placard-carrying children in Maryland to lobby for antirock legislation in that state.

A recent article originally published in the Christian magazine *Passport*, and later distributed nationally to law enforcement personnel by the Boise group, *File 18*, states that Satanic messages are, through rock music, being slipped past "that part of the listener's brain which rejects information," through the use of low-frequency sound waves. These waves can alter moods and behavior. The article goes on to say that the perpetrators of this conspiracy, as well as many of the fans of the music, are adept in occult matters, and that other secret "codes" than those employed in the music are being used as methods of communication. "Members of stoner gangs," the article asserts, "are quite adept at writing backwards and using the Runic, Theban, Hebrew, Pafsing, Malchim, and Celestial alphabets. That is why much of their graffiti is not recognizable to the untrained eye."[7]

They might be able to write backward and in Etruscan, but the so-called stoners often seem to have difficulty writing forward, in English, as was unintentionally and ironically pointed out on the May 16, 1985, ABC *20/20* broadcast "The Devil Worshippers." Pointing to the wall of an abandoned building, the commentator cited spray-painted graffiti as "proof" that a Satanic cult had been meeting there. There, writ large: SATIN RULES. Either the vandals were into fabrics or someone needed a refresher course in Basic Devil, illustrating that the superficial prevalence of a phenomenon does not necessarily indicate its seriousness.

However, the Devil did not make his rock and roll debut as a heavy metalist. The Rolling Stones, Led Zeppelin,

[7]John Frattarola, "America's Best Kept Secret," *Passport*, Special Report, 1987, p. 12.

Styx, and the Cars are just a few rock groups rumored at one time or another to be in league with the Prince of Darkness. In the 1960s the Reverend David Norbel (a preacher with Billy Lee Hargis's right-wing Christian Crusade), in his book *Communism, Hypnotism, and the Beatles*, wrote that the British performers were in reality agents of a Satanic-Communist plot to make the youth of America mentally ill by timing their musical rhythms to teenage pulsebeats.

The fact is that ever since Elvis Presley's pelvis-pumping antics scandalized viewers of the Ed Sullivan show in the 1950s, rock and roll has been deemed the Devil's music. In unashamedly expressing the narcissistic yearnings of youth, by exalting the pursuit of earthly joy and material rewards over those of a nebulous hereafter, rock and roll has consistently challenged existing American middle-class values of sex, work, religion, and politics. In expressing youthful discontent with the beliefs and practices of the political and religious Establishment, it has served as a catalyst for change.

Thus, in the 1960s, rock music not only affirmed the ideals of personal freedom and self-exploration, but San Francisco groups like the Jefferson Airplane and the Grateful Dead accelerated social change through a quasi-religious endorsement of mind-expanding drugs. It was during the era of psychedelic revolution, when dissatisfaction with accepted values peaked, when Eastern mysticism and alternate forms of consciousness were being explored, that a more darkly demonic element found its way into the music.

It was also in the sixties that be-ins, happenings, and outdoor rock festivals, all reminiscent of the pagan Sabbats, came into being. The resemblances were psychological as well as superficial. These events served as a cathartic release for the participants, with religious-like use of symbols and costumes by the performers, wild and hypnotic music, widespread use of hallucinogens, and orgiastic dancing. In addition, the celebrants experienced a feeling of loss of ego, of being mystically absorbed into a larger unity.

On Halloween, 1969, the old Sabbat and the new-style rock concert looked as if they were going to formally merge with the announcement of a "Black Arts Festival" at Olympia Stadium in Detroit. Scheduled to appear along with the headlining rock group the Coven, were clairvoyant Peter Hurkos, Timothy Leary, and Anton LaVey, who was supposed to perform a Satanic benediction. The event was canceled, however, when the promoters bowed to pressure from the Detroit Council of Churches.

It was just as well. A little more than a month later, at Altamont Race Track outside San Francisco, 300,000 fans attended a free concert given by the Rolling Stones. Things turned nasty throughout the afternoon as the security force of the Hell's Angels waded through the frenzied crowd, keeping the peace with sawed-off pool cues. Disregarding the building climate of violence, the Stones appeared on stage in wizard's robes and began a rendition of "Sympathy for the Devil"—a song about Mephistopheles nostalgically reminiscing about his meddling in human affairs—and before they finished, a young black man in the audience was stabbed to death. In the ensuing panic, fatalities mounted to three, and one hundred people were injured.

The Stones had gained a reputation for diabolic dabbling ever since lead singer Mick Jagger and drummer Keith Richards had become friendly with underground filmmaker Kenneth Anger. Jagger had composed the Moog synthesizer sound track for Anger's "Invocation of My Demon Brother," and Richards and his model-girlfriend, Anita Pallenberg, along with singer Marianne Faithfull, had played in his film *Lucifer Rising*. It was Faithfull who inspired Jagger to write "Sympathy for the Devil" after she read Mikhail Bulgakov's *The Master and Margarita*, a 1930s novel about a socially sophisticated Satan who returns to Moscow to obsereve the results of his work—the Russian Revolution. Anger was also the primary influence in Jagger's decision to use the Devil from the Tarot card pack designed by Aleister Crowley on the cover of *Their Satanic Majesties Request* album.

The tragedy at Altamont shook Jagger up enough to put an abrupt end to his flirtation with diabolism, and for some time afterward, he wore a large wooden crucifix, on stage and off. But it was too late: the innocence of Woodstock was dead. In the shadows of Kent State and the Chicago riots, the subtle niceties of sixties music began to change.

Heavy metal, with its thunderous volume, stage violence, and lyrics promoting sex and drugs, soon appeared on the scene. Love had failed to sweep the world; aggression ruled. If the songs of the sixties had reflected identity confusion, the new music was without any identity but raw, unbridled rage, destruction without any goals.

The Who smashed their instruments on stage to cheering and often violent crowds. Jim Morrison, in testing out his theory that he could hynotically control audience behavior through his music, purposely and successfully commanded a riot at a 1968 Chicago concert. It was just a matter of time before Satan, the personification of the violent, unbridled id, was formally asked to sing lead vocals.

Actually he already had, in the form of a British rocker named Arthur Browne, whose hit, "Fire," had swept the U.S. and Europe in 1968. During his performances, Browne would declare himself the "God of Hell-Fire," and set fire to his hair while climbing a ten-foot cross. His incendiary stage effects blazed the way for the spectacular shock-rock shows to come.

One young musician impressed by Browne's antics was Vincent Furnier, the son of a Phoenix preacher. A few years later his group, Alice Cooper, was packing in teenage audiences who laid down their money to see the ghoulishly made-up Furnier play with snakes, perform mock executions, and chop up baby dolls.

Sensing a new dark mood on the part of teenage audiences, other groups like Blue Oyster Cult and Judas Priest began to adopt semi-Satanic imagery. But the undisputed heavy metal kings in the early 1970s were Black Sabbath, a British group who appeared on stage showcasing nightmarish visions of the coming Apocalypse. Panned by music critics and ignored by radio stations, Black Sabbath sold seven million records and emerged as the main heavy metal group of the decade.

As audiences became more and more jaded, stage shows became more and more outlandish. Ozzy Osbourne, Black Sabbath's lead singer (who was later to split off from the group and go solo), took shock-rock Grand Guignol to new extremes when he began biting the heads off live bats and spitting them at squealing audiences.

Visual special effects reached dizzying heights at the

concerts of the group KISS. As if emerging from a world of sulfurous brimstone, the quartet would appear out of clouds of billowing smoke, wearing horrific facial make-up, exhaling fire, and shooting laser beams out of their guitars. "We wanted to look like we crawled out from under a rock somewhere in hell," bassist Gene Simmons said in an interview. "We wanted parents to look at us and instantly want to throw up."[8] Soon the rumors began to circulate that KISS was an acronym for "Kids in Service to Satan."

Denial by KISS of any Satanic connection fell on deaf ears in fundamentalist circles, where it had long been believed that Satanists were in control of the record industry and were seeking to subliminally subvert America's youth through "backward-masked" propaganda audible only when the records or tapes were played backward. The songs of Led Zeppelin, ELO, the Cars, Styx, and Black Oak Arkansas were "exposed" on such Christian TV shows as the *700 Club* for containing such insidious messages as "I live for Satan" and "Satan is God."

Even the theme for the old *Mr. Ed* series was alleged to be Satanic. Seventy-five teenagers participated in a mass burning of *Mr. Ed* records in April 1986, after evangelist Jim Brown claimed during a seminar at the First Church of the Nazarene in Ironton, Ohio, that "A Horse Is a Horse," when played in reverse, becomes "Someone sung this song for Satan."

It must be noted that the psychological effectiveness of forward—never mind backward—subliminal messages has never been established, and is still being debated by experts. In addition, back-masked messages are not easy to recover, taking much labor and, often, special equipment. Even when recovered, most of the "accursed" phrases found so repugnant by evangelism turn out to be garbled and unrecognizable.[9]

Still, the danger seems immediate enough to occupy the time of legislators. In 1982, California Republican Robert K. Dornan introduced a resolution in the U.S. House of Representatives requiring all records suspected of backward-masking to carry a consumer warning. In 1983, the

[8] *Hit Parader*, Oct. 1985, p. 34.
[9] Examples of specific back-masked transcriptions can be found in William Poundstone's *Big Secrets* (1983).

Arkansas State Senate unanimously passed a similar bill, the debate there taking on an unintentionally comic atmosphere when several of the senators presented arguments speaking backward.

As comedian Jay Leno sardonically once remarked on a television special: "You know what you get when you play Twisted Sister's 'Burn in Hell' backwards? 'Go to church and pray on Sunday.'"

Some groups, however, like the Parents' Music Resource Center, take the menace more seriously. Headed by Sally Nevius and Tipper Gore, wife of Tennessee Senator and presidential aspirant Albert Gore, the PMRC is a group of concerned parents who formed to combat what they see as dangerous violent and occult influences in rock music and videos. In 1985, the PMRC sent a letter to the Recording Industry Association of America urging the industry to start a rating system of concerts and to reassess the recording contracts of certain artists. The letter, signed by twenty PMRC members (including sixteen wives of senators and congressmen, as well as Susan Baker, wife of Treasury Secretary James Baker), also advocated plain wrappers for LP covers that display violent or sexually explicit themes, an "X" rating for albums that feature profanity, suicide, or homosexuality, and an "O" rating for those with occult references. The members argue that if we are concerned enough about the content of movies to install a rating system, we should be just as concerned about the content of recordings and videos to which our children are exposed.

Four months after the letter was sent, the PMRC repeated the suggestions to the Senate Commerce Committee hearings into "porn rock." Called to testify at the hearings, rock musician Frank Zappa suggested that the labeling request was simply fundamentalism in secular garb and asked PMRC members sarcastically if they were a "cult." Zappa noted that many rock performers were Muslim, and asked if the rating system should not be expanded to include "M" to designate possible nefarious influences by that faith.

Strangely, the man most often named as the prime mover behind the Satanic plot to take over the world, Anton LaVey, sees the heavy metal craze as a Christian—not a Satanic—creation. "Heavy metal has succeeded because its symbology is more appealing than that of Christianity, which is why Christians created it," he postulated recently, as he went through a medley of old ballads on the synthesizer keyboards that fill the kitchen of his home. "It's a convenient scapegoat because they can denounce it from their pulpits, while, at the same time, get the kids to buy, buy, buy, when they don't buy hymns to Jesus. It's the last big burp of Christianity."

True Satanic music, LaVey explains iconoclastically, is melodic and lyrical. And he cites tunes like "That Old Black Magic," "Taboo," and Irving Berlin's "Stay Down Here Where You Belong" as examples. The lyrics of these songs make the listener think, LaVey says, which is antithetical to the purpose of heavy metal—which uses repetitive rhythms, simplistic lyrics, and blistering volume to convert the kids into "nonthinking zombies."

At the crux of the debate is the issue of what propagandizing effect rock music can have on the mind. "You've got to get down to the basic thing," says rocker Frank Zappa. "There's no proof that any word that you hear on a record is going to turn you into a social liability or make you go to hell. That premise is wrong. And starting from that wrong premise and working their way outward, [PMRC] created something that in 1985 was verging on hysteria."[10]

Pamela Cantor, president of the American Society of Suicidology, recently expressed doubts that rock music, by itself, could truly influence a mentally healthy individual. "Kids who are disturbed to begin with will buy into this type of activity," she said. "Kids who are normal are going to look at it as a game, or music."[11]

Dr. Morton Kurland, a Palm Springs psychiatrist whose patient John McCollum committed suicide after listening to an Ozzy Osbourne record, is convinced that music and the media can exert an influence, but *only* if a person is already suffering from other serious emotional problems. "When a kid is at the breaking point . . . he is susceptible to other influences, like music or MTV," Kurland told me in an interview. "Sadomasochism, blood, and violence make big bucks for the producers of rock videos, but such things can push a kid over the edge."[12]

[10]*Rip*, June 1987, p. 53.
[11]"Satan Worship on the Rise?" *San Diego Tribune*, Jan. 23, 1986, p. B-11.
[12]Conversation with the author.

Most criminal psychologists deny that music in itself—no matter how blasphemous or violent—could create a Night Stalker or a Charles Manson. An individual who feels alienated from society will gravitate toward those groups and pursuits that support his own self-image, and herein lies the danger: in an imitative society, the heroes who are worshiped and imitated are not great men, but celebrities. And the androgynous, black leather-clad, ghoulish stars of heavy metal are natural idols for misfits.

To counter this, two Californians, Darlyne Pettinicchio, a probation officer, and Greg Bodenhamer, have established "Back in Control," to "de-metal" teens. Both of them act as "heavy metal and punk consultants" to law enforcement agencies; they offer lectures and seminars and also a four-week "de-metaling" course. A series of scare films they've produced is shown to "educate" juvenile officers. Furthermore, Pettinicchio has put together a twenty-nine page manual informing adults of the dangers of the music and of its ties to the Devil. Pettinicchio claims, for example, that "occult graffiti is frequently placed underground, under bridges, in flood-control channels and under freeway overpasses to be closer to Hell and the devil."[13] Among "Satanic symbols," she lists the pentagram, the inverted cross, and the swastika, as well as the Star of David. When a recent interviewer asked her to explain diabolic significance of the Jewish star, she replied: "The reason for the Star of David . . . if you know anything about the occult, you'll know that it's the exact opposite of Christianity. That's what the occult is."[14]

The scary thing is that this sort of misinformation has been taken seriously and accepted by law enforcement officials. After an April 1985 presentation by Back in Control, for example, the Union City Police Department compiled its own workbook, "Punk Rock and Heavy Metal: The Problem/One Solution," which echoes many of Back in Control's dicta. Similar volumes have been produced by police departments across the country.

To ACLU representative Barry Lynn, this definitely represents a dangerous trend. He observes that Back in Control seems to be using the probation department to

[13]*Rip*, June 1987, p. 56.
[14]Ibid.

promote a "sectarian religious viewpoint in the masquerade of rehabilitation."[15]

This secularization of religious ideas can lead to gross misrepresentation of data (a dead frog can thus become evidence of a Satanic cult) and a misappropriation of law enforcement resources. If there are dangerous stoner gangs out there—and there is at least some tangible evidence that there are—it would seem to be important to identify them and determine what is motivating their formation without confusing the issue with religious bias. From a social standpoint, for example, more significant than any so-called Satanic practices by such gangs might be the fact that juvenile authorities in Los Angeles, San Bernardino, and San Diego counties have reported that the members of stoner groups are being recruited by violent biker gangs, such as the Hell's Angels. Thus, according to these sources, young "temporary misfits" are being converted into "permanent misfits," and are becoming unredeemable threats to society.

The number of heavy metal fans that fall into such antisocial patterns is undoubtedly small. It strikes one that the principal danger for the great majority of the music's audience lies not in heavy metal's content, or its subliminal messages, but in its lack thereof. Just as a person could go stupid, as well as deaf, listening to amplified white noise or the sound of jet aircraft taking off, so might he go deaf and stupid listening to the mindless, boring inanity of heavy metal. As historian Jeffrey Burton Russell, who has written a four-volume history of the Devil, puts it: "The Devil no doubt has some interest in cultural despair, Satan chic, and demonic rock groups, but he must be more enthusiastic about nuclear armament, gulags, and exploitative imperialism."[16]

[15]*Rip*, op. cit., p. 56.
[16]Russell, Jeffrey Burton, *Mephistopheles: The Devil in The Modern World*, Ithaca: Cornell University Press, 1986, p. 257.

CHAPTER XII

The Call to Cthulhu

"We are fortunate that the Auschwitz taboo prevents people from looking too closely at . . . Nazi Germany, or from experimenting with any of its regular governmental doctrines. Because they work. They are the essence of true political power. Anti-Semitism is irrelevant to them. . . . It is ironically true that a right-wing backlash in the United States—which is what the neo-Nazis are hoping for—would wipe them out first. If an American Fuehrer does appear, he won't be wearing a uniform with a swastika armband. He will wear a business suit, and he will be calling popular attention to the patriotic virtues in 1776."
—Michael Aquino

Although a few Satanic cults have reported an increase in membership over the past four years, as a whole the move has not achieved the numerical or organizational strength it displayed in the mid-1970s. Marcello Truzzi puts it in perspective: "Satanism may be on the rise, but in the '60s, the Church of Satan had a much larger membership. The Church of Satanic Liberation claims to have a thousand members nationally. Still, that's not many when you consider that the Church of John F. Kennedy, which believes that Kennedy was the Messiah, has over 2,000 members now."

Although the vast majority of Satanists belong to the neo-Satanic churches and constitute no threat to society, certain gangs of adolescents have adopted various Satanic trappings and symbolism in the past few years, and there is some evidence that certain "outlaw" groups have gained in popularity, perhaps as a result of media attention. There is no evidence, however, that any of these cults are in contact with one another, or are part of any widespread conspiracy. Satanism appears to be a cultural phenomenon, what sociologist David Martin calls a movement of "parallel spontaneities."

Satanism, along with other occult belief systems, has historically made its appearance in times of social fragmentation, when the established system of norms and values is in a state of confusion. Sociologists Charles Glock and Rodney Stark have observed that religious cults, as well as radical political movements, tend to rise up in times of social dislocation as a response to psychic, social, or economic deprivation. As historian Ortega y Gasset put it: "The situation becomes extreme when man finds no solution in the normal point of view; this condition forces him to hunt an escape in a distant and eccentric extreme which formerly had seemed to him less worthy of attention."[1]

In ancient Greece, magic had a revival during the Persian Wars. Roman superstition reached its height when the Empire was in a stage of dissolution, and when Christianity was rising to challenge the old order. The savagery of the Inquisition increased drastically during the time of the Reformation and the Thirty Years War.

In America, Spiritualism was born in the years of social conflict preceding the Civil War, and occultism in general had a revival in the 1870s and 1880s, during times of great social unrest. The Ku Klux Klan, with its ghostly white robes and secret vocabulary, born during those postwar times, had a major revival during the 1930s when the country was in the grips of the Great Depression. During the social turmoil of the 1960s, interest in the occult and Eastern mysticism reached new heights, particularly among restless and disaffected youth.

But the conflict of social values and norms first felt in the 1960s did not end with the demise of the hippie "movement" and the psychedelic revolution. If anything, the new communications revolution has worsened matters. The rise of computers and depersonalized services, for example, can but add to the alienation of individuals.

The average American is the incredible shrinking man, growing smaller each day in the face of unprecedented

[1]Ortega y Gasset, *Man in Crisis*, New York: W. W. Norton, 1962, p. 147.

strides in technology and communications. His social frame of reference has increased a billionfold and he finds it suddenly difficult to isolate himself within his culture. His privacy gone, he finds little solace in the anonymous masses, his exposure to other cultures has loosened his firm grasp on his own, and he finds himself in a state of uncertainty. There is nothing unique or powerful about him; he is just part of the herd, performing meaningless tasks, bored by his job, the end product of his labor often being divorced and unrecognizable from that labor.

The traditional safety valves for these frustrations, such as religion and the secular moral codes of society, have broken down in the face of the new technology. Man has landed on the moon, but the churches still echo the same tired rhetoric. The gap between knowledge and theology has widened inexorably and shows no sign of narrowing. As traditional religion fails to supply the viable answers, and as man becomes more and more depersonalized by bureaucratization and a mass society, he will seek identity where he can find it.

The yuppie goals of material success, which in the late 1970s supplanted the counterculture's search for spirituality and social equality, have been profoundly shaken by an economic slump generated by industrial and technological competition from abroad.

Beginning in the 1980s, mysticism and magic, not surprisingly, began to find their way back into the culture as money-seekers began to experience uncertainty and dissatisfaction with the corporate world. The inner-directed values of the sixties have returned metamorphosed in the eighties, without the costumed trappings. Men and women in business suits consult Tarot cards, psychics, and pay $150 for "trance-channeling" sessions in which they talk to the spirits of the dead. Actress Jane Fonda wears crystals to "energize herself," and Shirley MacLaine regularly leaves her body to visit other solar systems. Neiman-Marcus, that bastion of posh consumerism, is currently pushing a line of fetish dolls billed as "representatives of another dimension."

The Stanford Research Institute International estimates that 34 million Americans are concerned with the burgeoning "inner growth" movement. Catholic theologian Andrew Greeley, in a 1985 survey for the National Opinion

Research Center in Chicago, found that 40 percent of Americans claim to have had contact with the dead, compared with 25 percent in 1972. Communes, holistic health centers, and meditation retreats are once more in vogue; the paranormal is once again normal.

Satanism, along with other occult and magical belief systems, is a response to social tensions. In his classic study of Trobriand Islanders, Malinowski found that the natives did not resort to magic when they had more effective methods of control but only turned to it when events were out of their hands. When prayers don't work and the economic picture worsens, people seek other means of controlling their lives.

In its ads, the Continental Association of Satan's Hope (CASH) includes a testimonial from a man who attributes his winning the British lottery to Satan's help. Lost your job? Your car being repossessed? Need a friend? Call Satan.

Just as the current state of social flux is deemed responsible for the attractiveness of cults, some social observers like Colin Wilson see it also as responsible for the current style of murder. The twentieth century, says Wilson, is unique as the age of the sociopath, the serial killer, and the sex murderer—a fact he deems the price we are paying for our high level of civilization. Wilson sees this new brand of homicide as a desperate and existential attempt by the murderer to assert its own reality: I kill, therefore I am. "The impersonality of society produces either revolt or contemptuous indifference," he writes. "Hence the age of centralization is also the age of the juvenile delinquent and the sex maniac."[2]

The escape into barbarity, as well as that into magical thinking, is an attempt by the individual to make himself feel powerful. When the two combine, it may make him feel doubly powerful. Thus, it is not surprising to find religious cults that practice violence to be springing up in recent years. We should be concerned about the fact, but not panicked.

Religious cults—Satanic and non-Satanic—that advocate and practice violence have always existed and continue to exist within society. When their presence is known to authorities, they should be carefully watched. A

[2]Wilson, Colin, *Encyclopedia of Murder*, New York: G. P. Putnam, 1962, p. 32.

responsible policy in this regard should be followed, however, to make sure that innocent religious groups are not persecuted simply for having unorthodox beliefs. We must also be careful that a reality is not created out of urban myth, as seemed to be the case with the cattle mutilations of the 1970s. We live in a copycat society, from the style of dress to the style of murder; there is always the possibility that we might create an abominable reality out of our own lurid imaginations.

Finally, it must be concluded that current claims of the existence of a child-molesting conspiracy of Satanists does not stand up to scrutiny. Despite a significant commitment of law enforcement personnel and technology, no evidence to back up the allegations has been produced. The theory seems to be the product of a sensationalist media abetted by a lack of skepticism among law enforcement, religious, and parent groups. But the failure of a conspiracy theory does not negate the social significance of its appearance. Such outbreaks of social-psychological contagion have crossed all cultural and historical lines. In the seventeenth century, convents throughout Europe were plagued by epidemics of demonic possession. It is possible that Satanic child abuse is the St. Vitus' dance of the 1980s.

In studies of primitive societies, anthropologists have often taken a functional approach to explain witchcraft beliefs. Clyde Kluckholn, in his classic work on Navajo witchcraft, came to the conclusion that witch beliefs serve as an outlet for repressed hostility within the culture. E. E. Evans-Pritchard, in his study of the Azande tribe in Africa, found such beliefs to be operative for the society as a whole, in that they explained away unfortunate events and fastened blame on the enemies of the afflicted. Witchcraft beliefs have been seen by these anthropologists as a way of relieving hostility generated through social tensions when other means are prohibited or inadequate. But the size of the fire may not always be commensurate with the amount of smoke it produces. "Even where witchcraft is performed by mechanical acts," writes Edward Norbeck, "ethnologists have often reported an abundance of accusation of witchcraft but little or no evidence of its actual practice. Secrecy is, of course, essential if the witch wishes to escape detection and punishment, but there is ample reason to think that in many societies accusations far outnumber practices."[3]

Studies of witchcraft among American Indian tribes have shown that the individuals most likely to be suspected or charged with sorcery are those who do not conform with the ideal patterns of behavior. That pattern was historically evident in the European witch craze of the sixteenth and seventeenth centuries, in which nonconformists, heretics, Jews, and lunatics were burned *en masse* for being in league with the Devil. More than one social analyst thinks it is a pattern that is still at work today.

"Such accusations identify the limits of acceptable behavior in a society," says sociologist R. George Kirkpatrick. "They are a way to clarify the norms and rules which hold a society together." Kirkpatrick believes that the current stories of a great Satanic conspiracy are the result of cultural *anomie*, an uncertainty about current norms and values. This, he says, is a result of the counterculture challenge to the "overarching values of the American civil religion," which, up until the 1960s, provided a set of guiding values and norms that permeates society. Now, in the face of normlessness, people are pointing accusing fingers, in order to define what is acceptable and what is not.

"Jews served as traditional scapegoats for such accusation in the past," says Kirkpatrick, "but it would be unfashionable in America today to be anti-Semitic. So Satanists are the ones committing the horrible crimes. In a way, Satanists are better scapegoats than Jews, because they don't exist. Every excess can be attributed to them."[4] In a world in which evil has become a nebulous concept, a projection of true evil is necessary in order to define parameters.

The argument that the new Satanic scare is a revival of the same old myth in updated form becomes even more viable when one notes the striking similarities between the so-called WICCA Letters, which are cited by advocates as proof of the reality of the conspiracy, and the *Protocols of the Elders of Zion*, a document that has been used to

---

[3]Norbeck, Edward, op. cit., p. 189–90.
[4]Conversation with the author.

"prove" the existence of a plot by Jews for world domination for the past eighty-five years.

The *Protocols*, which first made its appearance in Russia in 1903, was claimed by its publishers to be a series of lectures, which had been intercepted by authorities, to a secret Jewish government called the Elders of Zion. Although it was proven a forgery, it continued to have credence among anti-Semitic European intellectual circles, until it was picked up by Hitler and his principle philosopher, Alfred Rosenberg, who made it the official party line of National Socialism. It was the *Protocols*, plus *volkisch*, the mystical concept of a Germanic nation-race, which revived the medieval view of Jews as subhuman agents of Satan and set the rationale behind the new genocide that was to follow.

The Jews, the *Protocols* revealed, were responsible for the sad condition of the world following World War I. It was all part of the master plan for world takeover, and the document laid out the blueprint step by step. Discontent was to be fostered among the populace by discrediting authority, raising the cost of living, and crushing the people under a burden of taxes. Wars were to be promoted to bring about economic chaos. Gentiles were to be encouraged to become atheists, and to indulge in every vice and luxury. Drunkenness and prostitution were to be encouraged, and the Christian faith was to be destroyed by attacks on morality. In the midst of all the chaos, the Jews were allegedly secretly setting themselves up to take over and establish the Messianic Age, the coming of the Antichrist.

Now compare the alleged aims of this "Jewish conspiracy" to those of the Satanic one, as set out in the goals attributed to the so-called (and nonexistent) Witches International Coven Council, and reprinted in the Christian magazine *Passport*:

1. To bring about the covens, both black and white magic, into one and have the arctress to govern all—ACCOMPLISHED;
2. To bring about personal debts causing discord and disharmony within families—ACCOMPLISHED;

3. To remove or educate the "new age youth" by:
   a. infiltrating boys/girls' clubs and big sister/brother programs
   b. infiltrating schools, having prayers removed, having teachers teach about drugs, sex, freedoms
   c. instigating and promoting rebellion against parents and all authority
   d. promoting equal rights for youth—ACCOMPLISHED;

4. To gain access to all people's backgrounds and vital information by:
   a. use of computers
   b. convenience
   c. infiltration—ACCOMPLISHED;

5. To have laws changed to benefit our ways, such as:
   a. removing children from the home environment and placing them in our foster homes
   b. mandatory placement of children in our daycare centers
   c. increased taxes
   d. open drug and pornography market to everyone—NOT YET ACCOMPLISHED;

6. To destroy government agencies by:
   a. overspending
   b. public opinion
   c. being on the offensive always, opposing, demonstrating, demoralizing—NOT YET ACCOMPLISHED;

7. Not to be revealed until all else has been accomplished. Target date for revelation—June 21, 1986—the beginning of the Summer Solstice and great feast on the Satanic calendar.[5]

It is perhaps significant that the current rash of stories comes at a time when Christian fundamentalism is mak-

[5]John Frattarola, "America's Best Kept Secret," *Passport*, Special Report, 1987.

ing an intensive effort to reaffirm its beliefs. Lawsuits have been filed—and won—to prevent the teaching of evolution, and new efforts have been made to reintroduce prayers in public schools. Television airtime has been given over to an unprecendented amount of evangelical programming.

Since the 1960s, the Christian system of beliefs and values has been challenged. A majority of the public no longer accepts the concepts of Original Sin, Heaven and Hell, and God and Satan, at least in literal form. The old mythology would thus have to be secularized in order to ensure its acceptance and belief. A religious myth, thus, has been transformed into a law-and-order one.

Christian fundamentalists point to actual instances of criminal psychotic violence, as well as to the unproven charges of ritualistic child abuse, as proof of the existence of Satan and a demonic conspiracy. But others, like historian Jeffrey Burton Russell, believe that if there is a malevolent spiritual force alive and well in the universe, it has, in recent years, been at work in more subtle ways. "The huge collective forces of modern societies with their bureaucratization of responsibility have produced what Hannah Arendt called the banality of evil," he writes; "forms are filled out so that Jews may be herded efficiently into gas ovens, maps with anonymous coordinates are issued so that bomber crews may burn schools and hospitals without a twinge of conscience. In such a world the Devil surely finds it more effective to sit behind a desk than to roam the world like a lion."[6]

That sentiment is shared by Anton LaVey, whose Hobbesian vision of an inevitable Infernal Empire is more chillingly modern than any Christian nightmare of Hell. He has no objection to the finger-pointing and media hype about Satanic conspiracy and ritualistic child abuse; rather, he sees it as playing right into the Devil's hands. "We have been sold the myth of a homogeneous society," he says, "in which nobody is any better or any worse than anyone else. But everybody needs somebody to feel superior to, as un-Christian as that may be. People still have aggressions, but no means to vent them."

The Satanic answer to this dilemma he sees as obvi-

[6]Russell, Jeffrey Burton, op. cit., p. 252.

ous—androids. Artificial humans will be produced that will look, smell, and feel like people, except that they will have no conscious volition. Each person will be able to be hostile and prejudiced toward his android, be physically abusive, even have sex whenever he or she wants it without the fear of getting AIDS.

"Because of research and development, the automaton will be more stimulating than any human could be," LaVey guarantees. "Like an old Deusenberg sitting at the curb is more alive than the people crowding around it, drawing energy from its beautiful chrome pipes, the object will become more valuable than the people watching it."

He rubs his bald head and grins. "When things become precious and people expendable, that is the horror of the true Satanic society. That is when the nightmare begins."

BIBLIOGRAPHY

Anonymous. *Documents from the Walburga Abbey.* Amsterdam: Walburga Abbey of the Church of Satan, n.d.

Aquino, Michael A. *The Crystal Tablet of Set.* San Francisco: Temple of Set, 1986.

Bainbridge, William. *Satan's Power.* Berkeley: University of California Press, 1978.

Becker, Howard. *Outsiders.* New York: Free Press, 1963.

Bettelheim, Bruno. *The Uses of Enchantment.* New York: Vintage, 1977.

Brunvand, Jan Harold. *The Choking Doberman and Other "New" Urban Legends,* New York: W.W. Norton, 1984.

Bugliosi, Vincent. *Helter Skelter.* New York: W.W. Norton, 1974.

Carus, Paul. *The History of the Devil and the Idea of Evil.* New York: Land's End, 1969.

Cavendish, Richard. *The Black Arts.* New York: Capricorn, 1968.

Cohn, Norman. *Europe's Inner Demons.* New York: Basic Books, 1975.

———. *Warrant for Genocide.* New York: Harper & Row, 1967.

Crowley, Aleister. *The Book of the Law.* Xeno, 1961.

———. *The Confessions of Aleister Crowley.* New York: Hill & Wang, 1969.

———. *Magick in Theory and Practice.* New York: Castle, n.d.

Eliade, Mircea. *Myths, Dreams, and Mysteries.* New York: Harper & Row, 1960.

———. *Rites and Symbols of Initiation.* London: Harper & Row, 1958.

Evans-Pritchard, E.E., *Witchcraft, Oracles, and Magic among the Azande*. London: Oxford University Press, 1937.

Festinger, Leon, Henry Riecken, and Stanley Schachter. *When Prophecy Fails*. New York: Harper & Row, 1956.

Fratlarola, John, "America's Best Kept Secret," *Passport* Special Report, 1987.

Freud, Sigmund. *Totem and Taboo*. New York: W.W. Norton, 1950.

Fromm, Erich. *Psychoanalysis and Religion*. New Haven: Yale University Press, 1950.

Fuller, John G. *Are the Kids Alright?* New York: New York Times Books, 1981.

Glock, Charles, and Rodney Stark. *Religion and Society in Tension*. Chicago: Rand McNally, 1965.

Harrington, Walt, "The Devil in Anton LaVey," Washington, Post Magazine, Feb. 23, 1986.

Hogg, Garry. *Cannibalism and Human Sacrifice*. Secaucus, N.J.: Citadel, 1966.

Hughes, Pennethorne. *Witchcraft*. Hammondsworth: Penguin, 1970.

Huysmans, J.K. *Down There*. New York: Dover, 1958.

Jahoda, Gustav. *The Psychology of Superstition*. Hammondsworth: Penguin, 1969.

James, William. *The Varieties of Religious Experience*. New York: Modern Library, 1929.

Kagan, Daniel, and Ian Summers. *Mute Evidence*. New York: Bantam, 1984.

Kelly, Aidan A. "Looking Reasonably at Outrageous Religions: Satanism as a Stage of Religious Maturation." Paper, 1986.

King, Francis. *The Rites of Modern Magic*. New York: Macmillan, 1970.

———. *Sexuality, Magic and Perversion*. Secaucus, N.J.: Citadel, 1972.

Klapp, Orrin. *Collective Search for Identity*. New York: Holt, Rinehart, 1969.

Kluckholn, Clyde. *Navaho Witchcraft*. Boston: Beacon, 1967.

LaVey, Anton Szandor. *The Compleat Witch*. New York: Dodd, Mead, 1971.

———. *The Satanic Bible*. New York: Avon, 1969.

———. *The Satanic Rituals*. New York: Avon, 1972.

Lessa, William, and Evon Vogt, eds. *Reader in Comparative Religion*. London: Harper & Row, 1965.

Levin, David. *What Happened in Salem?* New York: Harcourt, Brace, 1960.

Lifton, Robert J.. *Thought Reform and the Psychology of Totalism*. New York: W.W. Norton, 1963.

Lowry, Shirley Park. *Familiar Mysteries*. New York: Oxford University Press, 1982.

Lyons, Arthur. *The Second Coming: Satanism in America*. New York: Dodd, Mead, 1970.

Malinowski, Bronislaw. *Magic, Science, and Religion*. Glencoe: The Free Press, 1948.

Mackenzie, Norman. *Secret Societies*. London: Aldus, 1968

Mannix, Daniel. *The Hellfire Club*. London: Foursquare, 1966.

Maple, Eric. *The Domain of Devils*. London: Pan, 1969.

Mather, Cotton, *Wonders of the Invisible World*, New York, 1950.

Melton, J Gordon. *The Encyclopedia of American Religions*, vol. 2. Wilmington, N.C.: McGrath, 1978.

———. *The Encyclopedic Handbook of Cults*. New York: Garland, 1986.

———. "Evidences of Satan in Contemporary America; A Survey." Paper presented at the Pacific Division of the American Philosophical Association, Los Angeles, Mar. 27–28, 1986.

Moody, Edward J. "Magical Therapy: An Anthropological Investigation of Contemporary Satanism," in Irving I. Zaretsky and Mark P. Leone, eds., *Religious Movements in Contemporary America*. Princeton: Princeton University Press, 1974.

Murray, Margaret. *The Witch-Cult in Western Europe*. London: Oxford, 1921.

Norbeck, Edward. *Religion in Primitive Society*. London: Harper & Row, 1961.

Norris, Joel, and Jerry Potter. "The Devil Made Me Do It." *Penthouse*, Jan. 1986.

Ortega y Gasset. *Man in Crisis*. New York: W.W. Norton, 1962.

Ouspensky, P.D. *The Psychology of Man's Possible Evolution*. New York: Alfred A. Knopf, 1954.

Parsons, Jack. "The Babalon Workings," "The Book of Antichrist." Personal papers, 1946–52.

Pauwels, Louis, and Jacques Bergier. *The Morning of the Magicians*. New York: Avon, 1968.

Perry, Charles. *The Haight-Ashbury*. New York: Random House, 1984.

Pielke, Robert. *You Say You Want a Revolution*. Chicago: Nelson-Hall, 1986.

Poundstone, William. *Big Secrets*. New York: Quill, 1983.

Rappeleye, Charles, "Satanism and Child Abuse," *FATE*, April, 1987.

Rhodes, H.T.F. *The Satanic Mass*. London: Rider, 1954.

Roszak, Theodore. *The Making of a Counterculture*. New York: Anchor, 1969.

Russell, Jeffrey Burton. *Mephistopheles: The Devil in the Modern World*. Ithaca: Cornell University Press, 1986.

Sanders, Ed. *The Family*. New York: Dutton, 1971.

Scott, Gini Graham. *The Magicians*. Oakland: Creative Communications, 1984.

Seabrook, William. *Witchcraft: Its Power in the World Today*. London: Sphere, 1970.

Smith, Michelle, and Lawrence Pazder. *Michelle Remembers*. New York: Congdon & Lattes, 1980.

Spence, Lewis. *An Encyclopedia of Occultism*. New York: University, 1960.

Starkey, Marion. *The Devil in Massachusetts*. New York: Knopf, 1949.

Summers, Montague. *The History of Witchcraft*. New York: Citadel, 1956.

Symonds, John. *The Great Beast*. London: Rider, 1951.

Terry, Maury. *The Ultimate Evil*. New York: Doubleday, 1987.

Trevor-Roper, H.R. *The European Witch-Craze of the 16th and 17th Centuries*. Hammondsworth: Penguin, 1967.

Truzzi, Marcello. "Towards a Sociology of the Occult: Notes on Modern Witchcraft," in Irving I. Zaretsky and Mark P. Leone, eds. *Religious Movements in Contemporary America*. Princeton: Princeton University Press, 1974.

Watts, Alan. *The Two Hands of God*. New York: Collier, 1963.

Williams, Charles. *Witchcraft*. New York: Meridian, 1959.

Wilson, Colin. *Encyclopedia of Murder*. New York: G.P. Putnam, 1962.

Wolfe, Burton. *The Devil's Avenger*. New York: Pyramid, 1974.

INDEX